Strange Bodies

Strange Bodies

Marcel Theroux

W F HOWES LTD

This large print edition published in 2013 by
W F Howes Ltd
Unit 4, Rearsby Business Park, Gaddesby Lane,
Rearsby, Leicester LE7 4YH

1 3 5 7 9 10 8 6 4 2

First published in the United Kingdom in 2013
by Faber and Faber Ltd

A CIP catalogue record for this book is available
from the British Library

ISBN 978 1 47123 970 0

Typeset by Palimpsest Book Production Limited,
Falkirk, Stirlingshire
Printed and bound by
CPI Group (UK) Ltd, Croydon, CR0 4YY

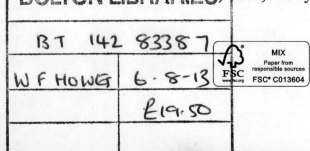

in nova fert animus mutatas dicere formas corpora.

OVID, *Metamorphoses*

Of shapes transformed to bodies strange I purpose to entreat.

ARTHUR GOLDING, *Ovid's Metamorphoses*

Now I am ready to tell how bodies are changed Into different bodies.

TED HUGHES, *Tales from Ovid*

PREFACE

Whatever this is, it started when Nicky Slopen came back from the dead.

The man who walked into my shop that day was solidly built, bearded, and had his head shaved almost to the scalp, but he knew my old nickname. He shuffled up to the counter and greeted me by it. 'No one's called me that for years,' I said.

'It has been years,' he said. 'It's me. Nicky.'

There was a rush of awkwardness as I flannelled to cover the fact I didn't know him, and then a much more unpleasant sensation when he said his last name.

'I heard you were . . .' I couldn't bring myself to say it. 'Is this some kind of joke? Because I don't appreciate it.'

'Calm down, Sukie, it's really me,' he said.

For a moment I just didn't believe him, but then he told me things that only he knew, things we'd said to each other, and gradually I saw that it was him. His eyes had a familiar intensity, and when he said my name, it had the same shape in his mouth that it had always had.

1

So of course I apologised: I was flummoxed, must have mixed him up with someone else. We had a laugh about it: reports of my death have been greatly exaggerated, that sort of thing. For over an hour all we did was chat about old times. Weekday mornings are so quiet in the shop that I generally use them for stocktaking and dealing with invoices.

When I signed the lease five years ago, I joked to Ted that I was staking my financial future on the existence of an innate human impulse that drives visitors to pretty market towns to stock up on butter dishes, preserving jars and other kitchen paraphernalia. So far it's been a gamble that's worked; at least, financially. That impulse does exist, and as Ted said, it seems to be countercyclical. It's even drawn a few old friends to the shop unexpectedly, and Nicky's visit felt like one of those: simultaneously warm and slightly awkward.

There was a clumsiness about him, a laboriousness in his movements that made me think he might have had a stroke, and a kind of neediness to his recollections that suggested he was going through tough times; no wedding ring, and I didn't ask about Leonora. He commiserated about my marriage and cooed over my pictures of Babette. He didn't have any of his own two, but men often don't, and he seemed a little choked when he talked about them.

We ate pad thai from the takeaway sitting on boxes in the stockroom and then when a coach party showed up he slipped away, promising to stop by again when he was in the area. The childminder called just as he was going, so we didn't get to say goodbye properly and I was too preoccupied to take his email. That evening I searched his name on the internet. That's when I found his obituary.

It wasn't enormously long, but then he wasn't yet forty, and still he'd made it into the 'Lives Remembered' section of the *Telegraph*, complete with a picture of him as I had known him at university: with that tall, spare frame that always seemed to typify a certain vanishing English body shape, even though his mother was actually Dutch.

> *Dr Nicholas Slopen, who died last Friday aged 39, was a scholar whose inspirational teaching style was matched by his outstanding abilities as an editor and critic. The first two volumes of the revised Oxford edition of the* Letters *of* Samuel Johnson *compiled under his guidance have been acclaimed as definitive. The third and final volume will be published later this year.*
>
> *Nicholas Slopen was born in Singapore in 1970 and raised in South London. He showed academic promise at a very early age, winning a Queen's Scholarship to Westminster and subsequently going on to Downing College, Cambridge, where he studied under the renowned scholar Ronald Harbottle.*

A fluent speaker of five languages, including Russian and Dutch, Slopen achieved the rare distinction of coauthoring two papers with Harbottle while still an undergraduate. Though Slopen's relationship with Harbottle was strained by the latter's championing of the controversial poet Matilda Swann, he always regarded Harbottle as a friend and mentor.

After studying for a time at Yale, Slopen accepted a post at University College London, where his work, both as a teacher and as a critic, was marked by a warm and idiosyncratic engagement with the texts, while still upholding the highest standards of scholarship. Jesting at Truth, *his 1998 study of Augustan satire, was regarded as a landmark. Reviewing the first volume of the* Johnson Letters *in the* Times Literary Supplement, *Darcus Millhouse acclaimed it as 'a gift for the ages'.*

He is survived by his wife, the pianist Leonora Kazemzadeh, and their two children.

Well, what to make of that? The thing gave me a creepy feeling. He didn't look the same – which of us did? – but there was no doubt in my mind that the man I'd seen was him. When you've known someone the way we knew each other, you just *know.* And yet the evidence of the obituary was right in front of me.

Reading it over, I was struck by what a lot he'd achieved, and also reminded why the two of us

4

were ultimately badly matched. I was an anomaly at Downing, a state-school girl who thought Goethe was pronounced 'Go-eath', and who got mixed up between China and Japan. On the few occasions I met his mother I could tell he was tense in case I said something stupid. It's odd, I suppose, for me to have a Cambridge degree and yet feel intellectually insecure, but that's how intimidating she seemed.

He won a fellowship to Yale at the beginning of our final year. He wouldn't take it up for another ten months, but I was hurt because he seemed to have written me out of his future. I ended things with him, hoping, I think, to force some acknowledgement from him that I would be part of his plans. I knew from our friends that it hurt him, but he took it stoically, like some bitter but necessary medicine. We hardly spoke that whole year, but we went to the May Ball together, because the previous year he'd promised he'd take me, and he was a man of his word. He'd started seeing someone else by then. My memory of the evening is shot through with a kind of sadness: that feeling I had perpetually when I was twenty-one that I was on the wrong side of the door to where the fun and laughter was. And I suppose I was still a little in love with him. But after graduation, we slipped out of each other's lives. We exchanged letters when his mother died. Then silence.

In the days that followed his showing up at the shop, I tracked down some old friends. A few had lost touch with Nicky altogether, but several had heard that he'd died and one said it was in a road accident. I didn't ask for the details. Something held me back from telling them about his visit to the shop. Everywhere I checked, the story was the same. University College London was even setting up a memorial fellowship named after him. But Nicky wasn't dead, and it seemed as though only he and I knew it.

The only way I could make sense of it was to assume that Nicky had got into some kind of trouble and taken a desperate decision to run away from it. It was completely out of character for him, but no other explanation fitted the facts. I knew I hadn't seen a ghost. He was too material for that.

And besides, I think men, even the good ones, are more apt to cut and run than we are. Ted walked out when Babette was six months old; he said he'd found someone who could make him happier than I could. This woman turned out to be a twenty-four-year-old Italian translator he'd met at a convention in Düsseldorf. That miserable period coincided with the date of Nicky's death, which might explain why it didn't make more of an impression on me. All the bad news got rolled up together in one big indigestible lump.

It was almost a year before I saw him again. I was closing up the shop at the end of one of those short December days, rushing because the book group was meeting at my house that evening. Just as I was about to leave, I remembered that it was Kath's birthday. I unlocked the front door and went back in to get her one of the ceramic Seletti jugs shaped like a milk carton. Sleet was rattling against the shopfront. I grabbed some wrapping paper and a bag to keep it all dry. When I turned round there was a dark shape in the doorway. I froze. The jug slipped out of my hand and smashed on the floor.

'Sukie?' he said.

I felt a little breathless. For an instant, the last twenty-odd years vanished like a trick of the light: no Leonora, no Ted, no kids, no break-ups and false starts, no ageing, only the two of us in the half-dark just like the first time I kissed him in Grantchester meadow.

Nicky stepped out of the shadows. He looked much worse than when I'd last seen him: unshaven, tired and badly dressed, but also more like his old self; he'd lost weight and his face had some of its shape back.

He told me he needed a place to stay. I explained about the book group and warned him that Babette was waking a lot in the night, but he didn't look like he had many other options. He sagged into the passenger seat like an old man.

From Ludlow to Barbrook is a twenty-minute drive, assuming you don't get stuck behind a tractor or a tourist. Nicky ignored my questions and didn't seem in any mood to talk. I found myself filling the silence by chattering on about my day, but by the time we got to Cleehill I couldn't pretend any more. I pulled over just beyond the pub. The locals call it the Kremlin because they claim it's the highest point between there and the Urals, and in the old days the jukebox used to pick up Radio Moscow. The rain had stopped. The moon was out and beyond the hills we could make out the vague orange glow of Birmingham. I turned to Nicky and asked him what was going on.

'It's a long story,' he said. 'I was in the Maudsley for a while.'

'Studying?' For some reason, I assumed it was a college.

'Sectioned,' he said. And then by way of explanation: 'It's a loony bin outside Croydon.'

Hailstones pounded on the roof of the car. We'd have to drive home the long way round, because the ford would be too dangerous to cross.

'Does Leonora know you're alive?'

'The Nicky she knew is dead.' He said it matter-offactly, with no real venom, but the hopelessness of it shocked me. And in the yellow rays of the Kremlin's outside light, his teeth looked crooked and broken. Suddenly, it struck me that he was, after all, really a stranger, and I was seized by a panicky feeling.

There was something unpleasant about his body in the seat next to me; it seemed oddly bulbous, like an overripe fruit. He smelled a bit sharp and foxy and I wondered when he'd last washed.

8

'Things have been difficult for me lately, Sukie,' he said. Without the reassurance of his familiar eyes, even his voice seemed rougher and strange. 'I don't want to drag you into it. I just need a place to stay for a night. It won't be much longer. This carcass is finally letting me down.' His voice tailed off and he lapsed into silence. The effort of speaking had exhausted him.

'I've got some of Ted's clean clothes that you can take, and you can eat and have a bath, but you can't stay,' I said. If I had lived alone, I would have chanced it, but I couldn't have him sleeping under the same roof as Babette.

Nicky just nodded. In that moment, I felt myself relent a little. He seemed so beaten down, and I remembered how tamely he'd acquiesced when I chucked him; not, I think, because he didn't care, but because that stoicism was part of his nature. It maddened me at the time, because I felt so sorry for myself that he was leaving; now I just felt sorry for him.

The book that night was by Tolstoy, *The Death of Ivan Ilyich*. I was a little distracted, wondering about the best way to get Nicky back to Ludlow and if I should offer to pay for a B and B. He sat in an armchair at one side of the living room, looking sick and hopeless, even after a bath and change of clothes. I could tell that his being there was making the others uncomfortable; it was making me uncomfortable. It didn't help that none of the others had liked the book. Ordinarily, we would have chatted about it for five minutes and then wandered off onto something else, but Nicky's presence made us self-conscious and we dutifully talked about the book much longer than we wanted to.

Louise was the only one who was openly critical of Tolstoy's book. It wasn't her cup of tea at all. She was hostile to all those canonical male writers anyway, and she was also fond of saying that the first rule of good writing is 'Show, don't tell'; she said Tolstoy didn't appear to have grasped this. Me, I liked the book. There's something of Ivan Ilyich in most men, I think, the way they shut down and turn robotic in middle age. It reminded me of Ted somehow and the way he'd become when we moved to Shropshire: forty, panicking inwardly, throwing himself into work and hobbies, and then this affair which had mid-life crisis written all over it. I was going to say this, but it struck me that it might sound like a reproach to Nicky. Whatever he'd been up to – and I didn't want to know – made Ted look like Father of the Year.

In my childhood, there was famously a British politician, John Stonehouse, who faked his own death to escape debts or marriage, or possibly both. He left a pile of clothes on a beach in Florida to make it look as though he'd drowned and then flew away to Australia to start a new life with his mistress. I understand the impulse to make a fresh start. That's why I came up here to open the shop. But to lie about your death – there's a level of deceit and desperation in that which made me wonder if I knew Nicky at all.

Glancing over at him, I thought how different he looked from the man I'd known. He was so old and weary. Then I noticed he was struggling to stand up. He was gripping the arms of the chair and his mouth was open and – shame on me for remembering this, but this is how it was – a big string of dribble was hanging from his lower lip. He managed to lift himself just clear of the seat, then keeled over on the floor. I got his shirt off and pumped his chest while Kath called an ambulance.

There was the strangest smell on him – like pear drops, but not as pleasant. Also, he had tattoos, clumsy ones, which, if you knew how squeamish he was about needles, made no sense at all. After a couple of minutes he was breathing on his own again and his eyes opened. His lips regained some of their colour. He was whispering something, but I couldn't make it out. Then he went again. This time we took turns to do CPR on him, but he was unconscious when the ambulance arrived. Kath stayed with Babette and I followed them back to Shrewsbury in my own car. There was a crash team waiting for them outside the hospital, but they'd given up trying to resuscitate him by the time I got there.

He had some money in his pockets and a coach

ticket from Carlisle, but no identification. I told them who he was, and the doctor wrote Nicky's name on the medical certificate and the cause of death as cardiac arrest. They left the body in their mortuary for Leonora to collect.

It turned out that Leonora was on holiday with the children at the time, and it took them a few days to get hold of her. When they reached her, she was, understandably, frosty. Her husband had been dead for months, she told them. And she faxed over the death certificate to prove it.

Exactly a week after Nicky died, two police officers dropped by the shop. I made two cups of tea in the back room and as I came back with them, I glimpsed the page of a notebook the younger one was holding. He'd written *dead white male* in a mixture of lower case and capitals and underlined it twice. In retrospect, I see I should have been on guard from then.

They explained there was confusion over the dead man's identity and they were trying to establish who he was so they could release the body to his relatives for burial. I told them that as far as I was concerned he was Nicholas Slopen. They asked me why I thought that, and I mentioned John Stonehouse and my assumption that Nicky had been running away from something.

Up to then, it had felt like a friendly chat, but at that point they became very aggressive. The older of the two policemen whipped out these awful autopsy photos from an envelope he was carrying

12

and pushed them in my face. He said that Nicky would have to be Harry Houdini to be alive after an accident like this. He shouted that Nicky had been dead for months and I should think about the pain I was causing his widow and his children.

They clearly thought I was a troublemaker: some crazy abandoned woman fixated on an old ex-boyfriend, tormenting Leonora with my fairy tales about her dead husband.

I was shaken by the photos, by their obvious hostility, by Nicky's reappearance and death, and I didn't have the stomach to argue with them. I capitulated. I said I hadn't seen him for almost twenty years and that I must have been mistaken.

Their aggression surprised me, but in retrospect, I see it shouldn't have. It's baffling to have the laws of physics subverted. Dead men don't go wandering round the Midlands looking up ex-girlfriends. And behind the woman who says they do is an uncomfortable archetype. It felt like those policemen wanted to stick me on a ducking stool or burn me at the stake.

'You don't *actually* know *anything*,' the older of the two policemen had said every time I had tried to explain why I'd drawn the conclusions I had. And part of me was relieved to be able to agree with him.

So that's how they left it. Officially, the man who died on my living-room carpet remains unidentified to this day. They preserved some DNA and cremated the rest of him.

Two months after Nicky died, I discovered that Babette had been posting her tiny rice cakes down the back of the sofa. We've had a rodent problem in the past here, so I went into overdrive trying to clear the place up. Sure enough, she'd been doing it for a while and I had to pull the cushions off everything to sort it out. Under the chair where Nicky had been sitting during book group, I found a tiny flash memory stick that I didn't recognise. I stuck it into my computer to see what it was. It didn't cross my mind that it would have anything to do with Nicky until I started reading it.

What follows is the text just as I found it.

I don't think a day has gone by when I haven't thought about Nicky's visits and asked myself why he came to me, particularly that second time. He must have known how close he was to his last hours. My feeling as I've got older is that human motivation is more opaque and more contradictory than we like to admit. But I've come to the conclusion that Nicky left that flash drive here on purpose; that he wanted someone to find it and make its contents public. I believe that Nicky felt a genuine connection to me and for that reason he entrusted me with his story.

Susanna Laidlaw-Robinson

From the impression of a foot in mud or clay, experts can precisely recreate not only the foot, but the species, gait, height, weight and likely age of its owner. By an analogous, but exponentially more complex procedure, we can use the methods demonstrated in this paper to recreate not only the generative linguistic capacity, but the intellectual, emotional and cultural complex in which it is embedded.

YURII OLEGOVICH MALEVIN, *Proceedings of the All-Union Soviet Academy of Sciences, Anthology of Closed Sessions*, June–October 1946

For Books are not absolutely dead things, but doe contain a potencie of life in them to be as active as that soule was whose progeny they are; nay they do preserve as in a violl the purest efficacie and extraction of that living intellect that bred them. I know they are as lively, and as vigorously productive, as those fabulous Dragons teeth; and being sown up and down, may chance to spring up armed men.

JOHN MILTON, Areopagitica

And this book is – instead of my body
And this word is – instead of my soul.

GRIGOR NAREKATSI, The Book of Grief

DENNIS HILL UNIT

MARCH–NOVEMBER 2010

CHAPTER 1

My name is Nicholas Patrick Slopen. I was born in Singapore City on April 10th 1970. I died on September 28th 2009, crushed in the wheel arch of a lorry outside Oval tube station.

This document is my testimony.

As will shortly become clear, I have an unknown but definitely brief period of time to explain the events leading up to my death and to establish the continuity of my identity after it. In view of the constraints upon me, I hope the reader will forgive my forgoing the usual niceties of autobiography. At the same time, I will have to commit myself to some details with a certain, and perhaps wearisome, degree of exactitude in order to provide evidence to support the contention contained in the first paragraph of this testimony: that I am Nicholas Slopen, and that my consciousness has survived my bodily death.

According to convention, I ought to give some account of my birth and childhood, but time is very short and little of that information is of material consequence to my narrative. The events leading up to my death began with the moment on 15 April 2009 when I arrived for lunch at the Green Gorse Tavern in Maiden Lane, Covent Garden, shortly before 1 p.m.

I had been invited there by Hunter Gould, who is, as I believe is well known, a figure of some notoriety in the music industry. It's not my intention to disguise or protect any identities in this document. Let them be answerable for what they have done.

Hunter, whom I had never met before, had approached me with an invitation for lunch through his secretary, Ms Preethika Choudhury. In a subsequent exchange of emails, Preethika explained that in addition to his musical interests, Hunter was a keen amateur collector of literary memorabilia and was seeking my help in authenticating a collection of letters which had been offered to him for sale by a private dealer.

Though it was a mild day, I had brought with me a precautionary raincoat folded into an oblong package under my left arm; in my right hand, I held a dented leather briefcase which was a gift to me from my wife, Leonora, and had belonged to her father, Bahman, who was himself a scholar of English literature, though his principal expertise was in early mediaeval Farsi poetry. I surrendered the coat to the maître d', but kept hold of the case, which contained a facsimile holograph letter written by the eighteenth-century lexicographer Dr Samuel Johnson, a back number of *Modern Languages Quarterly*, a crumpled copy of the *Evening Standard* and a sachet of anti-wrinkle cream.

I see already I have failed in my resolution to be as concise as possible.

Forgive me. It must be hard for anyone to imagine the degree of comfort I obtain from the vividness of these recollections.

If only I had the luxury of time there is so very much more I would like to add. It is hard to relinquish all that I once possessed: the person I once was and the people I loved, however inadequately; more than mere vanity suffers at the conscious abbreviation of so much that was important to me.

For the sake of full disclosure, I should explain that I am currently incarcerated in the Dennis Hill Unit of the Maudsley Trust. The DHU is a secure facility, for people who have been sectioned for their own or others' safety. The wags in here call it the Dangerous Humans Unit. It's located in the Royal Bethlem Hospital, itself a lineal descendant of Bedlam, the notorious insane asylum which provided nugatory medical care for its inmates, but a rather higher standard of entertainment for the fashionable ladies and gentlemen who came to laugh at them. I appreciate that none of these details enhances the plausibility of what I am setting down.

The awfulness of my position almost defies summary. I was detained two weeks ago after an incident that took place at the home of my wife and in the presence of my son Lucius. I am now being held for assessment under Section 2 of the 1983 Mental Health Act. Under the terms of the Section, Leonora is my nearest relative and has the right to request my discharge. However, as far as Leonora is concerned I have been dead for months. All she knows is that a total stranger burst into her house, berated her and tearfully claimed to have usurped her dead husband's identity. There's little doubt that I would, in her position, have called the police as well.

And yet, here is a paradox. While no longer myself, I have never felt so clearly myself. As grandiose as it sounds, I feel closer than at any time in my life to perceiving the truth of the universe – the penumbra of sacred feeling which rings the real. Which *constitutes* the real. Without which we are so much meat and bone whizzing through space. *Mono no aware*, the Japanese call it. That *feeling over things* which suffuses their art with stoic melancholy, the only true response to the transience and beauty of our existence. Oh my poor children. Did anyone care how I knew their names? How many times have these hands bathed their pretty heads? But force of habit misleads me. Not these hands, of course. Not once.

Having been assured that Hunter was yet to arrive, I took my seat and ordered a bottle of sparkling water. I was uncertain of the etiquette of business lunches and slightly nervous at the prospect of sitting through an entire meal with a perfect stranger. To take my mind off what was to come, I rummaged through my briefcase for a distraction and, since I had read most of its contents *ad nauseam*, pulled out the sachet of face cream.

The cream had arrived by post that morning in a parcel addressed to the previous occupant of our house in southwest London. It came with a letter from a Frenchman called Dr Ricaud who had an address on the Champs-Elysées. Dr Ricaud had also included a glossy catalogue of his beauty products, all manufactured at his *laboratoires* on the Channel Islands. 'Your BEAUTY never stops,' his letter said. 'Your skin defies time.' The doctor's bold claims were essentially unverifiable as the lady they were addressed to had been dead for fourteen years. Her legacy on earth was a marble urn near Streatham crematorium, a persistent smell of damp food in the room that had once been her scullery, and letters like this one which continued to offer her deals on cosmetics or inform her of her victory in prize draws.

At five minutes past one, Hunter Gould arrived in the restaurant and, being shown to the table, greeted me by my first name.

Although I knew Hunter from his colourful reputation as a bigshot in the music business, I had neither met him nor spoken to him before that moment. Preethika had extended the initial lunch invitation without explaining what it was for. Until

Hunter's motive for inviting me was belatedly made clear, the emails provoked a lot of speculation among my family. In fact, Sarah and Lucius, my children, amused themselves with the notion that Hunter was going to offer me a recording deal, and had proposed a number of titles for my first album, of which *Bring Me the Headphones of John the Baptist* seemed not only plausible, but possibly touched with authentic genius.

It was my wife Leonora who reminded me of our single previous encounter with Hunter Gould. About two years earlier, the two of us had been on a rare date at a cinema in Bayswater where, just as the previews ended, a stocky American stood up and lectured the entire audience about the need to switch off their mobile phones. I instinctively fumbled in my pocket as Leonora whispered: 'Isn't that Hunter Gould?' and the stranger on my left nodded at her with an expression of sheer delight. I can't recall the name of the film, but the audience behaved impeccably throughout it.

I told this story to Hunter by way of small-talk when we were seated at the table.

Up close, Hunter was big and toadlike, his face chubby and pugnacious and somehow a bit short of features, like an underdressed Mr Potato Head. I guessed, wrongly as it turned out, that he was in his early fifties. He had the build of a nightclub doorman and it occurred to me then that this was part of his success in business: his portly but muscular physique posed the oblique threat that, if it came down to it, he could send the lawyers out of the room and simply duff you up.

'I remember that,' Hunter said, refilling my glass and adding parenthetically, 'You sure you don't want wine?' With a fastidiousness that struck me as mildly eccentric, he had brought a special supply of alkaline mineral water with him in a copper flask. The waiter placed a fresh glass on the table for it.

Hunter went on: 'I mean, I don't remember that actual instance but it was a phase I went through. Eventually I saw a shrink who told me I was disinhibited and medicated me for it. I had a series of manic episodes, but they weren't so easy to spot because I'm naturally an exuberant personality.'

'I've always been slightly envious of people with mania,' I said. 'All that energy.'

'Yes,' said Hunter. 'I believe I've tried almost every legal and non-legal drug on the planet and manic episodes with disinhibition are right up there with the best.'

I added that it didn't seem all that crazy to ask an auditorium full of strangers to turn their mobile phones off, just a little unusual.

'That was the more benign side of my madness. In fact . . .' Hunter leaned forward. 'In fact, what's crazier, sitting in the movie theatre listening to some asshole talk on his cellphone or to make it clear from the get-go that these are the rules, we watch the movie in respectful silence, and insist that everybody abide by them?'

'That's right,' I agreed, wondering if he was still on some kind of medication.

'Unfortunately that wasn't the whole extent of it,' Hunter went on. 'There was some challenging racial stuff, which it turns out is very common as an element of delusional behaviour – and, you know, it was by no means racist, but it was open to misinterpretation. And working in the music business, there are lots of big and fragile egos. Humankind cannot bear very much reality. As the man said.'

Over the lunch (two courses, Caesar salad and fish-cakes for me, salad and wild salmon for Hunter; neither of us drank wine) we chatted amiably. I listened politely as Hunter extolled the benefits of his alkaline water and the low-glycaemic diet he was on. 'I can't remember the last time I had sugar,' he said, as the waiter handed me the dessert menu. While I ate sticky toffee pudding, Hunter drank green tea and explained in more detail the task he had in mind for me.

For some years, Hunter said, he had indulged a private passion for collecting memorabilia associated with famous English literary figures, particularly those of the Augustan and Romantic periods. He had established a collection of objects and letters that had once belonged to Alexander Pope, Jane Austen, Byron, Shelley and John Clare, but so far had nothing connected to his favourite author, Dr Johnson. Now some letters had been offered to him, and he wanted to confirm they were real.

As Hunter talked warmly about his cherished pieces, I confess I had to fight an inward spurt of resentment. At the age of almost forty, and after a lifetime's commitment to the study of English letters, I could barely afford to buy books in hardback; the last holiday I'd taken with my family had been spent on board a narrowboat on a rainswept canal in the Midlands; whereas Hunter, a hobbyist, a mere dilettante, was able actually to own unique objects of irreplaceable historic and scholastic value. I checked myself for an instant and recognised that my snobbishness was a defensive reflex. I was ashamed of my real reasons for coming to the lunch. While I may have insisted that I was simply curious to meet Hunter, properly, at root, I was hoping that it would be to my financial advantage. And so, with the forensic gift for nuance that had made me a talented literary scholar and virtually hopeless at everything else, I saw the truth was a horrible reverse of the stereotype: on this occasion, the rich man cared only for literature, while the scholar was just in it for the money.

'What you're asking is fairly straightforward,' I said to him. 'There's a lot of extant material in Johnson's own hand. I have a sample of it here. Comparing them would be a pretty good place to start.'

'Unfortunately, the seller isn't keen to have the letters copied as he says they're in a very fragile state.'

I said nothing, but my expression must have betrayed my scepticism.

'I know what you're thinking,' said Hunter. 'It

made me suspicious too. I've seen the letters, and they look like the real thing, but all I have for now is transcripts.'

He took a sheaf of A4 paper from the inside pocket of his navy blue jacket. It was folded longways down the middle and consisted of half a dozen closely typed sheets. 'I understand the limitations of what you can do,' Hunter said reasonably. 'I don't expect a cast-iron guarantee. I just want your professional opinion: is it likely to be Johnson, or not?'

As I glanced down the first page, I noted the faithful transcription of original spellings. I could hear an almost wistful note of surprise in my own voice when I remarked to Hunter that the letters appeared to be new to me. Although I would never have said it to Hunter, on reading the first few lines of the first document I caught a glimpse of something so clearly recognisable – the gait of a loved one on a distant hillside, the smell of my children's hair, the varied sensations evoked by my mother's cooking – that its authenticity seemed to me both undeniable and impossible to analyse. Out of habit, I began rationalising the feeling: it was something in the sinuosity of the sentences, a few familiar contractions, a pet word or two. But beyond that, there was something more; a quality which I embarrassed myself by wanting to call *soul*.

Hunter mistook my silent rapture for either doubtfulness or reluctance, and with no way to assuage the former, he used the only means at his disposal to deal with the latter. Withdrawing a Coutts chequebook and Mont Blanc ballpoint from his other inside pocket, he said: 'Naturally, I'm not expecting you to do this gratis. I was thinking, five or six, say six? And assuming it's genuine you'll write me a document authenticating it.'

On the other side of the table, I fought the astonished flush of pleasure that was brought to my face by the realisation that Hunter Gould was writing me a personal cheque for £3000. 'I'll give you the same on delivery,' Hunter added as he scrawled the jagged spikes of his signature.

I pocketed the cheque awkwardly and said I'd be delighted to help.

CHAPTER 2

I cannot make you understand what it is to look at the moon through this stranger's eyes and know that I will never hold my children again. Sometimes I wake up on the ward with a pain in my chest that feels like my heart breaking. Yes, *my heart breaking*. The description lacks either medical or literary merit, but it ameliorates nothing to know that my house of suffering is bricked and barred with clichés. *Tears, heartbreak,* pathetic fallacies of weeping skies and bleeding sunsets: these aren't lousy approximations of lived experiences, they're the nerves and fibre of human life itself. I was never a Whorfian, and yet I have woken up to find I am made of words.

And all that I am – the meat of me and the 167 key markers coded and recombined in infinite variation – can only express with more embellishment these seventeen syllables of Onitsura: *This autumn I'll be looking at the moon with no child upon my knee.*

Once in a while, if our therapeutic outcomes are consistently positive, we get permission to visit the museum. It houses artefacts from the old Bedlam and paintings and art works by our predecessors.

There are carvings from the former entrance: Melancholy and Madness as huge stone figures, old admission papers, a vitrine full of restraints – cuffs, a leather collar, gags, a harness.

Most of all, I am regularly astonished by the power of the art. In William Kurelek's *The Maze* I see a fleshy labyrinth that still feels like a good summation of my predicament. It shows the cross-section of a cranium, filled with tableaux of nightmarish memories. The works of the parricide Richard Dadd trouble me with their hints of buried violence. But my favourite is a huge piece by Jonathan Martin, the nineteenth-century arsonist who tried to burn down York Minster. It is a mad apocalyptic panorama of London in flames. In crabbed but legible handwriting on the reverse he wrote a long account of a dream he had. I found it so moving that I have committed it to memory:

> *2ndly I dreamt towards the morning that I saw 12 Rainbows in the heavens, they crossed each other, and I stood under the yard-shed, and the patients all around me observed it, and one said I count eleven rainbows. I thought when he said that, the rainbows moved from the heavens, and became like an army of soldiers engaging and intermixing with each other, they came direct from heaven towards me, and I felt*

the reflection of the fire and the patients made sport of it. I reclined upon one knee and prayed that God would have mercy upon their ignorance; and I thought the rainbows would have overthrown the Hospital: and I awoke out of my sleep.

Because I am an educated man there has been a certain amount of favouritism shown towards me at the Dangerous Humans Unit. One of the psychiatrists, Dr Fenella Webster, clearly fancies herself as a literary figure. She's had me in her office a number of times to discuss Jane Austen and to air her theories about the so-called question of Shakespeare's authorship. Like most anti-Stratfordians, she has no feeling for the poetry itself and the insights she offers are second-hand, but she has taken a shine to me and lobbied for me to have access to a computer. Strictly speaking, the internet is out of bounds, but I've found a way to connect. And though my faculty email account has been closed, my personal correspondence is still online. It's thanks to Dr Webster that I am able to work on this testimony.

Twice a week, she and I engage in wholly useless therapeutic wranglings in which she tries to make me admit that I'm not who I say I am. I've given up trying to make her understand the peculiar awfulness of my condition. I'm a demi-man, a simulacrum, *a tattered coat upon a stick.* And I can't escape the feeling that Yeats *knew*, in the vatic, unwitting way of poets. After all, he underwent a procedure of his own, the Steinach, to rejuvenate himself. *A mouth that has no moisture and no breath, breathless mouths may summon; I hail the super-human; I call it death-in-life and life-in-death.* Its exactness chills me.

Soon after my lunch with Hunter I was incapacitated by a mysterious illness which my dentist finally identified as trench mouth, but for three hours that first afternoon, sitting in the tiny study that had been carved out of the attic space above the house, I worked methodically on the letters. The skylights were open for the breeze and I could smell the scent of the horse-chestnut candles in the park and hear the faint chimes of an ice-cream van that trolled the streets around the house in the hour after school ended. That smell, those sounds, and my immersion in the writing of someone I had once loved like an old friend sent me into the kind of fruitful work trance that I felt I had lost the knack for. I read and annotated the extracts, trying to hold my initial certainty about their authorship in check, and to arrive at a verdict dispassionately, balancing the claims of style, vocabulary and subject matter.

Some time after five o'clock, I became aware of a presence in the darkening room. I looked up from the papers on my desk and saw my son sitting in the armchair with an anxious look on his face.

'Why did you call me Lucius?' he asked.

'Why?' I felt groggy and disoriented being roused from my work. My mind was full of balanced periods and quaint Johnsonian English: *irremeable, Cantharides, chymistry.*

'You're nearly fifteen. Aren't we both a bit old for these questions?'

'Really, Dad, why?'

'Your mother chose Sarah's name, so it was my turn to pick and I chose Lucius.'

'Yes, but why?'

'It's a lovely name, it comes from *lux*, meaning light. A bearer of light.'

'Dwayne Tennant says it's a pussy name.'

'Dwayne Tennant? Well, what does he know?' I opened my web browser. 'Look: see what it says here: "Lucius – Roman *praenomen*, or given name, which was derived from Latin *lux*, light. Two Etruscan kings of early Rome had this name as well as several later Romans, including Lucius Annaeus Seneca" – You've got the same name as Seneca –'

'Great.'

'"– A famous statesman, philosopher, orator and tragedian. Also three popes have borne this name."'

Lucius looked pained and unconvinced. I tried another tactic.

'Well, let's see if Dwayne's name is in the database. "Dwayne – anglicised from the Gaelic Dubhan, which means little and dark, derived from *dubh*, 'dark, black', combined with a diminutive suffix." So the next time Dwayne gives you any shit, you tell him his name means small and black.'

'That's half right, anyway. He's six foot two and looks like Sol Campbell.'

'Sol?'

'He plays for Portsmouth.'

'Sol? That's Spanish for sun. He's more or less got the same name as you!'

'Thanks, Dad. You've been a big help.'

Oh Lucius. In my next incarnation, let me forget your pained face as I pleaded with your mother to recognise me on my return. No. Let you forget. My first wish must be for your happiness.

You slipped out of the room and the hopefulness that I had felt a few minutes earlier seemed to vanish with you. The pages of notes I'd made and the transcripts that had evoked the sound of a sage, loved voice felt like a grotesque irrelevance.

Every morning you slunk out of our house after breakfast, leaving behind the books and the smell of coffee, and the sound of someone's voice on Radio 4 holding forth about Noh theatre or Medici Florence or house prices, and like a spy going deep undercover into enemy territory, you entered a world that was a terrible inversion of everything I had taught you to value: a world shaped by toughness, boastful ignorance, firm gender stereotypes, underachievement and the threat of violence.

Your mother, no doubt, would mock me for melodrama.

The school you were at was by no means the worst

in the area, but when I compared the education you were getting to the one I had received, I felt ashamed – of my failings as a father, of my insistence on sticking to an impossible, underpaid profession, and more primitively, of my inability to protect you from unnecessary emotional hardship.

You were like me at your age: slight, undergrown, sensitive, too small to be useful at sports or fighting. But unlike me, you shut down in the classroom. At open days, the bland generic comments of your teachers made me suspect they had difficulty remembering who you were. The needs of boys like you were crowded out by the educational emergencies, the budding sociopaths, the cultural insistence on loud and flash and don't care.

Your trick was to keep your head down. Did you see that I knew that? Somewhere between our front door and the school gates, you became invisible. That was your chosen method of survival. But now this snag: the name – *Lucius*, like a monstrous barnacle on an aerodynamic hull, like a pink feather in a forage cap, was blowing your cover.

What I would give – what wouldn't I give? – to be with you all again. As I was.

Leonora had invited Caspar and Hilary for dinner that night. I was silent for much of the meal, mainly preoccupied with Hunter's letters, though I had other reasons to be charmless, too.

One miserable Christmas, two years earlier, fossicking through my shelves for a top-up present to add to Leonora's exiguous pile (perfume, a diary, Wolford stockings), I opened, of all things, a copy of *Madame Bovary* and out dropped a photograph of Leonora and Caspar, not in a strictly intimate pose, but smiling and entwined, with their linked arms supporting the camera, in a way that made its implications impossible to deny; and, to her credit, she didn't.

Leonora told me at the time that the photo was an old one. We'd had some difficult years after Lucius was born. She said it had been a brief and thoughtless fling and begged me not to pursue it. I did as she asked and tried to be magnanimous about the affair, but it always hurt me the way Leonora lit up when Caspar arrived.

Lately, there had been no closeness between us. I was philosophical about it. The love in marriage turns like the lamp in a lighthouse, leaving you in darkness for long stretches, but it always comes back. I believe that, but I can't tell if it's a thought or a quotation. That's one of the anxieties about the Procedure. That it turns you into a kind of fleshly *Bartlett's*.

Caspar's money has always been part of the problem for me. Leonora doesn't suit the suburban grime of Tooting, or being married to an academic. There's something Notting Hill manqué about her. We battled on afterwards, but my feelings for her became complicated by a demeaning gratitude that she hadn't left me for Caspar; I'd paw at her futilely from my side of the bed, my desire sharpened by the knowledge of her infidelity.

I told the doctors here about it during one of my assessments. Could a total stranger have known that? The detail about *Madame Bovary*? Doesn't that prove I'm me?

There's literally nothing – and imagine my academic aversion to *that* adverb, but here it's justified – *literally nothing* that they will take as evidence. I've raged at them about it. At the formal hearing I tried everything. I harangued them with a desperate curriculum vitae of names, dates, pets, old teachers, addresses, first kisses and favourite colours; but the password to my old life is irretrievably lost. In the end, they forcibly sedated me: six of them held me down and I got a huge shot of Largactil in my backside. I woke up in a seclusion cell two days later with a chemical hangover that was almost as bad as coming round after the Procedure. I only exaggerate a little. I can't go through that again. Apart from anything, I haven't got the time to waste. I've seen how quickly the final lap comes on you when it comes.

Caspar brought the unfamiliar smell of money into our house. With him around – leaving aside for the moment the fact that he'd fucked my wife – you were always reminded that we were living through a potlatch of financial excess. Yet instead of feeling that there was something rather disgusting about the amounts Caspar was earning, I always felt that I was at fault. At that moment in history, to be earning as little as I did, after the education I'd had, seemed like a culpable incompetence.

Hilary said banal things all through the meal, which she barely touched. I think the striking flatness of her personality may simply be the lassitude of someone dwelling constantly in the early stages of starvation. Flushed away by so much colonic hydrotherapy, so etiolated by Bikram yoga that she looked like gristle, she had negated the very plumpness that once made her so attractive. And always the slightly amused glances between them at our unfashionable house and the mess.

'Interior design is not our strong suit,' I said, cringingly, after dinner as we went through to our front room to drink dessert wine.

'One would never have guessed,' Caspar said with failed and mechanical irony, raising an amused eyebrow at our bowing MDF shelves and stained sofa.

Somehow we got onto the subject of education. Caspar and I ended up arguing about grammar schools and the old canard of academic selection. I found myself attacking it in a way that left me shrill and shaky. Caspar was surprised by my vehemence, but then he was probably unaware of the subtext.

Leonora stayed up after they left listening to music and slipped into bed beside me while I was half asleep. She reached across to me, over the two feet of cold sheets that were made colder by our forlorn matrimonial acceptance that that side of things was just not happening at the moment. She touched my shoulder.

'You're grinding your teeth again,' she said.

I grunted an apology and pretended to sleep.

'What is the matter with you?' said Leonora. 'You hardly spoke all evening and then you tear a strip off Caspar for saying something perfectly inoffensive. Behaving weirdly. Sending off for beauty products. Do I have to draw the obvious conclusion?'

'What beauty products?'

'That fancy French face cream on your desk. I thought with your hatred of cliché you would have wanted to avoid anything that smacked of mid-life crisis.'

CHAPTER 3

from: nicholas_slopen@hotmail.com
to: hg@insideoutrecords.com
subject: Johnsoniana
date: 25 April 2009 18.06 BST

Dear Hunter,

I'm sorry it's taken me so long to get back to you, but soon after our lunch, I fell ill with a mysterious ailment that baffled my doctor but which my dentist says is trench mouth. I've finally felt well enough to assess the letters and am attaching a brief report on them. It's a fairly dry biscuit, I'm afraid, as I've used quite a lot of computer analysis to back up some of my assertions, but the results are pretty categorical and I thought I would give you a rough sense of them here.

Of the letters I examined, four are entirely new. Of those four letters, both stylistic and computer analysis strongly suggest that Johnson is the author. But, as your adviser, I have to say that it would be foolish to

41

part with any money unless there's an opportunity to carry out a more detailed examination of the letters themselves. It would enable us to clinch the case either way. There are lots of things that would either support or refute J's authorship – not just the handwriting, but the kind of paper, the postmarks, even whether the letters conform to the conventions of the period which were pretty exacting, partly because of the cost of paper and the expense of postage. I'd be more than happy to do this if you wanted to and were able to arrange it.

There's a further wrinkle to this, which I have only glanced at in my formal report, but which I wanted to share with you. As I said, only four of the letters are genuinely new to me, and the contents of three of them are hardly earth-shattering, but the fourth one has – I don't know exactly how to put it – let's just say there's something potentially exciting about it. Here's the text of it in full. It's undated, which adds to the mystery in my view.

Madam,

You were once so kind as to incourage my hope that you would offer me succour in my hour of dolorous imaginings. I pray that the gulf between us is not so irremeable that you would neglect a promised kindness. The black dog has come upon me. I find myself disordered in my wits. I am deprived of liberty and those who hold me insist that it is for my own good. The bearer of this shall give you directions to try what comfort you may to your most humble servant.

As I mention in the report, the spelling *incourage* and the reference to the 'black dog' both have precedent in other letters of Johnson, but what's interesting about this letter is that Johnson seems to have written it in the middle of a mental breakdown. That's intriguing enough, I think, to make the letter important to his biographers.

What makes it even more interesting is what I take to be its intended recipient and its likely date of composition. Now forgive me if this is all old hat to you. I know you have read widely in the period, but I'm not sure how much you know of Johnson's personal life.

The bulk of Johnson's extant letters were written in the last twenty or so years of his life when he was corresponding frequently with a woman called Hester Lynch Thrale. Hester Thrale was more than twenty years younger than Johnson. She was in her thirties when she met him and by all accounts very charming, and from what we have of her letters to Johnson, very smart. Johnson clearly loved her – whatever you take the word to mean. And when her husband died, there was a rumour that she and Johnson might marry. Now Johnson, as you know, was a deeply troubled fellow, probably suffered from Tourette's, definitely struggled with depression, was scarred from child-hood scrofula etc. etc. – however much of a literary lion he was, he was hardly a catch for a pretty and wealthy young, or youngish, widow. But what happened next scandal-ised the whole of London society. Thrale took up with an Italian music teacher called Piozzi and eventually married him. Johnson wrote her a thunderous letter when he heard the news and, to her credit, she fought back with a very dignified letter of her own. They were reconciled eventually, but never recovered the friendship which had clearly been one of the things that brightened Johnson's life. Johnson died in 1784. It's arguable, I think, that the loss of Hester Thrale's friendship hastened his death.

Again, I apologise if all this is familiar to you, but I repeat it because it seems to me that the letter fits into that late period of Johnson's life, some time after that rift had opened up between himself and Hester Thrale.

The potential importance of this letter makes me, however, suspicious. I'd like to know more about its provenance – are there more?! – and if possible see the original before I give it a clean bill of health.
Best,
Nicholas

CHAPTER 4

My eagerness to establish the authenticity of Hunter's letters wasn't entirely motivated by concern for Hunter. That parenthesis – *are there more?!* – with its jovial and uncharacteristic punctuation concealed a hope so profound that I almost couldn't admit it to myself. It was a silver cord tying me to the ethereal forms of my childhood dreams.

For as long as I can remember, I wanted to be an academic – even before I knew such a word existed. Something with the flavour of old books and libraries, ink, index cards and the silent ingestion of pure knowledge must have been marked on my consciousness at birth, the way a green sea turtle is imprinted with the topographical sense of the beach where it hatched and returns there to lay eggs as an adult.

All my life, I seem to have been trying to recreate some primal ideal of bookishness. While my peers at primary school were playing football, I declared myself the custodian of the tiny school library, embossed my name on a badge with the teacher's label-maker, and spent break time memorising the numbers of the Dewey Decimal System. I was nine. The lid of my school desk was unshuttable because of the books I'd tucked away inside it. And it wasn't just the books. Anything with a sense of ceremony and formality attracted me. My school had an optional uniform that was worn by only one family – Jehovah's Witnesses from Guyana – and me. The fashion of the 1970s meant that my peer group grew their hair long and wore polyester trousers and monkey boots. If a gown and mortar board had been available, I'd probably have worn them too. I insisted on a short back and sides every time I went to the barber. My appetite for books ruined my eyesight and I was delighted when I got my first pair of NHS spectacles at eight.

I sometimes look back at the eccentric figure I cut at school and wonder why I wasn't teased mercilessly. Partly, I suppose, it was because another boy, called Frederick, was the official class oddball. Frederick was being raised by a single mother who was German and who insisted on sending him to school in lederhosen. But even at my next school, a roughish comprehensive, I could count the unpleasant incidents on the fingers of one hand – dinner money stolen once; thumped on the ear and called a gay-boy; a treasured copy of *The Happy Prince* nicked at break time and kicked around the yard until its fluttering pages broke apart and flew upwards in a pathetic parody of escape.

Aged thirteen, I won an assisted place to a fee-paying school with a distinguished history. My baffled music-teacher parents were proud beyond imagining. The school was six hundred years old and maintained a unique pronunciation of Latin and an annual ceremony where boys fought over a giant pancake to win Maundy money. It should have been my Avalon; but I struggled. My wayward education in state schools meant I was behind everyone in languages and maths. I found it hard to make friends. The school boasted of its traditions and the achievements of its ancient alumni, but its ethos was worldly, knowing and fashionable. I was as out of step here as I had been at Spencer Park. I wasn't even particularly clever any more, the realisation of which eroded what had been until then the most reliable component of my identity. To make matters worse, I had terrible acne and yet a voice that stubbornly refused to drop out of its boyish treble until I was seventeen. English lessons, which I'd always looked forward to, I now dreaded in case I was called on to read. At school, my natural peers were the other misfits with whom I played Dungeons and Dragons, and Runequest. At home, I spent most weekends with Frederick, my old lightning conductor from primary school.

All this time, I felt I was in pursuit of something, something that I could not express exactly in words but that I knew was real because I felt it keenly in the stippled drawings of Robin Jacques that illustrated my favourite books of fairy tales; in graveyards and wintertime and the garden of my maternal grandparents' home in Winterswijk; in Tolkien and Carols and the lead figures of paladins and clerics that I assiduously painted for the sessions of D and D; it was on Wandsworth *Common* in a summer evening, and in the overgrown back garden of Frederick's house in winter; the chalk paths of Box Hill were full of it when we went bum-sliding in filthy clothes on our birthdays.

The faint traces of this scent seemed to be linked to a knowledge of life and of the past that was rooted in books and yet, beyond those, it shaded on its furthest side into some inkling of a spiritual life, something that a monk might feel as he warmed his hand over a candle and prayed for his pen to be steady as he copied the holy book. It wasn't until I reached university that this ineffable vibration was finally incarnated in a human being, and I experienced a sense of arrival, of paddling my armoured belly up the sand of a long-remembered beach.

Ronald Harbottle was then fifty-three; his big pompadour greying, but still thick. He had a bearish build and a rumbling bass voice. His cramped room in the corner of Founders' Court was infused with the smells of instant coffee, old book bindings and the honey-centred cough sweets that he ate incessantly. Here, amid a relaxed disorder – stacks of essays spilling off the low table,

49

a life-mask of Keats, invitations weighted onto the mantelpiece with fives gloves, a candle stub stuck on a clay head from Sumatra, uncorrected proofs for a journal article underfoot – Harbottle conducted his supervisions in an atmosphere of reassuring certainty: governments could change and fall, fashions ebb and shift, but this was the centre of the world; the eternal knowledge remained the same – *Piers Plowman*, the works of the Gawain poet, Chaucer, Shakespeare, the Jacobeans, the Metaphysicals, Milton, Pope, Fielding, Austen, Keats and, of course, Johnson. Ah Johnson! If there was a model for Harbottle's wry humanism, a clear and laughing eye fixed on the cold facts of life, scorning cant, embracing truth, refuting sophistry with the toe-punt of the self-evidently real, a vast appetite for food and conversation – Johnson was it. Ron Harbottle's life was shambolic, inefficient, totally lacking in any conception of career, and yet illuminated by his omnivalent curiosity, his spirit of humane endeavour and his generosity to those he taught.

It was Ron who encouraged my habit of keeping a diary in the very words that Johnson uses in the *Life*: 'He recommended to me to keep a journal of my life, full and unreserved. He said it would be a very good exercise, and would yield me great satisfaction when the particulars were faded from my remembrance.' It was a daily commitment I never wavered from, even in the darkest years to come.

My time at university passed in a dream of bliss. The deceits of memory are sometimes more instructive than the truth: every one of my recollected supervisions seems to have taken place at 5 p.m. on a Friday in late October, the gas fire sighing, Founder's Court outside the window slipping into a purple twilight, Harbottle scrutinising my essay through half-moon glasses, then casting it aside and calling on me to unpack my more sweeping statements, go further with my assertions, elucidate my vaguer points. Harbottle would pour us both sherry and keep me beyond the allotted hour to talk further. Flushed with alcohol and approbation, I would keep writing in my hardbound notebook, my handwriting growing more looping and intoxicated, noting down new directions of enquiry, suggested reading. Sometimes Harbottle would go to the shelves, pull off books and throw them at me – books from his personal library, for me to pore over later, trying to decipher the faded pencilled annotations of the master. I learned that he used alchemical symbols as a kind of shorthand and adopted them myself; for instance, marking a turning point in a narrative with the horned squiggle of Mercury in the margin beside it.

I studied to the exclusion of everything else. I was a pale, happy ghost haunting the libraries. I won an outstanding degree and went to the United States for a year. On my return, Harbottle supervised my MLitt and agreed to be my thesis adviser for my doctorate – *Johnson and Judgement: Literary Aesthetics in the Augustan Age*. We collaborated on the articles for the *Quarterly*. I seemed set fair for a glittering academic career at the university. Then disaster.

At three o'clock one morning of the Lent term, the clunky rotary phone which I, as a postgraduate, was now entitled to have in my room began to ring. It was Harbottle. He had made an extraordinary discovery. He needed to see me without delay.

Thirty minutes later, Harbottle arrived in my room, knock-kneed with agitation, and pressed on me a sheaf of handwritten verses. Reversing the usual pattern of hospitality, I had made us both cups of instant coffee. I handed Ron his and looked over the pages. I didn't recognise the handwriting. They were love poems. The first one was titled 'The Milkman of Love'; it described the eponymous milkman doing his rounds in fourteen ten-syllable lines that assonated ABAB . . .

'Extraordinary,' said Harbottle, shaking his head in bafflement. 'Don't you agree?'

I had never seen him in this mood and it disconcerted me that Ron, my mentor, a man of such steady, such Johnsonian discernment, should be unhinged by a handful of sophomoric poems that would have been rejected by any self-respecting student magazine; it gave me the unpleasant sense that the world had wobbled on its axis.

But worse was to come.

'I never thought I'd say it,' Harbottle said, 'but,

as sonnets, they're more achieved, more vital, sounder in aspiration and execution, than anything I've seen since Shakespeare's. They've got a simplicity that recalls the *Lyrical Ballads*. She's stripped the language down to its pith. Even with Shakespeare, we think of the sonnets as his greatest achievements, but did he ever write anything better than "When icicles hang by the wall"?' He sagged into one of a pair of battered armchairs that I used for supervisions – I had just begun to teach a little myself. 'I'm going to take them round to Owen.'

'Owen?'

'Owen Whitchurch, of course. Who else?'

I tried to dissuade him. Whitchurch – a friend to both of us – was emeritus professor of English Literature, and the most visible and public intellectual in the department. More importantly, he was undoubtedly sound asleep. But Ron was adamant. He swigged down his coffee and stood up.

'Do you have to go this minute?'

'Absolutely. This won't wait.'

I tried one last sally to make him reconsider. I directed my whole arsenal of critical weaponry – an arsenal that Harbottle himself had equipped me with – onto the poems and blasted them into smithereens. I pointed out the deficiencies in metre, the staleness of the imagery, the triteness of the rhymes – the spelling mistakes, for god's sake!

Harbottle's face grew stiff and masklike. When

he was quite sure I was finished, he moved closer to me. 'The trouble with you, Nicholas, is that you're too cold-blooded to ever understand real passion. These are the real thing.' He spat the words with a contempt that I had never heard from him before, then snatched up the poems and left.

The poems were the work of a first-year undergraduate called Tilda Swann, with whom Harbottle was having an affair. I, unlike most, was more able to forgive the grotesque conjunction of fifty-seven-year-old man and nineteen-year-old woman than Harbottle's betrayal of his literary judgement. That finely calibrated instrument, trained to measure the lapses of genius in microns, had been usurped by an old man's vanity.

While the affair ended quickly, Harbottle continued to insist on the poems' merit and, in the teeth of derision, proceeded to spend the credibility he'd husbanded over years on getting them into print. *The Milkman of Love and Other Poems* was published in 1993 by a small poetry press. Harbottle's championship of the book gave it a celebrity it would have otherwise lacked. There were profiles of Swann, one in a tabloid paper under the pull-quote 'Me better than Shakespeare? It's all a bit much'. Harbottle gave a special lecture to the faculty on the merits of the poems. I couldn't bring myself to go. The consensus was that Harbottle had lost his marbles. He continued to teach, and even included Swann's poetry in classes he taught on practical criticism, while the undergraduates smirked and nudged each other. But as an academic, he was finished.

More surprising, perhaps, was the effect it had on me. From the moment of our night-time encounter, something changed in me. I went for days without working. Having virtually lived in the University Library for the past four years, I didn't go near it for weeks. I fell ill with a succession of mysterious ailments that kept me from studying or teaching. Each time I opened a book, I felt sick and dizzy. I tormented myself with fearful self-diagnoses: ME, leukaemia, depression. I went back to live at home at the end of term and got a job in the furniture department at Arding and Hobbs. I worked my way up from the loading bays to actual contact with the customers, and after a while, the manager gave me the heady responsibility of arranging the second-hand books with which we dressed the empty shelves of the mocked-up living rooms that were supposed to seduce our customers into paroxysms of spending. Among the duff and tired volumes – mostly *Reader's Digest* condensed books – were now and again one or two of surprising quality. I date the remission of my nervous illness from the moment that I dug a copy of *Her Privates We*, Frederic Manning's wartime novel, and a pristine first edition of *The Ordeal of Gilbert Pinfold* out of a consignment which had been sent in from a charity shop. I sold them both to a rare book dealer for a fiver. It wasn't the money that motivated me to steal them.

Perhaps I felt their predicament resembled mine – their redundancy on the veneered shelves. But I think it was more than that. The Word is alive. We have always known it. But it needs to be uttered, aloud or in the mind of a reader. Without a consciousness to tickle them into life, those books were dead.

It was the stirrings of my recovery. I felt like a sickly patient recovering his appetite and gradually I formed the idea of returning to my academic ambition. I transferred to University College London. But my effortless gift for study had vanished for ever. In its place, there was only drudgery and the fear of failure.

I was like one of those sporting naturals whose talent is instinctive and unrationalised. Having lost something that I had once done wholly by intuition, I had no idea how to regain it. Long before I completed my doctorate – it would take a further eight years – I was sated with Johnson's work to the point of disgust. By then, I was the young father of two and scraping by on a junior lecturer's salary. Those evenings in Founder's Court seemed to belong to another life. I taught a module on the eighteenth century, dragging a class of indifferent students through *The Rape of the Lock*, *Rasselas* and *Gulliver's Travels*. Books which had once been vessels of life-supplying ether, flasks of rare and intoxicating wines, seemed now a vinegary irrelevance. I consoled myself with the specious thought that even if I had retained my

love for the subject, it would have made no difference. The currency of academic success has
changed. Academic departments aren't interested
in scholarship any more. Desperate for sources of
funding, they promote those men and women who
bring large research projects into the faculty.
Writing monographs is nowadays a less valued
skill than filling out grant applications. Solitude,
slowness, patience and exactitude are the opposite
virtues to the ones wanted now.

And yet – *are there more!?* – I hadn't given up
hope that something might turn up.

In the last few weeks of his life, Johnson and his
servant – a freed slave called Francis Barber –
burned bundles of Johnson's personal papers at his
house in Bolt Court. It's one of those terrible
literary autos-da-fé which keep people like me
awake at night. I've always secretly hoped that
someone might have had the presence of mind to
save or make copies of those precious documents.

Hunter's letter had made this hope flare briefly
into life. And the possibility, however remote, of
a cache of undiscovered letters was foundation
enough for a pleasing deskbound fantasy: a large
research project to raise my profile in the department, money from external bodies to fund the
necessary re-evaluation of Johnson's last years; a
professorship and a post teaching elsewhere,
perhaps beside a sighing gas fire, in the relaxed
disorder of Q6, Founder's Court.

CHAPTER 5

from: hg@insideoutrecords.com
to: nicholas_slopen@hotmail.com
cc: sinan@malevinart.org
subject: re: Johnsoniana
date: 26 April 2009 10.05 BST

Hi Nicholas,

Ouch! Trench mouth? I have no idea what that is, but it sounds awful . . .

Thanks for the report. I've passed on your points about the letters to the seller and he's happy for you to take a look at the originals. I'm in NY for the next couple of weeks so I'm copying you both in to this message.

Sinan, Nicholas Slopen is the scholar I told you about who is helping me with my collection.

Nicholas, Sinan Malevin is a very old and dear friend with whom I've worked in the past.

I'm going to let you gentlemen arrange a time for Nicholas to inspect the letters. See you when I'm back from the States.
  Cheers, H

CHAPTER 6

The day after the first May Bank Holiday, I travelled to Green Park by tube to meet Sinan Malevin. The address I'd been given was in St James's Square, which surprised me since, though I knew the area well, I wasn't aware that it housed a rare book dealership. My puzzlement deepened when the destination turned out to be a large Georgian town house on the eastern side of the square that appeared to be a single private dwelling. A discreet closed-circuit TV camera was mounted above its portico and surveyed the handsome patterned tiling that led up to the entrance. As soon as I stepped up from the pavement, the huge glossy black door opened without warning. A tiny woman with a pale face emerged from the gloom behind it. 'Professor Slopen?' she said, in an accent that might have been Russian but that I couldn't at that moment place with certainty.

'It's just Doctor, in fact, but I'm grateful for the promotion,' I said. I was momentarily distracted from the grandeur of the dim interior by the oddness of my host. She was strikingly small and plain, not more than five feet tall, with a plump, unlined and oddly ageless face. Her frizzy hair was pinned up behind her head in a shiny brown corona.

She bustled across the vestibule, her heels clattering on the black and white marble of the floor. I followed her up the staircase, silenced by the vastness of the entrance hall, the profusion of mahogany and marble, gilt mirrors, oil paintings and rococo bronzes, and most of all by the realisation that this building was indeed a private residence.

The woman ascended rapidly, but with a slight limp. Her asymmetric steps beat a muffled iamb on the carpet, which was held in place by glistening brass stair rods. I tried to engage her in conversation by asking her name.

She came to a sudden halt and turned to me, favouring her good leg. 'Telauga,' she said, then once more turned abruptly and resumed her brisk and lurching ascent. When she reached the first-floor landing, she opened a door and gravely announced: 'Dr Slopen is here to see you.'

We entered a room whose scale suggested that it must have once been a ballroom. The three sash windows that gave on to the square seemed almost twenty feet high, and the ceiling above us was at least double height; the room's walls were newly panelled with oak.

'You must be Mr Malevin,' I said, stepping forward to offer my hand to an olive-skinned man of about my age. Malevin was slightly built, with the round-shouldered posture of the bona fide bibliophile, but a slightly dandyish demeanour; he had on an expensive-looking dark blue suit with almost imperceptible jags of white stitching on the collar, and was wearing his rather coarse black hair in a shoulder-length bob.

'Sinan, please,' said Malevin, leaving his hands by his sides and glancing somewhat disapprovingly at my offered hand: 'We will be handling fragile manuscripts. For the same reason, I'm sorry I can't offer you something to drink. Perhaps afterwards.'

'I understand,' I said. 'Is there somewhere I could wash my hands before we start?'

'Vera, take Dr Slopen to the washroom,' said Malevin.

The washroom was of the same baronial opulence as the rest of the house; the faucets of the tub-sized washbasin looked like capstans and dispensed twin geysers of scalding and icy water. Everything was new. The designers had clearly been briefed to recreate the grandeur of a stately home, but without the dog-eared and faded quality that the British upper classes prize as the imprimatur of old money.

When I came back, Malevin was standing with his back to the door, unpacking manila folders from an archive storage box laid out on a long table parallel to the side wall. 'Hunter tells me you are sceptical about the provenance of the letters,' Malevin said, turning towards me with a disarming smile.

'I'm a scholar,' I said, 'and I always like to work from primary sources if they're available.'

'Provenance is everything,' Malevin said, laying the folders out in sequence along the table. I was silent for a moment, noticing for the first time Malevin's white-gloved hands.

'Gloves,' I said.

'A precaution. But one I'm afraid I'll have to insist on. The paper, as you know, is very old.' He handed me a pair of cotton gloves.

'Of course,' I said, conceding to Malevin's request after a hesitation so brief that I hoped it was imperceptible.

'Here they are,' said Malevin, indicating the table spread with its cargo of folders.

I slipped a magnifying glass out of the right hip pocket of my jacket and approached the table. As I opened the first folder, I said casually, 'I hope it's not rude of me to ask, but I've been trying to place you and I can't for the life of me figure out where you're from.'

'Provenance again.'

'Just curious,' I said absently, peering at the handwriting in front of me.

'My family is from Dagestan.'

'Dagestan?'

'It's part of the Russian Federation. We are a republic in the Caucasus,' Malevin said.

'I know. I've read Lermontov. Mountains and vendettas, right?'

'Something like.'

The first folder of letters was indisputably Johnson. It's strange how modern his handwriting is, especially compared to the Jacobeans and the scribble that passes as Shakespeare's signature – the trail of a beetle meandering through inkblots. Johnson's handwriting looks almost contemporary: firm and decisive, like an old-fashioned CEO, or a reforming public-school headmaster. Of course, it altered through his life, weakening and growing more illegible as his health failed. But these were in the mature hand from the years of his fame; the drudgery of his dictionary behind him; some measure of financial security gained; he'd befriended the Thrales and spent restorative weekends at their grand house in Streatham, eating forced peaches and being lionised; he'd acquired Boswell, the friend and biographer whose work would make him immortal.

Absent from the collection was the letter that had most intrigued me: the undated one that I had referred to in my email to Hunter. When I mentioned this omission, Malevin scrutinised the folders on the table and agreed that it appeared to be missing. He went across the room, unlocked a low cherrywood cupboard and wheeled out a trolley packed with a single row of storage boxes. As he began to examine them, the calm of the room was broken by the chirruping of a mobile phone. Though the ring was low and discreet, there was something jarring about the sound in these surroundings, which the furnishings and the technology of scholarship seemed to place in an older and slower century. Malevin took a nickel-coloured device out of his jacket pocket and answered in Russian. He paused with his back towards me, then excused himself and walked quickly out.

For five minutes I sat and listened to the systole and diastole of the large antique wall clock at the rear of the room. I had satisfied myself that the genuineness of the letters I had been able to examine was beyond dispute. Now, with no sign of either host returning, I turned my attention to the trolley of new material. The boxes were numbered with Roman numerals from VI onwards in a sequence that continued from the boxes I had already seen. With scarcely more thought than I would have given to helping myself to mashed potato at my own table, I took the next two boxes in the series and brought them across to the long table for perusal.

It was a moment that I would relive many times over and which would stitch itself to my consciousness like that handful of other moments – my belated first smoky French kiss, proposing to Leonora in the hills above Thrang, cradling Sarah's purple and ventouse-distended head in the operating theatre – that seemed not just to make up the life I have lived, but to constitute the person I have become.

One Christmas, when I was nine and at a loose end around the house, I opened the door of the spare room next to the one I shared with my sister and spied the glistening handlebars of a brand-new bicycle: specifically, a silver Raleigh Chopper accessorised with rear-view mirrors and tassels fixed on the handgrips. Aware that I had violated some kind of taboo, I shut the door immediately, breathlessly, but with the after-image of the bicycle burned on my eyes in such detail that I felt I could have drawn it exactly. For my perennially impoverished and proudly middle-class presents, the Chopper was an uncharacteristically lavish and fashionable present. It surprised a desire in me so deeply felt that I wasn't even aware of it until I opened the door. After that, I could not forget it. I questioned my mother all afternoon about my Christmas presents in the customary way, while she stonewalled me with riddles, which only enhanced my pleasure in the secret possession of my new knowledge. At bedtime, after brushing my teeth, I permitted myself one last peek at the bicycle, this time opening the door to the spare room wider. The bicycle had gone. Baffled, I waited fruitlessly for it to turn up on Christmas Day. The process of disillusionment was gradual, but it became painfully clear that the vanishing bicycle had in fact never existed; it was a kind of hallucination.

Now, opening the first folder from the first of the new boxes, I experienced the same shock I had on opening the door of the spare room and seeing the hallucinatory bicycle. Fortified with decades of adult disappointments, I waited for the elation to pass, for my blast of astonishment to resolve itself into something more trivial, but it only deepened. There in front of me was an autograph manuscript written in Johnson's mature hand entitled 'On Nightmares'.

'Of the evils that afflict a distempered imagination, none chafe with such asperity as the conviction that the seat of reason is itself undone,' it began, and continued on both sides of a dozen closely argued foolscap pages. The next box revealed another cache of undated letters, some of them close to inarticulacy in their heart-rending pleas for assistance. 'These men – nay, pray, do what you can.' And the next, a diary on scraps of paper that reminded me of something out of Gogol in its sense of disorder and persecution. This was a Johnson that everybody knew existed but revealed with an unprecedented clarity and in his own words: melancholic, existentially terrified, trying to beat away the shadows of his own unreason with logic and conviviality, and finally being left on his own to confront the darkness. The writing on the final page tapered away unfinished after the words 'left with little hope, nay none' with a smeared and dwindling line of ink as though the writer had collapsed over the piece of paper.

I gave an involuntary shudder. The two centuries between me and Johnson telescoped to nothing. It came to me forcibly, and for the first time that I could remember, that behind the famous words that had turned Johnson into a monument was a living man who smelled of sweat and woodsmoke, feared death, hunger and madness; whose literary afterlife could be no consolation for the suffering he had undergone in the poor and far-off country of the past.

In my rapture of discovery, I had left my magnifying glass to one side. I collected the glass from the chair where it lay and as I did so, for the first time, I was troubled by the stirring of doubts. Why had Malevin not shown Hunter the prizes of his collection? Why be silent about them? And where had they been for the last two hundred years? Was it really credible that a vein as well worked as this one could contain so much unknown, unimagined material? And it brought up something that had been bothering me from the start: the white gloves. Among library conservators, they are regarded as useless at best. The slight protection they offer is more than offset by the additional clumsiness they impose on the wearer. Malevin was bluffing. The gloves were a piece of theatre.

With a growing sense of anxiety, I scrutinised the papers under the white light of a halogen pocket torch that I had brought for the purpose. My stomach gave a lurch – the door pushed open; this time, no bicycle.

It's a troublesome detail for would-be forgers to remember, but the good ones are usually aware of it: the bulk of paper in the eighteenth century was still what's called *laid*. Laid is the paper of antiquity, it's made using preindustrial processes that produce distinctive rib-marks in the surface. These kinds of markings were absent from most of the Johnson pages. They were smooth and blemish-free. It was unlikely, if not unthinkable, that Johnson would have had access to this quantity of wove – like a writer of the 1960s using a word processor.

Turning over more pages, I was sure now that I had let my hope trump my judgement. And yet the material still rang so true. The forgers had gone to elaborate lengths to fake the text, but there was an extraordinary incongruity between the sophistication of the material and the amateurishness of the physical forgery. Whoever had done it had forgotten to take into account the huge technological shifts that were occurring in Johnson's lifetime. It appeared that the pages had been created by someone working from a job lot of old paper, some eighteenth-century, some early nineteenth-century. Now the ink suddenly looked suspect, and the ageing of the paper had an amateurish feel: tea bags? Candle smoke? There was an absence of dating on all except the most uncontroversial letters; the headings of the diary entries gave only the days of the week, as if the forger was unwilling to risk committing to dates in a verifiable year.

The room suddenly felt close and overheated. I clicked off my torch and stood up. I had a sense of dislocation, as though I had just seen the eyes in a portrait move. Phrases from the pages were still running through my head, yet now I knew the living, suffering man who had been speaking to me was no more than a trick of the light. That figure who had just seemed so close suddenly receded into a familiar image: quaint old periwig-wearing Johnson: '. . . should my testimony from this dark place spare another from a sojourn here.' Amid all the other sensations was a feeling of loss. It reminded me of the quality I had always loved in Johnson: the solace of his fierce, suffering intelligence. Like a rare handful of characters in books, Johnson seems to project a vast empathy back out to the reader; he seems to know what it is like for the reader to live. Wholly pessimistic, he admits and grapples with the dark, unresolvable facts which everyone knows in their hearts to be true, but every age finds its own ways of avoiding: that life is a painful, chronic illness lightened by brief bouts of remission, that death comes stalking remorselessly down every corridor, that the extraordinary disjunctions of human suffering are tragicomic at best, and at worst entirely meaningless. And yet, his preparedness to hold onto these dismal truths performs a kind of alchemy. His moral courage is transformative, a guide and comfort, but also a kind of protection: Virgil leading Dante through Hell, Tinkerbell swallowing the poison meant for Peter, Christ at Golgotha. Like them, his example seems to say: You shall face these things, but you shall not face them alone.

I suddenly heard voices in the hall. It sounded like Telauga. I wondered if Malevin knew about the forgery. He must – and yet the sophistication of the material seemed beyond him. Could Malevin be a victim of the hoax? It seemed unlikely. There was something not right about the whole enterprise. I knew more about Dagestan than Malevin probably suspected. I knew it was a benighted republic full of Islamists and sheep rustlers. The idea that Malevin had made his personal fortune dealing rare books rather stretched credulity. For the first time, it dawned on me that I had uncovered something that might put me at personal risk.

Working as quickly as I could, I returned the pages to the folders, the folders to the storage boxes and then placed the boxes on the trolley at the far side of the room. As I did so, the sounds on the stairs grew louder. This time they were two male voices: Malevin's tenor and a gruffer deep bass. The two men paused outside the door of the drawing room, talking animatedly in Russian.

I sat back down at the table and composed myself. I put the torch back in my pocket, smoothed my hair, and then took out a lens cloth and began polishing my magnifying glass. When I looked up, I noticed with horror that a loose page from the diary had fallen out and was lying among the genuine letters.

The door swung open. 'Did you satisfy yourself?' Malevin asked. Beside him was standing a bull-necked, squat, muscular man in a boxy double-breasted suit and extraordinarily long, pointed Italian shoes. The man walked with a muscle-bound waddle and was holding a gold mobile phone.

'It was a privilege to examine this material,' I said in a tone that I hoped sounded sufficiently awestruck. Malevin beamed, revealing a set of sharp white teeth and a slightly vulpine overbite.

'I'm pleased you say so,' Malevin said. 'This is my associate, Mr Bykov,' he added. 'Mr Bykov, this is Dr Slopen, a famous scholar and *literaturoved.*'

Mr Bykov acknowledged me with a nod. In Russian, he told Malevin that I was puny enough to be a genuine *intelligent* – the Russian word that covers a range of meanings from intellectual to member of the chattering classes. 'Mr Bykov is saying you have the physical characteristics of a real intellectual,' said Malevin, boldly spinning the insult into a compliment as Bykov stood beside him, rolling his neck and shoulders with the loose menace of a wrestler.

'*Ya ponyal,*' I said. '*Nemnozhko govoryu po-russki.*'

Bykov's snap to attention made me glad I hadn't waited any longer to reveal that I understood the language. I didn't want them to say anything compromising in my hearing. It was a lazy asssumption of Bykov's to think that I couldn't understand him.

Malevin felt obliged to massage Bykov's words further. 'What he is saying is in fact correct because anyone can have muscles, but to train the mind is a much longer process. Old Soviet Union was understanding this. My family too are *intelligent*. My father was famous academician.'

'I expect that's where you got your love of books,' I said. I had manoeuvred my body to screen the rogue page from the two men. There was no hope of returning it to its proper place with the rest of the diary, but perhaps I would get a chance to slip it in a folder with some of the other letters.

Malevin flashed another foxy grin. 'In some sense, you are right. And are you perhaps Jewish?'

'No,' I said. 'Are you?'

Malevin laughed, as though instead of merely batting back the question I had made a hilariously implausible assertion of my own. He translated the question for Bykov, who found it funny too.

'We are laughing,' said Malevin, 'because both Mr Bykov and myself are very typical Dagestani men. Very typical physical type, especially for our ethnic group. So for you to say this is a funny suggestion.'

I looked from one man to the other; from Malevin with his slight build and effete hair to Bykov beside him with his dorsal muscles built up into huge meaty flanges. 'You're both typical Dagestani men?'

'Yes!' said Malevin. 'Typical Avar, but one ectomorph, one mesomorph – not same body type. You understand? And because, as you said before, we are a mountain people, Avari are a very

73

pure race. Soviet racial science defined the Avars as purest example of Caucasian type. Very long-living people, because genetic endowment very strong on the whole, but also having predisposition for certain disease because base of DNA not wide like in your country with many invasions and immigration.' Malevin flicked his hair out of his face with his hand. 'Now, if you have finished your work, we shall put papers away and have a drink?'

'I'd love to,' I said, 'but I still haven't had a chance to check that letter we were talking about.'

'Of course. One moment.'

Malevin crossed the room and riffled through the boxes on the trolley. As he did so, Bykov's phone cheeped, and in the second it took him to turn his back and answer it, I slipped the loose page in between two sheets of acid-free tissue paper in the folder of letters nearest to me. Having done that, I felt the immediate danger had passed. I could simply profess ignorance if it turned up, and claim I'd been less than thorough in my examination of the letters.

'Here it is.' Malevin opened the folder and laid the letter in front of me.

It was, as I had suspected, one of the bogus documents; correctly laid out in terms of the period's conventions, which were largely governed by the necessity for squeezing as much as possible on a single page to save on postage – paid, in the eighteenth century, by the recipient – but wholly unpersuasive in terms of the paper it used and the way it had been aged. And yet, even knowing it was a fraud, I was moved again by the pathetic terms of the plea. Estranged from Hester Thrale since her decision to marry an Italian music teacher, Johnson was trying to rekindle the memory of their friendship, begging for her help as he sank towards insanity and death. Writing these words, he may have had only days to live.

I had to check myself. It was a mirage. The figure faded again – and yet, the powerful sense remained that the words were sincere, that behind the ink was a suffering heart. It was an extraordinary deception, simultaneously elaborate and shoddy; as mystifying in its shortcomings as in its strange potency, and clearly beyond the linguistic talents of Malevin and Bykov to pull off.

'Please to stay and have drink with myself and Mr Bykov,' Malevin said, as he returned the letter to its home.

'I would love to,' I said. 'But I need to get home early.'

'On another occasion then.'

Malevin saw me out himself. As we walked downstairs, he quizzed me about my Russian – I learned it at school, choosing it because it was wholly new to my peers and the only subject I wouldn't have to play catch-up in – and I asked him what had sparked his interest in English literature.

'From childhood I loved these writers,' Malevin said expansively. 'Byron, Shelley, Shakespeare, of course – you know Pasternak translated? Johnson I am admiring more and more. His dictionary is very impressive. He is like English Lomonosov. You know? Lomonosov our Russian Johnson, but perhaps more talent because also scientist.'

'*Our* Russian?' I said, emboldened by my proximity to the front door.

Malevin caught the nuance instantly. 'This is an old Soviet habit that I have not eradicated. As you know, Dagestan was part of Russian Empire even in Czar days. Russia export to us Lomonosov, Pushkin and Dostoevsky. In return, they take all Dagestan oil and mineral wealth.' Malevin opened the door onto St James's Square. 'So, if I say "our Russian Lomonosov", it's because my people have paid a lot of money for him.'

There was something unmistakably hostile in the way he said the words, as though he had decided to forgo the polite theatre that had characterised the visit and to leave me in no doubt that I was dealing with a man of great will and acuity. The point was underlined when I looked back across the square from beside the steps of the London Library and saw Malevin waving to me from the portico. In the context of our last exchange, the location and the surreally vast house, the gesture seemed not only an assertion of wealth and status but also, even if only subliminally, a threat.

CHAPTER 7

from: nicholas_slopen@hotmail.com
to: hg@insideoutrecords.com
subject: Emergency
date: May 5 2009 16.43 BST

Dear Hunter,
  Something's come up and I need to
speak to you ASAP. Can you call?

from: hg@insideoutrecords.com
to: nicholas_slopen@hotmail.com
subject: re: Emergency
date: May 5 2009 16.50 BST

Hi Nick,
  Phone coverage very patchy here. What
up? Sinan emailed to say you loved the
material, best, H

from: nicholas_slopen@hotmail.com
to: hg@insideoutrecords.com
subject: re: re: Emergency
date: May 5 2009 23.45 BST

Well, yes, I told Sinan exactly what I felt – which is that I spent the most extraordinary hour of my life examining the letters. There is stuff there that could blow a hole through our current ideas about Johnson: new letters, an essay in manuscript that is completely new, a diary that Johnson kept during a prolonged bout of mental illness, as well as the material we'd seen the transcripts of. It's fair to say that any Johnson scholar would give their right arm for this stuff. I've been waiting my whole life to discover something like this. And you know what? I'm still waiting.

I'm sorry to have to say this, but it's my belief that your friend Sinan is a party to fraud.

I feel very far out of my comfort zone with this. I think we should call the police.
Nicholas

CHAPTER 8

S arah. My firstborn. My sacrifice. You were conceived in love. I was twenty-four years old when I held you for the first time, and by the standards of the middle classes in our era, a child myself.

You were prematurely wise and verbal. No blessing, I can assure you. When you were barely four, you looked at me one bedtime and asked, 'Dad, am I just a body?' I fobbed you off with equivocations: '. . . some people believe.' Now, finally, I am in a position to answer properly: not even that much. I am a living refutation of Descartes. I am a codable sequence of proteins. I am a mind's shadow. *Someone is building God in a dark cup.*

Once your mother was pregnant, there was really no alternative to marriage. Her parents had fled the Iranian revolution and considered themselves very westernised, but a termination was out of the question. The truth is, we never considered it. I felt blessed by you. And lucky to be with your mother. My sentimentality now sounds so conventional. All fathers feel this. As though we've been coded for the Procedure. Malevin's dad was right. What we think of as unique in us is infinitesimal. We can be coded in a few days. That's the madness of this. Instead of propelling our tiny differences into an infinitely extended future in carcass after carcass – and please, Hunter, could we discuss the ethics of *that*? – oughn't we to celebrate our sameness, our commonalities? The truth is we are virtually identical. We are interchangeable. That is the true beauty of humanity: ant beauty, not peacock beauty. We persuade ourselves that we are unique, but the typologist of human experience would have his work done in an afternoon. Every father weeps at his daughter's wedding, knowing that the tiny sugar plum he held at her birth is being entrusted to another man. Though, come to think of it, Bahman was dry-eyed at ours. Always the slow-burning disapproval. Even my editorship of the letters failed to impress him. He said it was a political decision to award it to someone so young, adding belittlingly that it was the unflashy kind of scholarship that gets you nowhere nowadays.

It was Bahman's sloe gin that I got drunk on on the night I sent that email to Hunter. I didn't drink much ordinarily – a lot less than my nominally Muslim father-in-law – but those letters had lit a fire in my heart that could only be doused with alcohol. I turned a sticky shot-glass of the sloe gin in my fingers and held it up to my desk-lamp. It was an inky purple colour and smelled like cough medicine. Away from the cone of light that shone on my desk, the room shaded into a sloe-coloured darkness. The house was so quiet that I became aware of the breath sighing through my nostrils. It sounded like a prelude to weeping.

I'm sorry . . . I had written, but for whom was I sorry? For Hunter? For my children, whose private education would not now be paid for by a ground-breaking reassessment of Johnson that I would not now write based on the new material that didn't actually exist? For Leonora, whom I seemed doomed to encumber forever with my miasma of failure and gloom? For myself, most fundamentally. That old dream of beauty had flared up again. For those first seconds, those yellowing pages had been gold leaves in a pharaoh's tomb, feathers on a new genus of bird, golden sand on an undiscovered shore, as if – I rubbed my eyes and poured another glass of sticky gin – as if I lived to be redeemed by a fistful of two-hundred-year-old letters.

Fifteen minutes after I had sent the email, the phone in my study rang.

'Nicholas, it's me.'

If I had been sober enough to notice at the time, I might have found it faintly sinister that Hunter had been able to get hold of a phone number which only a handful of people ever used and which, moreover, was unlisted. As it was, my overriding emotion was one of relief.

'I'm slightly alarmed by the tone of your email,' Hunter went on. In spite of his profession, Hunter has no actual musical talent that I'm aware of, but he has a gravelly ex-smoker's voice which he can modulate like a cello; now he played its warm brown tones to evoke the reassuring hug of a big brother. 'I know Sinan very well and I can tell you, Nicholas, he's absolutely on the level.'

'I'm glad you say that, Hunter, but there's something odd going on. He's sitting on a big stash of forged material. Most of it's on wove paper. He's using these pointless gloves. I don't like it one bit.' Somewhere inside me, a sober Nicholas listened aghast to the drunken, nasal sound of my own voice. I struggled to order my thoughts and vainly took swipes at them: Telauga, the house, cherrywood cabinets, Bykov, the missing letter; but I sensed I was thrashing at the point I wanted to make, and only burying it deeper.

'Listen,' said Hunter, 'I finished my business ahead of schedule. I think the best thing is if we meet tomorrow. Get some sleep. Don't do anything hasty. And let's put our heads together on this over lunch. I'll meet you at the Wolseley at one.'

The next day, like a pair of boxers who are unwilling to engage in the unpleasant business of trading blows, Hunter and I spent the first fifteen minutes of our lunch circling each other. He asked about my trench mouth and I explained the condition owed its ghastly name to its frequent occurrence in soldiers in the First World War. It was also known as Vincent's disease, I said, and was

82

caused by an overgrowth of certain bacteria that are normally present in the mouth but which in large quantities cause tiny ulcers to appear all over the soft tissue of the gums and tongue. The upside, I told him, was that I'd lost half a stone because I hadn't been able to eat solid food.

'The upside to any illness', said Hunter, 'is that you feel close to it.'

'Close to the illness?' I was only half listening because I was very hungover and reading the menu to see which, if any, of the foods I could contemplate eating without my stomach giving a wrench of disgust.

'To IT.' Hunter's eyes scanned me eagerly for a response. 'Do you have any idea what I'm talking about?'

'No,' I said. 'None.'

'There's a thin membrane between this world and our real spiritual lives, and when you become ill, that membrane gets stretched very thin.'

'If you say so,' I said pettishly.

'Not because I say so.' Hunter smiled and picked up his menu. 'I get it: this conversation is embarrassing you.'

He was only partly right. I was preoccupied with the issue of the letters, but in general there was nothing I felt like discussing less than the alleged membrane between myself and the spirit world. It smacked of table-tapping, ectoplasm, gimmicky séances, sad people who find reality insufficient, and I said something along these lines to Hunter.

My scepticism not only did not put Hunter off, it positively incited him, the way coquettish indifference is supposed to provoke ardour in a would-be lover.

'Reality isn't insufficient,' he insisted. 'Reality is greater than you can have any inkling of. I'm speaking only of the real. The *réal* – you know what it means in Spanish, of course. *Réal* is royal. Reality is king.'

Then he said something strange, the significance of which didn't dawn on me until much later. He looked me straight in the eye and said: 'Have you known much death, Nicholas?'

It was a question I didn't feel like exploring with him, not then, probably not ever.

My father was technically a Victorian. He was born in 1899 and was in his seventies when I was conceived. I remember him in my early childhood as he subsided into old age, playing the piano less and less, but always taking pleasure in his teaching. He died in 1985, peacefully, at home.

It was a relief for me to learn that while women are born with a full complement of eggs in their ovaries, men generate fresh sperm throughout their lives. But I have often wondered if a lot about my sister and myself is explained by the fact that we were the belated product of nineteenth-century testicles.

My mother was more than forty years younger than my father. At his funeral, my sister and I met various middle-aged half-siblings, who

84

had children around our age. My mother died suddenly when I was at graduate school. She had been predeceased by my sister Emily who died of leukaemia at the absurdly young age of nineteen.

Since I was very young, I've known what it is to live under the shadow of death, in the expectation of bereavement; to look ahead and experience the vertiginous sense of being suspended in time. For all our differences, Hunter and I had this in common. And it was only much later, when I began finally to acknowledge our unexpected kinship, that I began to understand him.

But for now I brushed his question aside.

'Speaking of reality, Hunter,' I said. 'We need to discuss these forgeries.'

That word, *forgeries*, caught Hunter in the act of swallowing a sip of water. He pursed his lips as though he'd been surprised by something extremely hot and wagged his finger at me until it cleared his throat. 'Not forgeries.'

'Not forgeries? What are you talking about? I've seen them.'

'I just want to reassure you, there's no question of their being forgeries.'

'Now I'm puzzled,' I said. 'I thought *I* was supposed to be advising *you* about that.'

'It all depends what you mean by a forgery,' Hunter said mysteriously.

We suspended our discussion while the waiter came to take our order. I declined to order any food, as much from principle as indisposition: I had already resolved to tear up Hunter's cheque. Hunter said he'd have seared scallops and rack of saltmarsh lamb. Looking back, I'm certain he was rattled, because he'd forgotten to bring his copper flask of special water.

'What I mean by a forgery', I said, when the waiter had gone, 'is a falsified document that is intended to deceive someone. I saw box after box of bogus Johnson material in Malevin's house.'

'But none that he was actually intending to sell,' said Hunter, doing his best to assume a got-you face.

'Well, one of the letters was intended for you. I've no idea who the other material was intended for.'

'If it's not intended to deceive anyone, is it still a forgery?'

'You think Malevin is creating this stuff as a kind of hobby? To amuse himself ?'

'I understand your anger,' said Hunter, bowing the lowest, most soothing strings of his voice. 'And I respect it. I give you my word that Sinan's deceit – if that's the right word – wasn't intentional. You really don't need to worry about it any more than that. You've been more than conscientious. Nicholas, I've got to ask you to just let this go.'

'Let it go? This is serious counterfeiting. As an academic, how could I live with myself if I let Johnson's legacy be cheapened by a load of fakes? I respect reality as much as you do. More, apparently.' I found myself surprisingly invigorated by my sense of outrage.

Hunter rapped his fingers on the table top and sighed through his nostrils. 'Okay. Look: frankly, I was hoping that a night's sleep and my reassurance that this is all above board would be enough to persuade you to ease up, but I see you've decided to play the crusader card.' He pulled his phone out of his jacket. 'Give me one second.' He turned away slightly from the table to make the call. 'Hey. I'm with Nicholas now. He's still worried about the stuff.' There was a pause while he listened. 'We'll be straight over.'

He stood up. 'Let's go.'

I was impressed in spite of everything that Hunter was able to settle the matter of the pending food order with a single glance to the maître d'.

'We'll walk,' said Hunter. 'It'll give me a chance to explain.'

The sun was breaking through after a morning of heavy showers as we negotiated the slick, rain-darkened streets between our abortive lunch on Piccadilly and St James's Square. Duke Street and Jermyn Street seemed to grow taller in the sunlight, stretching skywards like the nave and transept of a gold-roofed cathedral.

Finally, something in Hunter seemed to relent. He lowered his head. 'You're absolutely right, of course,' he said, disarmingly. 'The bulk of that material is not by Johnson at all.'

'Then you know who forged it?'

'It wasn't *forged*. It was *written* by Vera Telauga's brother Jack.'

'Come on, Hunter.' I rolled my eyes at him. 'Don't insult my intelligence. That's pure sophistry.'

'I spent two semesters at law school before I signed my first band,' said Hunter. 'For a crime to be committed, there has to be *mens rea*, criminal intent. Sinan never intended to sell any of those documents. I think you'll understand all this better once you've had the chance to meet Jack Telauga.' Hunter refolded his silk scarf and tucked its ends inside his overcoat. 'He's a savant. I've never seen anything like it. You can't get a word out of him in conversation. He sits there doing nothing, barely able to do up his own laces – I think Vera has to bathe him. But put a pen in his hand and this is what comes out.'

'I know what a savant is,' I said tartly. 'But I don't believe you.'

'Which is why Sinan and I concocted our story about the papers. I wouldn't buy anything from Sinan – more to the point, why would he need to sell? You've seen his house. Sinan is a good guy. He's taken care of Vera and her brother for years. Jack's been checked out by all kinds of specialists. He's physically fine, but he's barely there mentally. Sinan didn't even know he could read. We have no idea how he's able to produce this work. It was my idea to show the material to a Johnson expert, to see what a professional made of it. I got Googling

88

and a few names came up. You were the first to bite. So, we had our lunch. You know the rest. Sinan and I never wanted you to look at the originals, but you're so conscientious.'

'And the fake paper? The white gloves?'

'Jack will only write on certain kinds of paper. And, yes, we aged some of it to look more plausible when you decided you needed to see them. And of course, at some level, I think Sinan wanted you to see the handwriting, to see how really amazing this guy is. He writes at full speed, Nicholas, it's beyond incredible. He's a phenomenon.'

This time, when we reached the house on St James's Square, Malevin answered the door himself. He was wearing a pale linen suit and a lilac shirt. He greeted Hunter with obvious warmth.

'Sinan, this is what happens when you leave curious people unsupervised,' Hunter said, embracing him and giving him a bearish back-slap.

Malevin waved us over the threshold.

The opulence of the house seemed even more pronounced on this visit, but the mood was oddly relaxed. Malevin escorted us into the study on the first floor. 'Happily,' said Malevin, 'I am able to offer you coffee on this occasion.'

'No valuable manuscripts to damage?' I asked.

Hunter had picked up an auction catalogue from one of the shelves and was flicking through it. 'I'll take an espresso, Sinan,' he said.

'You are quite correct', Malevin said, 'that we

have been guilty of some deceptions.' He leaned towards the intercom on his desk and asked someone to bring in three espressos.

Hunter closed the catalogue and put it back on the shelf. 'Nicholas, I want you to know that when we embarked on this, we had no notion that we'd end up here. In fact, if we had, I doubt whether we'd have gone ahead with it. Your doggedness has put us in a difficult position. The fact is that the truth of this situation is much stranger and more complex than you can imagine.'

A few moments later, the door opened and both Bykov and Vera Telauga came in. Vera clumped across the room with her stacked heels and stood by the fireplace. Bykov was carrying a tray with four espressos on it. He gave a coffee to each of us, starting with Vera and finishing with his employer. Malevin emptied his in a single gulp and looked at his watch. 'Vera, is your brother awake?'

She set her cup on down and turned her blank moon-face towards him. 'He is.'

Malevin stood up. 'Come, you will see for yourself.'

Behind the main staircase was a concealed door leading to a narrow and undistinguished set of stairs into the basement. For a moment, it crossed my mind that I was walking into a trap. While I dismissed the anxiety at the time, hindsight reveals it to have been, in the broadest sense, prescient.

The basement was spacious but devoid of natural

light and clearly intended as a kind of servants' accommodation. It was paved with granite and lit with fluorescent tubes.

Malevin led us all to a door and then stood aside to let Vera Telauga unlock it with a key she carried in a pocket of her dress. 'It's better if Hunter and I stand here. The room is not spacious and . . .' He tailed off briefly. 'And Jack has a sensitive disposition.'

You always forget the aura a living body has, even a carcass. He sat on a narrow bed along one edge of the room, his body turned away from the door. It was his shoulders I noticed first, rocking protectively over a crumpled sheaf of papers, stirring and twitching, like an animal in a stable. He gave the impression of great mass. He was powerfully built and the confined space exaggerated his physical presence, his slumped muscularity. He was wearing dark tracksuit bottoms and a navy blue sweatshirt. He didn't look up, but from what I could see, there was no family resemblance to Vera Telauga. He had a huge shaved head like a granite boulder and slack grey cheeks. The most astonishing thing of all, of course, I wasn't aware of – we never are: he had life in him.

Looking at that lump of man, ostensibly Telauga's brother, I felt a chill come over me. Or is that image, which verges on cliché, simply a proleptic interpolation of mine, knowing as I do that he was not Telauga's brother, and the man I was then is

91

now dead? I derive no comfort from these awful paradoxes.

The room was brightly lit. The smell, faintly faecal, with an overriding note of disinfectant, is one that I have grown familiar with in the Dangerous Humans Unit. There was a lamp on a low table. A tiny barred window onto an internal courtyard. A chair. A jug of water. An old prayer book. Vera spoke to him in a cheery voice, telling him he had a visitor, but there was a wariness in her movements that spoke more eloquently of some residual fear. I sat opposite him in the chair and greeted him. There was no indication that he'd even heard me.

'Don't be offended by his silence, Dr Slopen,' Vera said. 'My brother is mute.'

I tried again to talk to him – nonsensical stuff. I said I had heard a lot about him, that we shared an interest in the works of Johnson, but I felt self-conscious and false – as though I were talking to a gerbil or a hat-stand. He continued to rock slightly back and forth, as if he found the motion soothing. The papers were gathered in his left fist. In his right was a bunch of pens – a fountain pen, some biros and a Pentel.

All the while, Vera was busy around the room, pretending to tidy, but clearly listening to our conversation. I asked her if I could be with him alone for a moment. She assented, and pointed out the panic button under the light switch. Then she left the room.

Naturally, I didn't think the two of us had any real privacy. I was sure we were being eavesdropped on somehow, but I wanted to be with him without the distraction of Vera's physical presence in the room.

I repeated some of the things I'd said before. Nothing altered in the rhythm of his rocking, or his slow, open-mouthed breathing. I believe it crossed my mind then that he'd been heavily sedated for my visit. The grip he had on the papers was unnaturally tight, as though he was clinging onto them to prevent himself dropping into unconsciousness.

Not a word I said made any impression on him. I tried to think of a poem that he might recognise. The only poem I could summon up at that moment was by Milton:

> *For Lycidas is dead, dead ere his prime,*
> *Young Lycidas and hath not left his peer:*
> *Who would not sing for Lycidas? he knew*
> *Himself to sing and build the lofty rhyme.*
> *He must not float upon his watery bier*
> *Unwept, and welter to the parching wind,*
> *Without the meed of some melodious tear.*

I don't know if I remembered it exactly. The poems that mean most to me are from the centuries closer to my own – and tend to be ones that I've kept separate from my academic studies. But 'Lycidas' has always had a resonance for me because of a friend of mine who drowned in an accident in Cornwall a long time ago. And I've always loved the downright eeriness in Milton that disappears from the mainstream of English poetry until the Romantics. *Comes the blind fury with the abhorred shears and slits the thin-spun life.*

And the truth is that reciting a poem was a restorative for me. There is something talismanic about familiar words. Once or twice, I've mumbled a prayer or a poem over my sleeping children as a clumsy form of blessing. I think I wanted to give this poor, broken madman something, even if it was only words. Which, in a way, is exactly what Milton was doing: the meed of some melodious tear isn't much, in the circumstances, but sometimes it's all we've got.

Of course, Johnson hated 'Lycidas'. In a story of many ironies, it's not the biggest, but it's worth remarking on. He was, *pace* Boswell, cool on Milton generally, found the Parnassian arrogance unattractive – who doesn't? – and the republicanism unforgivable; but he singled out 'Lycidas' for the big guns of his critical displeasure.

I was about halfway through, stumbling a bit over the words, when I noticed that the man had stopped rocking. I slowed down, because I knew I was reaching the end of what I remembered. As I came to the last line of the passage, he turned his body and stared at me. I was seized by a kind of panic as I saw that he had the haunted and knowing eyes of a caged ape. He opened his mouth and a low, strangulated sound came out. Then he raised his huge body slowly from the bed and moved towards me with his big arms outstretched.

The door opened before I could reach the panic button. Bykov tackled the man and threw him onto the floor. The papers and pens flew out of his hands. I felt Malevin guide me out of the room. As I glanced down, I could see one of the crumpled pages under my foot. In a faultless imitation of Johnson's mature hand, the first two words read: 'Abhorrent machine'.

Malevin was very apologetic about the outburst. He said Jack hadn't been himself lately. Those were his actual words, and, in a way, the truest ones he'd spoken. The hangover of adrenalin in my bloodstream made the floor feel rubbery under my feet. 'I'm sorry if he frightened you,' said Malevin.

Upstairs, in that vast ballroom, there seemed little to add, but I wanted to know why they had bothered with the authentication.

Malevin looked unaccountably pleased with himself. 'We were curious to know if the pastiches he produced were capable of fooling an expert.'

'And did you get your answer?'

'We did. Of the twelve letters you certified as genuine, eleven were Telauga's work. Only one was by Johnson.'

'I didn't authenticate them,' I said, suddenly aware of a thin, shrill note in my voice.

'You didn't raise any questions about them. On

the basis of the content and the handwriting, you assumed they were by Johnson himself,' said Hunter.

I stared at him, suspended somewhere between outrage and disbelief. I've never been good at being wrong. The juggernaut of my intellectual vanity stops slowly and backs up even slower. The shame of it induced a strange hallucinatory sensation of disembodiment.

'Our priority is Jack's well-being,' Hunter went on. 'The third volume of the Johnson letters must be scheduled for publication pretty soon. Sinan and I have no intention of embarrassing you, Nicholas. I think it's best for all of us if we quietly bury this episode.'

'I have no objection to that,' I said faintly.

Somewhere outside, above the leaden clouds, I seemed to hear the ghost of Ronald Harbottle laughing at my discomfiture.

CHAPTER 9

Extracted from Dr Webster's Journal

Patient Q. Sectioned for assessment last month. Admitted to DHU with paranoid psychosis and severe ideational disturbances. His name and identity unknown. Maintains he is an academic called Nicholas Slopen who in fact died last year in a road traffic accident. Originally detained under Section 4 after a pattern of stalking and threatening behaviour directed towards deceased's wife.

Client is in fact extremely knowledgeable about English literature, and educated to at least degree level. In our first interviews, he comes across as lucid and articulate – and somewhat patronising. He clearly regards me as his intellectual inferior. I'm uncertain whether his arrogance is a pre-existing personality trait or a component of his manic defence. It's only when pressed on the question of his identity that he begins to exhibit the pronounced delusional behaviour.

I point out that the man he claims to be is, undoubtedly, deceased.

Q remains silent for some time. Then says: 'I could a tale unfold whose lightest word/Would harrow up thy soul, freeze thy young blood/ Make thy two eyes like stars start from their spheres.'

Q seems pleased when I recognise the quote as Shakespeare; less pleased when I refer to the large body of work that raises questions about the identity of 'Shakespeare' and the likelihood of his being the author.

He becomes agitated. Maintains loudly that 'Shakespeare is Shakespeare, and I am Nicholas Patrick Slopen.' His intransigence over Shakespeare possibly a reaction-formation to manage anxieties over own false identity?

Our interview degenerates after this. He exhibits marked contempt for my opinion, then rounds on me and attacks me as a quack scientist. Maintains violently that he is the deceased man and repeats a number of slurs about the dead man's wife. Eventually the restraint team intervene and the interview is terminated.

Two days later, Q approaches me in the common area and apologises for his outburst. This time he offers of his own accord to submit to testing. I subsequently administer Rorschach tests, Minnesota Multiphasic Personality Inventory, Thematic Apperception Test, Rotter Incomplete Sentence test, and further quantitative tests of my own devising to establish degree of psychosis.

Client clearly enjoys tests, and though he tries, he's not quite able to hide the grandiose and manic behaviour that accompanies high scores on standard IQ and word association tests.

Q presents an administrative dilemma for the ward as, at the time of writing, we are yet to establish his true identity. Police have checked his fingerprints and DNA against all existing databases.

One week later, Q returns confidently and tells me he is willing to 'come clean'. He proceeds to give a long and detailed account of what he now says is his true identity. He claims his name is Paul Noble and that he is a single, childless teacher of English as a foreign language. He says he returned from a TEFL school in Turkey after falling out with the headteacher. On his return he became depressed and began drinking and gambling. Claims he had the idea of taking on the dead man's identity to avoid consequences of paying gambling debts.

The story seems superficially plausible, but doesn't explain pattern of psychotic behaviour towards Ms Kazemzadeh.

Informal checks with TEFL reveal no record of a Paul Noble, a Philip Paul Noble, or any of the permutations of the name that Q suggests.

Q becomes quite crestfallen and attempts to talk his way round various discrepancies in his stories.

I tell him that TEFL do have a record of a Patrick Philip Noble teaching in a school in Istanbul.

Q maintains this is him and that the record-keeping at the school was notoriously slack.

I reveal that Patrick Philip Noble is a made-up identity of my invention and tell him he's clutching at straws.

Q becomes angry and abusive. Reverts to previous claim that he's Dr Slopen. Repeats a number of slurs about a prominent record producer. Restraint team forced to intervene and medicate.

Q responds well to medication. Subsequently displays contrition for outburst. This time, when questioned on identity, says he thought he was Dr Slopen, but clearly can't be as Dr Slopen is dead. Q offers the conclusion that this must mean he, Q, is suffering from mental illness. Q suggests no alternative theory as to his identity. He seems open to suggestion that he may be suffering from amnesia or head trauma. MRI and subsequent tests all negative for abnormalities, though recent scar tissue around occipital cranial area suggests some kind of contusion within the last twelve to eighteen months.

Q avoids socialising with other clients, but issues surrounding his identity aside, his condition has stabilised. As a reward for amelioration, Q is offered and accepts computer privileges. No workstations within DHU so I suggest he uses mine for an hour a day. I ask him what he will work on. He is resistant to answering initially, but then concedes he is interested in learning more about debate over Shakespeare's authorship. His progress continues to be satisfactory.

CHAPTER 10

For the last five minutes, Dr Webster has been skulking around her office looking for 'some papers', but clearly spying on me. I wonder if her interest is purely professional, or connected to the fact that I hacked into her account yesterday, from where I copied and pasted the above notes on her poor, loopy – and *surely* composite – patient Q.

It's taken me a few weeks to figure out what her password might be. Incredibly, it's this: *bacon*. That's the level of imaginative deficiency you've got with the anti-Stratfordians.

The strong temptation is to begin every session here with the words 'The irony is . . .' I'm poor in everything but ironies, and to be truthful, I've forgotten what's so good about irony in the first place. It's just the resting state of the universe. Johnson puts it best in a section I *can* recall from memory. 'The real state of sublunary nature,' he calls it, 'in which, at the same time, the reveller is hasting to his wine, and the mourner burying his friend; in which the malignity of one is sometimes defeated by the frolic of another; and many mischiefs and many benefits are done and hindered without design or purpose.'

But the truth is that the irony he describes in those easy pairings – revellers sharing the world with mourners, Wile E. Coyote foiled by the Road Runner's cheery energy – is simply the last available meaning before the significance of anything decays to random chance. *Many mischiefs and many benefits are done and hindered without design or purpose.* Good becomes bad, bad good; love degenerates to dullness and senseless animosity. Irony is not order, but it gives a shape to things. We can't believe that a rational God had a hand in this chaos, but we're not quite ready to sign up to the devastating truth of Johnson's last line. Our faith in irony is a sticking plaster to restore our loss of Faith in its larger sense. God is not just, perhaps, but his grasp of irony shows that at least he has a sense of humour. That is supposed to be comforting.

I've tried to tell the truth since the moment I got here, but the baroque involutions, the doublings and false corridors of my story have clearly done me no favours with the chumps who run this place; even to me, as I relive it, it resembles some half-understood allegory – a form that I loathe. I know it partakes of the comic – necessarily: the conventions of genre are not shared by the true state of sublunary nature – but it is not funny. In the end, only two facts stand out to me with absolute clarity: I love my children and I'm going to die. And then again, of whom has that not been true?

The first week of my incarceration, I began a letter to Lucius and Sarah in which I attempted to set out briefly what I believe has happened to me. I had to stop after a few paragraphs. Now, addressing myself to the same question in this longer form has led me to wonder whether, even if it were possible, it's *desirable* for them to know my story. Better perhaps for them to believe what the world believes: that their father died in a road traffic accident. Although there is a larger ethical principle at stake. What was done to Jack was wrong. Whichever Ivan or Mikhail or Dimitrii they have parked me in must have been taken by force or deception and dispossessed of everything he had. I may be, broadly speaking, the beneficiary of the deed, but that doesn't make me blind to its depravity.

The three hundredth anniversary of Johnson's birth involved me in a host of academic obligations, colloquia, symposia, *festschriften* – even television programmes. I gave a talk at Johnson's house in Gough Square and addressed the Streatham Historical Society when they unveiled a plaque outside the Samuel Johnson, a pub with no connection to the man, and whose illiterate and violent clientele present us with another joyless irony. There was a slew of new biographies, capitalising on the rare currency of their subject; and the third volume of my edition of the *Letters* was due to be published in December. In the end, the book would miss its deadline and publication would be set back to the following year, but I spent the second half of May revisiting the letters as I began the slow work of proofreading and finalising the indexing.

The last section of the book includes a number of undated letters that have turned up since the Hyde edition of 1992–4, as well as the letters of 1784 which Boswell suppressed because of their unpleasant content. In them, Johnson recounts at painful length his struggles with asthma, dropsy and insomnia. I was working off new transcriptions in many cases, some of which I'd made during a two-month sabbatical in America. One was a defective fragment that I had found in the Beinecke Library. I give it in Chapman's 1952 version as my own is unavailable to me:

> *. . . bleeding, and Physick, and . . . innumerable Miseries. There are many Ups and Downs in the world, and my dearest Mistress, I <have?> been down, and up, and down again. When you are up again, keep up.*

As I pored over it in mid-May, a week or so after the encounter at the St James's Square mansion, it struck me how inferior it was *qua* Johnson to Jack Telauga's work. And yet it is undeniably the real thing. Where are the sonorous Latinisms of Johnson in his pomp? All gone; all lost; instead only weak little words, and the desperate, failed attempt to think up a sustaining apophthegm – and is there a scoutmaster or an agony aunt on earth who would demean themselves to the point of offering *when you are up again, keep up* as counsel to the bereaved and hopeless? The wisest man in English letters is reading us the contents of a fortune cookie. It is tragic in the truest sense: the young lose their youth, the beautiful their beauty and the wise their wisdom.

I had mentioned nothing to anyone about my work for Hunter or the meeting with Jack Telauga. The episode was simply too humiliating, too redolent of failure, too reminiscent of Ron Harbottle's catastrophic lapse.

From here, the DHU, fetid antechamber to the afterlife, I see that one of the most harmful patterns in my previous existence was my pose as an emotionally invulnerable intellectual. It flattered me and concealed my hurt and resentment at the world; but like all such damaging routines it was barren and self-perpetuating. How different things might be today if I had been able to admit someone else to the sanctum of my fear and worry.

But over the next few days, the immediate sting of embarrassment lessened. I found a new freshness in Johnson's writing; there was less drudgery and more horripilation. As I read, I thought of Telauga's wounded eyes, and the ghostly voice of the forged letters: *abhorrent machine.*

★   ★   ★

106

On the weekend of the second May Bank Holiday, Leonora took the children to visit her parents in Oxford. I stayed in London, ostensibly to catch up on work and marking. On the Monday morning, I cycled across Clapham and into the West End with a leather-bound copy of Fanny Burney's *Evelina* and a box of alphonso mangoes. There were Bank Holiday crowds along Piccadilly and outside the Royal Academy, but St James's Square was quiet.

Vera Telauga answered the door in slippers. I told her that I was just passing by and wanted to drop off some small gifts. Her face betrayed no surprise. She invited me in.

'My brother is asleep,' she said, as she led me into that enormous drawing room.

'I hope you don't mind my visiting,' I said. 'I've been thinking about your brother a lot. Johnson takes up a large part of my waking life. It's rare to find such commonality of interest with anyone. Even among scholars. Last time I was at a conference, all anyone wanted to talk about was *The Wire*.'

'I don't know to which wire you are referring,' she said. 'But then I am a stranger in your country.' She tucked her feet under herself as she sat. Bykov slouched in carrying two espressos on a tray and some Spanish biscuits. 'You were impressed with his work?'

'More than impressed. It's extraordinary. I'm very curious to read some of his other writing. Does he only write in that style?'

'Yes, only Johnson,' she said. 'It's a form of savantism, as Hunter explained.'

'How did it come about? I mean, his first language is Russian, right?'

She looked slightly uncomfortable at my questions.

'That is correct. This particular interest emerged a few years ago. Before that, it was others.'

'Others?'

'His first enthusiasm was for Pushkin.' She dispatched her coffee in a single gulp and began looking at her watch. 'I'm sorry, Dr Slopen . . .'

Her body language and tone was intended to hasten our interview to its close, but I was determined to press on. I told her I had a favour to ask of her. 'I hope you don't think it's forward of me,' I said. 'Last time, unfortunately, our visit was cut short. I wondered if I could watch him – Jack, your brother – working.'

'That won't be possible, I'm afraid.'

'I understand,' I said. 'I'm sorry to seem pushy. It's just so incredible to think that your brother is capable of that extraordinary work.' I set my cup down and stood up as if to leave.

She understood immediately what I was driving at: I was calling their whole story into question. 'One moment,' she said. 'Please sit.'

About ten minutes later, she returned.

'This way, please,' she said.

★　★　★

Bykov and Vera led the way as we descended the back stairs to the cellar passage. Bykov was the first to the door. There was a circular window of reinforced glass about the diameter of a grapefruit which he looked through. '*Vot tak. Nam udalos'. Mankurt pishet,*' he muttered, almost to himself. *There it is. We're in luck. The mankurt is writing.*

I was a step or two behind them, but I heard him clearly and I saw the icy look that he got from Vera.

'*Chto?*' he asked – *What?* He was too dim or insensitive to read her admonitory glance.

Vera signalled for me to join her at the tiny window.

There was something sordid and zoological about the scene inside the room. The brightness of it. The aliveness of him. One thinks of writing as meditative, an act full of repose, but Jack was sprawled over his desk, shirtless, twitching and fidgeting, the flesh of his back all wax-coloured and loose. A piece of rejected paper was scrunched in his right hand; his left moved steadily across the page.

He was, he was, he was . . . I want to call him a brooding immensity, but I realise I'm plagiarising Conrad's description of the Belgian Congo. I don't know whether that's a coincidence or a side-effect of the Procedure: there must have been at least one essay on *Heart of Darkness* in the batch that Vera coded.

Poor, poor Jack Telauga. Would it have been any

kinder, I wonder, to rebuild a less melancholy personality?

I don't think it's hindsight that makes me recall, from this distance, feeling that he was like a huge malfunctioning machine. But the truth about him – about me as I am now – was unguessable.

'Come,' said Vera, unlocking the door and knocking three times on the pane of glass to forewarn him. We went in together. He glanced up from his work.

His face was expressionless. There is no surprise left in you after a month of reawakening, only stoicism alternating with rage. He turned away and continued to write.

Knowing, as I do, the pain of coming to in a carcass, I understand now some of what he must have undergone. The physical agony is severe, but the sense of psychological dislocation is unimaginable, and in his case probably fatal. Someone recovering from a stroke or floundering in the shallows of progressive dementia might have an inkling of a fraction of what we felt. And keep in mind that the world that generated him, the world he had been coded for, bore no resemblance to what he found. It's a wonder he was as sane as he was.

I watched as his pen formed the letters on the paper. To my eye, there were slight differences between Jack's and the hand of the forged letters, but it might have been the pen – a fat Mont Blanc fountain pen on this occasion – or some change in his physical condition. He set down the pen for a moment to pause for thought and rubbed his big hands against the bristles of his shaved dome.

Vera took a page from the discarded ones at his feet. 'You see: Milton has been much on his mind since your meeting.' In that eerily Johnsonian hand, he had quoted Johnson's own judgement of 'Lycidas'. 'The diction is harsh, the rhymes uncertain, and the numbers unpleasing . . . its inherent improbability always forces dissatisfaction on the mind . . . where there is leisure for fiction there is little grief.'

'Was he always like this?' I asked her.

She looked at me. 'You pity him?' she said, as though surprised.

'Who wouldn't?' I said. She turned away abruptly. I thought at the time that I'd offended her.

'So, have you seen enough?' she asked, with her back still to me. I hadn't, but I couldn't think of a reason to prolong the spectacle and I felt faintly uncomfortable about the prurience of my interest in him.

As we returned to the ground floor, I made some polite comments about the large oil paintings in the stairwell, and Vera proceeded to identify them for me.

'Malevich, Repin, Goncharova. Over there Aivazovskii.'

I paused at the Aivazovskii. I'd seen his work at the Hermitage. Russians often compare him to Turner and his paintings sell for millions, but I had never been a fan. This one showed Pushkin on a craggy Black Sea shoreline, ankle-deep in water that was as flat and shiny as icing sugar.

'I can't forgive Aivazovskii for boasting that he had never read a book,' I said, truthfully.

Vera gave me a strange look. I noticed again how smooth her forehead was, and the alert intelligence in her blue-grey eyes. Something in them seemed to soften slightly. She handed me the page that she'd picked up off the floor. 'A souvenir.'

I thanked her. In the last yard or so of hallway, I remembered something that I'd meant to ask. 'By the way,' I said, 'what does *mankurt* mean?'

She smiled thinly. 'Russian slang.' She thanked me for my visit and I left.

It was one of those English spring days which are as fresh and green as a spear of asparagus: the plane trees rustling in the light wind, the sky unimprovably blue.

I wheeled my bicycle back along Piccadilly and through Green Park. American students were playing Ultimate Frisbee in a clearing.

Sitting in a deckchair, I turned over the strange events of the morning in my mind and looked again at the page Vera had given me; the ink on it seemed almost purple in the sun. The handwriting had an entirely natural flow. It had been written without hesitation. I thought how odd it was that Jack had achieved that fluency at all, never mind the fact that he was working left-handed. There was something about the ease of it, its *wu wei*, that was surely beyond a willed act.

I had never come across anything like it; but then again, it didn't seem to be far outside the bell curve of human giftedness. The few savants I knew of by name had, if anything, greater talents: the artist Stephen Wiltshire could reproduce architecturally correct pictures of whole cityscapes in a matter of minutes and from memory; the linguistic savant Daniel Tammet learned Icelandic in a week; Kim Peek could read two pages of text simultaneously by scanning separate pages with each eye. Even at my old school there was a boy called Dave Crabcock – a nickname derived of course from the operations of schoolboy logic on his actual name and surname: David Babcock – who memorised all the hexadecimal commands on the ZX Spectrum and could calculate *pi* in his head to fifty places.

So where did my unease come from?

Vot tak. Nam udalos'. Mankurt pishet.

Sooner or later, every student of Russian who visits the country gets taken aside and coached, usually over vodka and always by a man, in the art of *mat*: foul language. Russians pride themselves on the variety and complexity of their swearing and the many shades of meaning that can be coaxed from a handful of root words. It's been said that much of the vocabulary of *mat* is of Tartar origin: so that part of the words' offensiveness is that they recapitulate the humiliation of those centuries when the country was subjected to Tartar rule, when Russian virgins were left outside villages as tribute along with gold and furs.

Mankurt, however, is no part of *mat*. *Mankurt* is a word of Central Asian origin which means, roughly, 'slave'.

I came across the word for the first time as an undergraduate when I read Chingiz Aitmatov's long novel *The Day Lasts Longer than a Hundred Years*, which is a strange blend of science fiction, socialist realism and Kirghiz folklore. One of its key elements is the legend of the mankurt.

The mankurts Aitmatov describes are prisoners who have been captured in battle and subjected to a bizarre and degrading cryptoscientific procedure. Their heads are shaved and the skin from a camel's udder is fastened to their naked scalps. The men are manacled and fitted with collars to prevent them removing the grafts either with their hands or by rubbing their heads on the ground. They are then left in an isolated place on the steppe in the baking summer sun. Most of the victims of this process die, but in those cases where the graft takes hold, the men lose their memory and identity to the point where they become robotically obedient, a kind of steppe golem.

In Aitmatov's book, the process is described in great detail. Clearly, it has no scientific validity, but Aitmatov makes the legend function as a veiled criticism of the Soviet suppression of Central Asian culture. The mankurt is, by metaphoric extension, the person who has lost touch with his own cultural origins.

I didn't imagine that Misha Bykov was using the word to express such a complicated idea. I took it to mean something more simply disparaging, like one of those discredited categories of human intelligence that only survive as insults: *moron*, *imbecile*, *cretin*. And I understood why Vera would have bridled at his remark.

But all the same, I couldn't help thinking of the awful image it evoked. And it left me with a lingering sense of disquiet.

Over the succeeding weeks, I visited Vera and Jack about half a dozen times. On each occasion, I found a different pretext to drop round: I brought a copy of *Pilgrim's Progress* the first time, then a brass-tipped calligraphic pen and some ink. The third time I brought Vera some chocolates and an inscribed copy of my Augustan satire book. She seemed genuinely touched by the gift.

Gradually, Vera opened up to me. I suppose I must have flirted with her a little to begin with, but she seemed immune to that variety of flattery: Vera was an intellectual snob. She boasted that five generations of intellectuals preceded her on both sides of her family. Her father was Lithuanian, she told me; her mother Jewish. She had a sister in Perm who was a gifted pianist. I told her about Leonora. In retrospect, I think I may have shared more than I intended about the state of our marriage.

I found her compelling company. What you got with Vera was either melodrama or fierce intelligence, sometimes both at the same time; she had no capacity for or interest in small-talk. She would have been exhausting to live with, but it made a refreshing change from the glib and shallow irony that was the dominant note of my interactions with colleagues and students. The week after I gave her the satire book, she took issue forcefully with a number of the assertions I'd made in the chapter on Swift. I'd have to say she was largely right.

She was very rough in argument. I like an intellectual scrap myself, and I found it stimulating too, but not, I think, in the way she did. It was intimate and almost physical. Once or twice, after fierce disputes – none of which I won – I remember her staring at me, her eyes very bright, her face flushed and her upper body moving very slightly in time with her breath.

One of her particular interests was Ada Lovelace, Byron's bluestocking daughter and pioneer computer programmer, who once lived in a house on St James's Square. Vera spent about two hours one afternoon trying to make me appreciate the elegance of Lovelace's procedure for calculating Bernoulli numbers.

I pleaded with her, telling her, only half-jokingly, that her explanation was wasted on an arts graduate.

She looked thunderous. I had hit some intellectual

sore point. 'Don't be proud of this false specialis-
ation that is killing wisdom,' she said. 'There is no
natural distinction between the arts and sciences.'

'Well, one deals in facts,' I said. 'The other
doesn't.'

'So history is an art or a science?' she countered.
Before I could reply, she added: 'Tolstoy and
Dostoevsky have also discovered the laws of nature!'

'They were novelists, Vera. By definition, they
made things up.'

'You are so limited! Bill Gates also makes things
up. Is he a novelist? Science, it's a process of creation too. Literature itself is a species of code. You
line up symbols and create a simulacrum of life.'

She was now breathless with excitement and
talking so loudly that I worried someone would
hear us. She took a step towards me. 'Close your
eyes!' she commanded.

Her tone was so peremptory that my instinct
was to refuse. She must have realised, because she
said it again, this time softening her voice, making
it into a request.

I looked at her. She nodded. I closed my eyes.

'*The bulrushes waved at the side of the river,*' she
said. She spoke very slowly. It reminded me of
when Leonora would practise one of her pieces
Largo, and the way the pulse of it would fill the
house. '*A bee moved lazily among them. The small
child slept in the basket of reeds. On the bank sat a
woman, curling a ringlet around her ear.*'

I was still a little overexcited from our argument,

117

and it took a moment for my mind to slow down and match Vera's delivery, but as it did a strange thing happened. It was as though a complex flavour began to unfold in my mind. There was a distinct sequence of changes. First, that initial resistance, then a feeling of relaxing, joining to the stream of her words, and the sensation that they had taken over the image-making centres of my brain. I saw the fat, brown heads of the bulrushes, heard the bee. Then I felt the sun overhead – which she hadn't mentioned – and I knew that the woman's shawl was blue.

Vera stopped. There was for a moment such peace in my inner world that I didn't want to open my eyes.

Another level of intimacy was reached on the day when Vera finally condescended to speak to me in Russian. I had wondered if I would glimpse a little more of the real Vera when she spoke in her native language, but my Russian wasn't good enough to intuit anything profound from her squeaky Moscow accent and when she spoke quickly I could barely follow her at all.

Whenever the conversation returned to Jack, she seemed to deflate a little. It was odd, I remember thinking at the time, because she had had his whole life to reconcile herself to his strangeness.

After the first visit, she always found some excuse to keep me away from him: he was sleeping, or poorly, or irascible. But my attentions must have gradually worn her down. The fourth or fifth time I turned up, I brought with me an engraving of Streatham Place, the Thrales' mansion (now demolished), which I'd bought from a Cecil Court dealer about ten years earlier and though she warned me he was feverish, she consented to my giving it to him in person.

We found him asleep on his bed. At Vera's suggestion, I called out 'Jack' to him until he opened his eyes. He gazed blankly at me for a second.

'Jack. It's me. Remember?' And then, because he clearly didn't, I mentioned the poem that had provoked his reaction on our first encounter. 'Remember? "Lycidas"?'

As soon as it was out of my mouth, the word seemed to work on him like *Open Sesame*. There was a deep, chthonic rumble in his vast chest, as though the door to a tomb was opening. His eyes widened. He echoed me in a low, sonorous voice, half swallowing the sibilants of the name: *Lyshidash*.

That was all I got out of him. That one word. It was obvious there was something amiss with him. He was, quite possibly, mad. But he wasn't as inward as you'd expect a savant to be. Just as I'd noticed the first time, there was a lively connection to the world in his pained eyes.

As soon as he had woken up he signalled to Vera for a glass of water. She poured him water from his jug and he drank it greedily, panting thirstily into the glass and spilling drops down his clothing. 'Might I trouble you, madam, for another?'

Vera nodded and left the room to refill the jug.

Bykov, who had relaxed his earlier vigilance after my third or fourth visit to the house, was nowhere to be seen, and I decided to take the opportunity to address Jack directly. 'My name is Nicholas,' I said. 'What is yours?'

Without lifting his eyes to me, he said, 'I am a man who lives in a dream of despondency. I am out of my wits, sir. Forgive me.' He had a big basso voice like Hunter's, but with none of Hunter's seduction; it had a funereal gravity and trailed into silence as he finished.

He sank back onto the bed and it creaked under him. Then he seemed to shut down. His body went very still. Even the twitching stopped. I said a few words to him and, when I could get nothing in reply, touched his hand. It was burning hot. When Vera returned with his water, I told her he seemed feverish. She felt his forehead and opened his window slightly.

I glanced at Vera. Her face was stony and pale. 'You said he couldn't speak,' I said.

'He speaks.'

As June wore on, my visits continued. Malevin was never there and the vast house was echoing and unoccupied. Once or twice I saw a Czech or Polish housekeeper manoeuvring a huge vacuum cleaner through the hallways. There was a cook, who I think may have been Spanish, but the house was evidently maintained with the bare minimum of staff.

Whenever I asked where Malevin was, Vera would tell me variously that he was away on business, in the south of France, or in Moscow, and offered no further details. She was more forthcoming, however, on the subject of her own life. She told me how she had dreamed as a child of becoming a dancer, leaving me to conclude that her physical abnormality had made it impossible. She had learned English at school, she said, and explained that memorising Shakespeare's sonnets had kindled her love of the language.

'All of them?' I said, with polite incredulity.

She opened her hands towards me and invited me to pick a number.

I chose 44, more or less at random, and because I was sure it wasn't one of the famous ones.

She set down her coffee cup, brushed something out of her left eye with her knuckle and recited without hesitation in a low voice that was salted with the Russian cadences of her accent:

'If the dull substance of my flesh were thought,
Injurious distance should not stop my way;
For then, despite of space, I would be brought
From limits far remote, where thou dost stay.'

In mid-June, Sotheby's had a rare book and manu-script sale which included a Fourth Folio and some bona fide Johnsoniana. I went to the preview, half expecting to run into Hunter or Malevin, but if they had any interest in the items they were bidding by proxy.

One of the Johnson letters was reproduced, actual size, on a gatefold page in the auction catalogue and I took it round to show Jack.

Unusually, he was up and about, actually wandering around the house in tracksuit bottoms, a velvet shirt and bare feet.

'Dr Slopen,' he said. 'I am very pleased to see you. Give me your hand.'

This time it was icy and the skin on it papery dry.

He held my gaze for an uncomfortably long time, staring unblinkingly into my eyes until I was forced to turn away, discomfited. I mentioned the auction catalogue. He didn't take the hint until Vera intervened, telling him that I had brought something for him. He let my hand drop and I took the catalogue from my bag and opened it to the marked page. He touched the paper, as if befuddled by the nature of the image, which had all the look of manuscript and yet was glossy and smooth.

'Truly,' he said to himself in a voice barely above a whisper, 'the madman dwells in a world of wonders.'

I believe that my first visit was motivated by a combination of curiosity and wounded pride. The sight of Jack writing, the proof that he really was the author of the letters, diminished my sense of shame about the forgeries. Somehow, being deceived by Jack – if *deceived* is the right word

– was more tolerable than being bested by one of my peers. Jack was so vulnerable, his confusion so profound, that I couldn't be envious of him, or even consider him an adversary.

But what drew me back? Certainly, I'd grown to like and respect Vera, and I felt a kind of fondness for her brother. But there was something else as well: an uncanny fascination with the man. It was as though his pained eyes held some knowledge that I'd lost. I saw in them something that I dimly knew: an unplaceable recollection, the stirring of old memories, a fragment of a half-remembered dream. And in my imagination his hopeless voice seemed to bubble up from the very depths of the underworld.

CHAPTER 11

I was certain at the time that Hunter and Malevin knew of my comings and goings. I assumed that Vera had cleared it with one or both of them before admitting me to Jack's room to watch him work, and that she reported to them after my subsequent visits. But I never imagined they would come to feel threatened by my interest.

The next I heard from Hunter was in the third week of June. As part of his larger self-deception that he is somehow a patron of the arts, Hunter had commissioned the creation of a limited edition of a new work by a writer and artist called Pascal Sheldon; his assistant sent an email inviting me and Leonora to its launch at short notice.

It was a gesture of conciliation. Hunter was smooth and wily enough to see that after shaming me with the fakes it would be politic to pour a little balm on my injured ego. And he did so in a way that was intended both to flatter me and to remind me of the gulf in status between us.

From where I sit, all my recollections are precious ones, but when I met Leonora that evening she seemed to shine on me with a radiance I hadn't seen for years. We had arranged to meet in the Portuguese cafe that had been one of the back-drops of our courtship and both came straight from work. I complimented her on her new dress.

She shrugged. 'It's an old one.'

'We used to meet here,' I said. 'Remember?'

'Yes. Back in Roman times.' She glanced up as she stirred her coffee and there was humour and a kind of excitement in her brown eyes. That turning lamp had finally revolved back on me. Being loved: it's the opposite of the Procedure. It's like finding your way back to your original carcass. Restoration. Redemption. Home.

The evening was so warm and humid it was like wearing wet clothes and Leonora's legs were bare. Her Asiatic skin – Sarah has it too – is sallow through the long dark English winter, but it turns golden at the slightest suggestion of sun. She would be forty soon – she is one year older than me – but the mellowness of her middle-aged beauty had a sweetness and a plangency that moved me more than ever.

'Shouldn't we be going?' she said.

I remember thinking: we should treasure this moment. After the series of crises we'd lived through: an abrupt marriage, sudden parenthood, the pangs and disappointments of raising children, two demanding careers, the affair: after all this, finally to fetch up in the landscape where we'd courted, still young enough, still healthy enough for love; solvent, working, absolved of the harshest demands of childcare. I thought to myself: I am blessed.

'You never said what happened to those papers you were working on for Hunter,' said Leonora, as we walked though the dusk. 'Did they turn out to be real?'

My astonishment at her curiosity was compounded by my amazement that she'd paid enough attention in the first place to know what I had been doing. I must have looked surprised.

'What's the matter?'

'I didn't know you were interested.'

'I'm interested in your work.'

'That, to make an understatement, is an overstatement.'

'Oh fuck off, Nicky.'

'I was joking.'

'There's no such thing as a joke.'

It's odd to think we must have uttered each of those sentences to each other on dozens of occasions. It was a dance we'd done a hundred times before. The phrases were boiler-plate, like the obligatory epithets of legal documents. 'I'm sorry,' I said. 'I got overexcited. It's so rare to feel like we might be getting along.'

'There you go again. Veering wildly between contempt and melodrama.'

Terrifying, really. It's as though the words own us, funnelling us back down the channels of old experiences.

'Please, Leonora. This is important.'

126

The hint of frank desperation in my voice jolted her out of the familiar script.

'You asked me about Hunter and I want to tell you.' I had never previously contemplated owning up to my embarrassment over the forged letters, but I knew I was about to. 'A very strange thing happened,' I said.

'Strange?'

'Strange. And embarrassing.'

'Embarrassing?' Those odd echoes had more real life in them than anything we'd said up to that moment. At this instant, on the point of sharing my humiliation with my wife, I felt on the brink of a kind of renewal; new possibilities were opening in front of us.

Just then, her phone rang. She hesitated for an instant, then paused my anecdote with a consolatory tap of my arm. *One of my students*, she mouthed. I walked beside her in silence as they rescheduled a lesson. By the time they'd finished talking we'd reached the shop and we were swallowed up by the party. On such chance occurrences, the shape of a life turns. The light had revolved again, casting its beam towards a distant shore. *Many mischiefs and many benefits are done and hindered without design or purpose.*

The launch was held in a rare-book shop on Ledbury Road that specialises in modern first editions. There was a display of Sheldon's creation, *The End of the Book*, in the front window. Hunter was on a chair in the back of the shop. He was clearly the eminence of the launch. On his lap lay a gold-topped cane, which enhanced his kingly bearing. His assistant, Preethika, controlled the flow of well-wishers who came to pay obeisance to her boss, letting them through one at a time. I found myself looking at one of Sheldon's books as I waited for a slot to approach Hunter.

'It's vellum and goatskin. Feel it,' said a rasping, upper-class voice beside me. It was Sheldon. He held one of his books towards me. He was about my age, cadaverous and effeminately handsome, wearing a bespoke suit, a cravat and a skull ring. I recognised him from his pictures in the papers. He'd famously had himself crucified in the Philippines about five years earlier as part of a previous artistic project.

The book sat weightily in my palm. It was a beautiful thing, redolent of ink and freshly tanned leather.

'Every one is completely unique,' Sheldon said proudly. 'I write them by hand. The printed book is over. This is about getting back to its artisanal origins, pre-Gutenberg. I take my inspiration from the Luttrell Psalter. You've heard of it?'

I told him I had. The boards were held together with an emerald-coloured binding so new that it creaked open reluctantly, as though shamed by its bathetic contents. The inside pages had been written entirely by hand. I could see messy handwriting, badly drawn stick-men with thought bubbles coming out of their heads; one of the pages was stuck all over with penny postage stamps; another contained what looked like a recipe for apple crumble.

'I thought it was a novel.'

'It is.'

'What's it about?'

'You'll have to buy it to find out, but it's got everything: love, death and an amusing dog.'

'This one's got a recipe for apple crumble,' I said.

'Don't you love that about the novel? The capaciousness?' he said, waving to someone at the other side of the room. A woman teetered over to kiss him on both cheeks.

When my turn came to see Harper, I noticed his clothes were hanging more loosely and I asked if he'd lost weight. He said he'd had keyhole surgery on his knee and his doctor had put him on a new diet. He got to his feet, put his arm around me and turned us both away from the throng. I could feel his newly skinny forearm pressing sharply into my back.

'Sinan not coming?' I said.

'He's in Moscow on business.'

Out of the corner of my eye, I could see Leonora talking animatedly to Hunter's girlfriend, a striking Chinese American woman called Candy Go.

'No hard feelings about the whole letters thing?' Hunter said.

'As far as I'm concerned it never happened.'

Hunter gave me an approving pat. 'Listen. I have some sad news about Jack,' he said.

Because of his suddenly sombre tone, I was already framing his next sentence in my mind, and yet the words still came as a shock.

'Jack passed away last night.'

The room seemed to contract around us. Sheldon was laughing uproariously. A waitress passed me bearing a tray of blinis.

I was so befuddled by the news that I asked him when it happened, forgetting that he'd already told me.

'Last night,' he said. 'It was very sudden.'

'I saw him two days ago,' I said. 'He seemed fine.'

Hunter shook his head regretfully. 'He was in terrible physical shape. The drugs he was on were highly toxic. His kidney function was impaired. It was only a matter of time.' But in the inflection of his voice, I seemed to hear him saying: *one fewer problem for both of us.*

'I'm so sorry,' I said. 'He was . . .' But I couldn't think what to add. 'I should call Vera.'

'Maybe drop her a note; to be honest, I think what she needs now is space to grieve.'

He gave my shoulder a valedictory squeeze and sailed out into the party.

The strength of my reaction took me by surprise. I couldn't call Jack a friend, but his life seemed to have touched me quite profoundly: his vulnerability, the sense of displacement. I remembered his pained, knowing eyes and the touch of his hand. Poor Vera,

I thought, poor Jack. It was hard to believe that that big body was now inert, its light extinguished. My vision swam with tears. I couldn't understand it. Even then, my sense of loss struck me as disproportionate. I wasn't sure why I cared so much. I thought perhaps it was a symptom of low-level depression: overinvesting in some alien misery, like Byron in his letter to Hobhouse, crying over the goldfish.

Our plan had been to leave the launch at eight and go to dinner, but it was closer to nine when we extricated ourselves from the party. Candy and Leonora had struck up a friendship in the way that pretty women seem to do in order to neutralise the threat of each other.

'Hunter's talked a lot about you,' Candy said to me when I brought Leonora her coat, in a way that let me know he hadn't. There was a – I don't want to call it a smell, but it struck me like an odour – let's call it an *emanation* coming off her. It oozed from her skin, and her boots and leather miniskirt and her silk scarf, and her impeccable hair. It was the aura of money. Ordinarily, that realisation would have been enough to set me fretting over my impoverishment and my life choices and pity my wife in her old dress, but the news about Jack Telauga shamed me out of all that. I felt profoundly grateful to be alive and to be taking my wife out to dinner.

I had booked a table at an expensive Japanese

restaurant. They'd grudgingly altered my reservation when it became clear we were running late, but the place was only half full.

The dinner was a piece of financial recklessness made feasible by my decision to cash Hunter's cheque. I'd given myself various rationales for my change of tack, but the true one, I think, is that I wanted to show off to Leonora. I wanted to reconnect with her, and this was the only way I could think of doing it. Lately, I've wondered if I was right. I think of the other things that I failed to give her, and it strikes me that slight financial embarrassment was the least of our worries.

Leonora gave me a look as we took our seats that was full of the triumphant and bitter I-told-you-so of a person who has come to relish the predictability of their partner's disappointing oversights. Leonora is allergic to fish. A number of evenings have been spoiled because I failed to remember this simple fact, but I was confident that she'd find something else agreeable on the menu. 'They have wagyu beef,' I said.

'I'm off red meat.'

'Since when?'

'Since Christmas.'

I examined the soy sauce bottle. 'Chicken?'

'Chicken it'll have to be. Order for me.' She headed for the Ladies.

I was philosophical about her sharpness. We had been doing the old dance for so long that she had lost her ear for anything but prickliness and sarcasm. But the gloomy news about Jack Telauga had crystallised something in me. I felt oppressed by my secret history with Hunter and the humbling misattribution of the fake letters, but more than that, the presence of Jack Telauga in my life, his isolation and strangeness, had begun to make me conscious of my riches. For the first time in a while, I felt lucky. I *was* lucky. And I resolved to tell Leonora as soon as she returned. I wanted to apologise to her, and share my secrets, and ask if we could turn over a new leaf.

It surprises me to learn in my fortieth year that underneath everything, I am an incorrigible optimist. Until my barrel reaches the lip of the falls – perhaps even in the giddy moments after-wards – I will continue to believe that everything will turn out for the best.

After a few minutes, Leonora reappeared. I watched her walk the length of the restaurant. Our eyes met, she smiled, and there was something so modest and contrite in her face that I was certain she felt as I did.

She took her seat and flapped her napkin out over her lap. I reached over to grab her hand. It lay inertly in my fingers.

'I need to tell you something,' she said.

'You took the words out of my mouth,' I said.

'Please, Nicky. Be serious. Don't make this harder than it is.'

Well, I knew then, of course. Of course.

★   ★   ★

It's part of the job description of the cuckold that he's always the last to know. To this day, I believe that Leonora was telling the truth after the *Madame Bovary* incident. She and Caspar had resolved to end things. But then, by coincidence, they had bumped into each other at a recital in Aldeburgh. God bless her, Leonora tried to spare my feelings as she explained what had happened, but there was a flame in her eyes when she recalled their meeting.

It was all arranged. I think this is in a woman's nature. A man would have presented a dilemma, or a bargaining position, but Leonora came to me with the done deed. She was moving to a flat with Caspar and taking the children. Accommodation, new schools, packing their stuff: all taken care of. It was the revelation that Lucius and Sarah had been party to the arrangements that threw me into the abyss. I understood the guilty pity behind Lucius's uncharacteristic recent willingness to accompany me to Homebase to buy a new lawn-mower. I burst into tears and told Leonora that she and the children were my life.

'That's never been true, Nicky,' she said. 'I've never been able to understand what would make you happy.'

'But I am happy! You make me happy!'

'No, no, no. Happiness is much simpler than this . . . All this self-torture and angst over things. Barely touching each other. We're like brother and sister.'

'Not because of me!'

In all the startling discomfort of coming to my senses in a new carcass, I don't recall a more agonising moment than this. All the shame and the pain and the pitying eyes of strangers. My awareness of myself as weak and hopeless. What made it harder was my perception that while I was broken and tearful, Leonora was speaking with a voice of reasoning tenderness. I was the one clinging to a fantasy about our marriage as insane as Roger N's delusion that Mossad has implanted a radio transmitter in his brain.

It would have taken someone of more than saint-like forgiveness and tolerance to sit through the rest of the meal. I couldn't bear to watch what happened next. Would Caspar come and get her from the restaurant? Were my children already installed in their new flat? Was Lucius playing his PSP in some Notting Hill duplex?

I left, angrily, and walked all the way home. Inevitably, because of the geography of the city, I was compelled to revisit scenes from my marriage from its inception to its apparent end: the lamplit rise of Kensington Palace Gardens where I used to cycle with Leonora on the crossbar of my bicycle. The hotel porch where I pleaded with her to stay with me. The bar at the Royal Court where she'd told me she was pregnant. The party shop on Wandsworth Bridge Road where I bought a tiny Batman costume for Sarah to wear to her first birthday party. Lucius's orthodontist. The shop where we ordered our kitchen table together as I fought Leonora's reluctance to move south of the river.

On Trinity Road, just after midnight, there were two boys in hoods loitering outside the garage. One approached me to ask me the time. It was all wearily predictable. But I looked him straight in the eye, and, seeing the rage and hopelessness of someone with even less to lose than him, he must have thought better of it.

It was almost one o'clock when I got home. I've returned after a burglary and this was similar: the hint of strange feet, something indefinably altered in the atmosphere. But all my possessions were intact. It was my family that had gone.

There's no skirting the ugliness of what happened next. I had two or three grim telephone conversations with Leonora. She was adamantine in her resolution. We agreed not to involve lawyers if it could be helped. She hinted that Hilary was in an even worse state than I was, as though that would cheer me up.

At this stage there was no real acrimony between us; perhaps because the children were relatively adult and there was no money to fight over. With an attention to the minutiae of the split that, to my mind, bordered on the sociopathic, Leonora had found both Sarah and Lucius places at a private sixth-form college near their new home. I didn't ask, but it was obvious that Caspar was paying.

I took Lucius and Sarah to lunch at a restaurant near Borough Market a week later. I seemed to have turned into a superfluous and pitiful character like someone in a William Trevor story, but it seemed right to go along with Leonora's desire to maintain the fiction that the wish for the separation was mutual. 'Mum says it's what you want too,' Lucius said. I didn't disagree.

Touchingly, when Lucius was out of earshot, Sarah gave me a concerned look and asked: 'Dad, you know about Caspar, but, you know, with you, is there anyone else?'

The truth – my unblemished record of fidelity – seemed like an admission of failure. So I said, 'No, sweetheart. No one important.' We talked about the new school, and their set books, and, after a walk along the river, I put them on the train at Embankment and walked back over the Thames at Hungerford Bridge under a grey sky, thinking: no one tells you this, how having children multiplies your capacity for suffering.

The gloom that moved into my house after Leonora took the kids made a poor companion and a worse colleague. My work suffered. Deadlines slipped past. I was terribly behind on the *Letters*. My head of department, a good friend, saw the state I was in and gave me two weeks' compassionate leave. I got in the habit of going for solitary walks to the South Bank and along the Thames to Southwark, half hoping that I would bump into Lucius skateboarding with friends from his old school.

Outside the Globe, one Sunday, I watched a woman in her twenties pretending to be a clockwork ballerina. Her dark hair was in a chignon, she had a drawn face, an unmistakable look of sadness, and a large rotating key attached to a battery in a box on her back. She moved in sad, jerky moments to music that was playing on a Dansette; only the rise and fall of her chest spoiled the illusion of her lifelessness.

The two commonest delusions among my fellow-inmates in the DHU are that their thoughts are being tampered with by government agencies, and that they are surrounded by human-seeming robots. I'm fully aware that neither of these ideas conforms to objective reality. They are the beliefs of the insane: brought on in a surprising number of cases by a predisposition to psychosis exacerbated by hallucinogens or strong cannabis. Of course. And yet, and yet. My lunatic companions have hit on a kind of truth. The soul that's left in them rages at the petrification of what once was living tissue.

Malevin *père* said a hundred thousand words was the minimum to reconstitute a core complex; but I sometimes feel that you could reconstruct an entire marriage in ten sentences.

That spark of new creation, the new phrase that genuinely surprises, the act that bears the impress of a live consciousness: these are astonishingly rare.

Human beings are everywhere overcome by rituals and dead language, by threadbare notions about what is real.

We think of ourselves as creatures with agency, but by middle age we are as habituated to our patterns of behaviour as zoo animals, the infinite possibilities of our childhood crimped and shut down as though we've undergone a botched and back-street version of the Procedure. But just beyond these bars, tantalisingly, are real feelings. If only we had new words to net them.

Of course, these madmen express it insanely, but they're right, aren't they, to fight the loathsome repetition of old postures? There is nothing false in their agony. Their question is my question: *How do I become real again?*

CHAPTER 12

Extracted from Dr Webster's Journal

Supervision with PW yesterday to discuss cases. Much of the session [. . .] spent on Q. PW says that even after thirty years he's still regularly surprised by the tenacity of the *idée fixe*. Important to remember, in his mind, that factual content is less important than the significance Q ascribes to it. That is the very moving aspect of this work. How awful must reality be for the psychotic to take refuge in this? He compares it to someone jumping out of a burning building knowing there is no hope of surviving the fall. One element of the psychosis, paradoxically, is a will to live.

I try to emphasise Q's obstinate commitment to his story. What's surprising about it is the particularity of it. I say I have checked some of the minor details of Q's account and found he's oddly precise about circumstantial stuff, even while being delusional in a larger sense. PW maintains this obsessive construction of the protective fantasy is absolutely conventional. I say that while it's conventional for a client to claim falsely to be the son of God, it seems strange for someone to claim falsely to be the son of Fred Bloggs, 23 Acacia Avenue, Tooting, SW17 or whatever. PW looks at me slightly oddly. Turns the subject back to my father. The whole weary manoeuvre suddenly so predictable and crude. Yes, family history of mental illness. Blah blah blah. Did you feel powerless as a child watching your father destroy his life? Blah blah blah. I get it! Q's my dad and I've lost my sense of professional detachment. So I'm going bonkers too. PW suggests reassigning Q. Suddenly, I loathe PW and want to punch him. Shame that I never experienced any of this in my training analysis.

Still, am a bit baffled by the texture of Q's delusion. For example, Googling the woman Q claims he was married to, a classical musician, throws up a number of articles, one of which is an interview. It mentions in passing that this woman is allergic to fish. This I also know from Q. What a strange thing to be accurate about. I find various instances of the same thing. I know PW is right, but feel strangely torn. PW asks about Roger moving in. I say it's going well so far. Then of course, last night have a full-on Technicolor dream about Dad and wake up crying at 3 a.m. Rog has taken a sleeping pill and is out of it and frankly not interested, but at least the dream restores my faith in analysis. Bought PW a cake today to say thanks. He looks at it wryly as if to say, 'Restoring your injured objects?' The sense of uplift lasts until now.

CHAPTER 13

I've cut and pasted the above from Dr Webster's journal. I was going to write something sarky about her – my relief that she has an interior life – but the truth is I'm overwhelmed by gratitude that she's experienced even a scintilla of doubt about her diagnosis of me.

Funny though – I don't remember telling her about the fish.

But how conscientious of her to check my story! I remember that article. It was two years ago, for *Gramophone*, at the time of the Poulenc recital. They sent a photographer almost as an afterthought. Leonora was rushing off to teach in Marylebone, he had time for five pictures at the most and they ended up using one of them for the cover. She has an extraordinary radiance, still. I remember coming out of a cinema with her once when we were courting and being taken aback by her beauty. Her face without makeup was flawless. We were standing on the pavement of the Fulham Road at six o'clock one summer evening and it was like watching the sun rise. But I was twenty-three and I didn't have the words for it then.

I didn't fall in love with Leonora's insides. I wonder, in the end, if that was one of the reasons for her contempt for me. She mentioned, sometimes with bitterness, how the world had begun to treat her differently when she grew breasts. I myself saw Sarah's shyness about her pubescent body after all the unselfconscious extroversion of her childhood. It is a kind of Fall.

Imagine Leonora in another carcass and what would she have? The music, of course. A headstrong nature. But nothing to make men fall at her feet. How many doors opened for her because of the cut of her jaw, her hair, her Asiatic eyes? That feeling that our bodies lead separate lives. In my case, inarguably so.

The tattoos on my chest and upper arms are reminders, if any were needed, that someone was here before me. No doubt Hunter and Malevin or their clients have pristine carcasses lined up for their own use. Or perhaps the whole venture is at a more speculative stage. Jack's quick deterioration doesn't inspire confidence in the proprietary technology behind this. We definitely have the feeling of prototypes about us.

I wonder at times about the previous tenant. What traces are left of him that I don't know about? Holding his stubby cock to piss, I feel strangely intrusive. I know I ought to feel sorrier for him. I'm sure he was younger than I was. Sturdier. Circumcised. I've studied the tattoos for hints. They're crude and rather blurry. There's an acronym under one that looks like it might be in Cyrillic, but the ink has bled too much to say for sure. The oddest of them is on the top of my right thigh. It's a big roundel with intersecting rings and a cross through it: just like Jack's. It looks like a target seen through rifle sights, and it's relatively fresh: as though it was applied shortly before the poor fellow got – how can I put it? – borrowed.

He has an odd smell, this stranger. It was Assia Wevill, wasn't it, who said Ted Hughes's hands smelled like a butcher's? There is something of the abattoir on me, something ferrous and musky.

I've grown fond of him. But there's no getting away from the fact that I miss the old one, the body I grew up in, with its chicken-pox scars and marks that were mnemonics for bits of my past. I liked my narrow feet. The ones I've got now are huge with big splayed toes. They're the feet of a peasant. If I had to guess, I'd say I was some farmer's son. There's a useful heft in my upper arms and it feels like he could handle himself. He has a prodigious appetite too.

Some of these tattoos are from military or naval service; others, I think, from doing time. The likeliest occupation? *Kontraktnik*, probably; one of those professional soldiers who bulked out the cannon fodder in the Chechen wars with a bit of military know-how. Too old to be a conscript. I imagine him back in the Caucasus for another tour of duty and drinking with the wrong people, or following the wrong woman back to an

145

apartment. Bosh. Out go the lights. The next thing he knows he's being held in a farmhouse in the middle of nowhere. They keep him dangling. Days of fear and boredom. At least they've got an incentive to treat him well. Constant misinformation about the state of the ransom demands or the prisoner exchange, or whatever they tell him. Things are finally looking promising. Only a few days now, *druzhok*. *Skoro domoi*. Bosh. Out he goes again. They unscrew his consciousness like a bulb from a standard lamp and put Nicky Slopen inside.

Lucius stacking toy cars in the front room; Leonora pulling sheets out of the tumble dryer; Sarah making faces at herself in the bathroom mirror, thinking that she's unobserved: these are *my* memories. But when I dream as I did last night and see a courtyard splashed with the bloody stains of fallen mulberries, a dusty mountain road, a barking dog – is that mine, or *his*? Who is this stranger inside me?

In the first week of July, I went to the twenty-four-hour chemist's in Balham to pick up some antidepressants. My GP had written me the prescription at least a week earlier. I had hoped to manage without them. Someone once told me that you're most at risk in those seven days when you first start taking them, but I'd had a terrible night and finally caved in to the desire to blot out the pain. I'd had a dream in which Lucius was a baby again. Pink-cheeked, a big grub wiggling in his sleeping bag, he was saying 'Watch Thomas!' through a mouthful of pacifier like a Punch and Judy Professor talking through his swozzle. I felt desolate on awakening and took the prescription from where I'd attached it to the fridge with a magnet.

The pharmacist, a grey-haired man with blue eyes and steel-rimmed spectacles, handed over the pills with an easy cordiality, as though I were a customer in a fashionable restaurant of which he was the maître d', and not just one more inadequate who wasn't up to facing the rigours of the twenty-first century without chemical assistance.

I washed the first one down with a caffe latte in the Starbucks opposite the supermarket and leafed through the Sunday paper. The colour supplement was full of recipes for swiss chard. I envied the exasperated young families juggling their coffees and tiny children. From my seat at the window, I could see the Pizza Express where Lucius had got his finger trapped in the door to the men's loos as a toddler. The Dutch component of my psyche – my mother's side – was slightly ashamed at my weakness. I knew at some level that I had to hold myself together for Lucius and Sarah; that I couldn't be destroyed by this; and that people had got over much worse. But on the way home, the thought *I have lost everything* was like a heavy object that I knew I'd be carrying forever.

It must have been something about the symmetry of our bereavements that made me think at that moment of Vera. It came to me with a pang that in the midst of everything I'd failed to send her a letter of condolence. Even in my downcast state, I was capable of grasping that her loss exceeded mine by some order of magnitude. I sat down at my desk and began to write: *Dear Vera . . .*

Perhaps I was being hypersensitive, but I found the letter impossible to write. If I didn't mention Leonora's departure the dilatoriness of my condolences seemed unforgivable. *Dear Vera, I was so sorry to hear the news about Jack two weeks ago.* And if I did mention it, I seemed clumsily to usurp her right to grief. *Dear Vera, I would have written sooner but I've had some bad news of my own.*

I decided to call her instead, but her phone was off, so soon after lunch I travelled into town with some flowers, planning to leave them at the house with a brief note.

The mansion was shuttered and dark, but on the second or third ring, I heard steps in the hall and a bolt slide open across the door. It was Vera. She asked me in.

Preoccupied as I was with my own burden of grief and loneliness, I still couldn't fail to notice that Vera was unusually pale and that she had the tense visage of someone under great mental strain.

I told her how sorry I was about Jack. For a while, we sat together in the half-dark of the drawing room, saying nothing. Much of the furniture was under dust covers and the place had taken on an oppressive, morgue-like atmosphere. It was more than I could stand being there. I told her I was going to an exhibition at the Royal Academy and, almost as an afterthought, I invited her to come. To my surprise, she immediately assented and rose to fetch her coat.

Of course, I'd actually intended to do no such thing, but now I was trapped by my lie and the two of us traipsed round room after room of insipid eighteenth-century watercolours by the painter and engraver Thomas Sandby. In my frame of mind, it was actually worse than being in Malevin's gloomy mansion. There was something utterly devastating about being confronted by the flatness and gentility of Sandby's landscapes. I looked in vain for something that would speak to my inner turmoil: something wounded, gothic and monstrous. But all there was were neat Augustan houses, tidy buildings and watery English sunshine. By the third room, I'd had enough. It wasn't that I needed someone to confide in, but that I needed to say the facts out loud, to do something to break through a terrible sense of depersonalisation. 'My wife left me,' I said.

Vera took my hand and, turning slowly towards me, looked me straight in the eye. It is the first time that I can recall being exposed to the full force of her extraordinary charisma. 'I'm so sorry,' she said. Something so tender, so understanding in her voice drew out a wave of desire in me that was as abrupt as it was bewildering.

For a while, we stood in the courtyard while Vera

smoked and the crowds queued for the Anish Kapoor sculptures. Then, when it became clear that neither of us was in any hurry to go anywhere, we walked to an odd restaurant bar behind Jermyn Street that was painted in bright harlequin colours. Over the genial hum of the afternoon drinkers, Vera listened to me and I drank most of a bottle of red wine.

If I'm doubtful about Dr Webster's abilities, perhaps it's because of this: my recollection of Vera that afternoon. Her capacity for empathy was astonishing, and I don't mean to diminish it in any way when I locate its source in her consciousness of her own odd physical appearance. To be listened to in the way Vera listened to me then was a profound and redeeming experience. I began by telling her about the immediate crisis: the loss of Leonora and my family. There was something active and almost physical about her mode of attention. She seemed to draw my story out of me with a hypnotic softness. The scope of our conversation widened: Ron, Lucius, Sarah; and the bereavements that had blighted my adolescence and youth.

And yet she didn't just listen in a validating silence. She probed, questioned, was sceptical about some of my conclusions. I remember, in particular, her insights about my relationship to Ron. I found myself drunkenly reciting my usual litany of his virtues: *his omnivalent curiosity, his spirit of humane endeavour, his generosity towards those he taught.* I waited for her approval, her sympathy. Rather coldly, she said it sounded like an obituary. 'Perhaps this is significant,' she said.

I asked why.

'From the moment of your severance, he was dead to you.'

'I know, it was awful.'

'It was intolerable,' she agreed, 'because it fulfilled your deepest, most guilty wish.'

I looked at her with some perplexity.

'Think of Hamlet,' she went on. 'What appals him is not the terrible death of his father, but a guilty glimpse of the dark part of him that willed it.'

I tried to pooh-pooh the suggestion, telling her that I too had read Ernest Jones's essay on the play, but she waved my objections aside. 'Harbottle and you were not mentor and disciple, you were father and son, with all the shades of Sophocles that entails. You resented the joint authorship. The bulk of the work was done by you. And on a psychic level, you wished him dead. Long before Tilda Swann, you wanted to usurp his throne. But when he – as it were – took his own life, the guilt almost destroyed you.'

The barman darted inscrutable glances at us from his station. From time to time, Vera would go outside to smoke, and I would sway to the Gents and encounter the wondering eyes of my unsteady reflection in the mirror. Every time I came back, Vera seemed more lovely; her eyes behind their thickly made-up lashes tender with sympathy, her broad mouth with its liverish lipstick, the touch of her gloved hand on my knee fierce and protective like the raised wing of a mother swan. The waitress silently renewed the empty bottle and brought the calamari that Vera insisted I eat to temper the alcohol. And, for what felt like the first time in my life, I tasted the joy of self-revelation to a compassionate intelligence, of constructing a workable self out of all the dissonant parts of me: a transaction that eerily foreshadowed the Procedure.

We returned to the St James's Square mansion together. I babbled about Johnson, recalling the nights he had spent with Savage in this very square, railing against the hardships of a writer's life. We had linked arms and she watched me in silence, with her all-seeing, all-forgiving smile.

Our first kiss was of an extraordinary, breathless intensity. I remember the leather calliper she wore on her crooked leg. I remember her womanly shape and her skin which smelled of rose petals. I remember calling her name in the darkness.

She woke me up gently just after 4 a.m. There was birdsong in the square. 'You must go,' she said. She came downstairs in her dressing gown to let me out. I paused in the hallway.

'I feel I should say something,' I said.

'We are both terribly lonely, Nicholas.' Her voice was deep from sleep and cigarettes, and her rumpled face looked almost monkey-like under her tangled hair.

'About Jack . . .'

'Things will go on much as they always have,' she said. 'Goodbye, Nicholas.'

I bent down to kiss her and she pecked me on the cheek.

Later that morning, I sent her a rather perfunctory text. I was taken aback by the turn of events and it seemed easier to behave as though it hadn't happened. I knew it wasn't quite right, but I didn't feel she could expect much else from me.

CHAPTER 14

There was a new orderly handing out the evening medication last night and I managed to palm my sedative. I'm sick of this chemically aided sleep that deprives me of my dreams. For a while I lay awake, listening to the noises of the ward: shoes squeaking on the lino, trolley wheels, snoring, shrieks and howls. Someone – surely Caiaphas, our resident Jehovah's Witness? – cried out: 'Forgive him, Jesus!' Someone else laughed. Then it began to rain outside. There was a subtle change of pressure inside the unit. The soul quickens in the aftermath of rain: an inkling of redemption. All the lost children in this place. Their unbearable sadness. At least I had . . . What *did* I have?

The dreams when they came were almost intolerable: a hideous mish-mash of Nicky's and *his*, and a flashback to the Procedure itself. The awful intensity of it, the *redness* of everything, that bucket with its unspeakable contents.

Caiaphas yesterday with his *Watchtower*s: 'God has a plan for you too, Nicholas!'

★   ★   ★

154

Every July, as one cohort finished its exams and moved off into the world, the university opened its doors to the summer students. I was predictably contemptuous of them – tourists, dabblers – when I started teaching at the summer school five years ago, but by selling six weeks of my holiday, I could earn an unignorable six grand. Then I began to enjoy it. I liked the older, widely read enthusiasts whom the school attracted. They wanted exactly the kind of unfashionable courses on Jane Austen, or eighteenth-century poetry, that had fallen out of favour with the faculty. I looked forward to teaching them. And in the summer after Leonora left, the contact with my students restored a sense of balance to my life. We mixed the classes up with theatre visits and sightseeing: Chawton, Stratford-upon-Avon, Richmond. One of my students, a man from Iowa, was ninety-seven years old, and had been stationed in London during the war. He walked unsteadily on and off the bus himself, unaided, followed by his grey-haired children. Through the eyes of the visitors, London recovered some of its charm for me.

In my free time, I worked on a paper I'd been invited to give at a conference in Italy about methodological issues raised by the late letters. On July 18th, a Saturday, I flew to Florence.

Italy was, initially anyway, a restorative. They'd put us in university accommodation, but we were near enough to the city to walk in. I was a guest of honour at the dinner on the first night. We ate and drank like Borgias. Best of all was being with my peers in academia. I had a taste of camaraderie.

The second night, Erik Betsen, Saul Lumsdaine, Horst Schnittingen and myself went out to get *bistecca* – that huge Florentine cut of meat the size of an Old Testament sacrifice. We resembled rowdy middle-aged brothers. Saul was the provocateur: teasing us, goading us to drink more. Erik was reading a paper the next day, so Saul, Horst and I ended the evening together, wandering drunkenly around the streets by the Duomo, whose lamplit marble facade looked as though it was made out of peppermints. It was a weeknight but high season, and the place was jammed with tourists and language students and hawkers selling knock-off designer handbags on the street corners.

Saul and Horst are both divorced. Saul's first marriage ended years ago. He is in his late fifties now and shamelessly cohabiting with a former student in Boston. He was gratifyingly effusive about the *Letters* and my satire book. Loosened up by his praise, I found myself confessing some of my involvement with Hunter. Horst had disappeared into a back alley to pee. 'When did he get in touch?' Saul asked. I told him it had been in April. 'He tried me first!' he said with a note of triumph.

I turned to face him on the pavement. My drunken vision moved blurrily and took a moment longer to stop than I did. 'He came to you?'

'Don't sound so surprised, Nicky. There aren't that many of us. And technically, I am your senior.' Saul drunkenly rattled one of those huge iron horse-hitches cemented into the walls of a palazzo.

The approach had been identical to the one they'd made to me. Saul remembered that it had been towards the end of February: an email to his academic address from Hunter's assistant, suggesting lunch.

'And what did you do?'

Saul put his hands in the pockets of his leather jacket and shrugged as though the answer was obvious. 'I said I was too busy.'

'Were you?'

'Not really, but I had better things to do and besides, there's something a little unsavoury about the guy, don't you think?'

'Which guy?'

'Hunter Gould.' He said the name with a falling intonation that made it sound like an unpleasant medical condition.

'Then what happened?'

'He pestered me for a while. Someone sent me transcripts of some letters. I had a look at them to get him off my back.'

'And?'

'They looked pretty sound to me. But how can you be sure without seeing the originals?'

Horst came back from the shadows and Saul seemed reluctant to continue the conversation.

'Do you remember who sent them?'

He shook his head.

Horst rejoined our party and the conversation turned towards academic politics and the disappointments of middle age.

And then the gloom that I thought I had outrun during the flight over Europe seemed to catch up with me. I started missing Lucius and Sarah. I left the others drinking at a table inside an unlikely plastic tent near the Palazzo Strozzi and walked back to my room to try and sleep.

While I was away, I had switched off my mobile phone to save money on roaming charges. As soon as I arrived back at Heathrow, there was a text message asking me to call; it had been sent from an unfamiliar phone number which I assumed was Leonora's. I rang it from the train into Paddington. Vera answered. It had been several weeks since our last communication. Through crackly, tunnel-hampered reception, she informed me a bit briskly that she needed to see me about a medical matter.

I remember the journey in with a peculiar vividness: the texture of the fabric on the seats of the train; the rosacea on the face of the man opposite who was reading Kerouac; the dusty trees of Green Park; the glint of chrome in the Audi showroom; garish sugar peaches in the window of the Japanese confectioner's where Vera was waiting for me, upstairs, in a private tea-room.

She was kneeling serenely in front of a low table when I arrived. In a blather of guilt and embarrassment, I apologised for not having been in touch.

A hostess poured green tea for both of us. 'I'm not so young to expect you to send me flowers,' Vera said. She thanked the hostess in Japanese and the woman discreetly withdrew.

'I apologise for imposing on you, but there is some news I must share. It appears that I am pregnant.' In the pause that followed, I began to speak. She held up her hand. 'Before you say anything, it is undoubtedly a consequence of our liaison,' she said. 'Of course, there is no question of my keeping the child.'

Even then, it struck me that her icy detachment conflicted with that word: *child*; but she gave no indication that the decision had caused her any pain.

I felt that some response was demanded of me. There was a ghastly symmetry between this and Leonora's accidental pregnancy all those years earlier. 'That's . . .' I began, and trailed off. In the alcove behind her hung a scroll-painting of a white crane. 'That's your decision.'

'This is a seasonal *wagashi*,' she said, passing me a plate holding a single sweet. 'It's made with bean paste and cherry blossom.'

It was the colour and texture of uncooked pastry. I took it and ate it. I have no recollection of its flavour.

'I never foresaw this happening,' she went on. 'Because of my unusual physiology, it's important

159

to act early. I have consulted my own doctor in Moscow and he has agreed to oversee the procedure.'

At that moment, I experienced a surge of relief: Vera was presenting me not with a problem but with a solution, and one so elegant and simple that it seemed to have been arrived at using formal logic. My anxiety gave way to a deep sense of magnanimity. 'If there's anything you need from me, Vera, just say the word.'

Vera sipped her tea with tiny, pecking movements. It was impossible to reconcile the woman in front of me with my fragmentary recollection of the night we had spent together. She glanced up at me. 'You may ask why I bother telling you at all.'

'Not at all,' I said. 'It involves both of us.'

'I'm letting you know as a courtesy, in case you have strong feelings to the contrary.' She set down her cup and let the implications of her words sink in. There was an unmistakable challenge in her eyes. I felt the profound insincerity of everything that I had said and I looked away.

'No,' I said, 'I don't.'

'Then that is decided.' She poured more tea. 'I will need, therefore, to ask your assistance.'

'Whatever it is, I'll do it.'

'I have obligations here that must be attended to in my absence.'

Rather blithely, perhaps, I promised her my complete co-operation.

'Given the delicacy of this matter, it's of the utmost importance that I can speak to you in total confidence,' she said.

'Of course.' I couldn't imagine a bigger secret than the one we already shared.

'You must *swear*, Nicholas,' she said, and her nostrils flared with a passion that brought a chastening flashback of our entwined bodies.

'I swear,' I said, though the intensity of her voice was making me nervous.

She glanced towards the door as though she feared another intrusion, then leaned forward and paused. She was clearly waiting for me to do the same. Hesitantly, I extended myself towards her across the low table. I moved closer with some trepidation and averted my eyes to the jade brooch on the lapel of her coat. Her breath provoked a strange tingle on my neck as she lowered her voice to a whisper. 'Jack is not dead,' she said.

For a moment, I didn't know how to respond. 'Hunter told me . . .' I began.

'Hunter had reasons for telling you what he did. Your continued interest in my brother is potentially awkward for Hunter and Sinan.'

'Why? They seemed pretty certain that I'm the one who should feel awkward: I couldn't tell your brother's work from Johnson's.'

'My brother owes his livelihood to a certain facility for pastiche. Let me say that there are papers extant . . . There are papers whose value has been . . . compromised.'

'Johnson papers?'

'Not only Johnson.'

'Your brother can do other writers?'

'My brother is simply the only such savant that you are aware of, Nicholas. The work is not of a kind that I can easily explain. Nor would it be in your interest to know more.'

As I recall the conversation now, it strikes me that the word 'savant' was bracketed by the tiniest hesitation.

'Meaning there are others?'

The look she gave me left me in little doubt that the answer was in the affirmative. She seemed to want me to understand that whatever Malevin was up to had been wider in scope than I had ever conceived of. More savants like Jack Telauga? A factory of forgers, working like Victorian copy clerks in the bowels of the St James's Square mansion? I told her she was embarrassing herself, but even as I said it, I regretted my choice of words.

She levelled her gaze at me. 'As you can imagine, I am not easily embarrassed.'

You have to marvel at her sleight of hand. Her frumpishness and built-up shoes, her whole odd being that spoke of some chromosomal abnormality, she had suddenly magicked into a source of strength.

'I don't trust Hunter or Sinan to take care of Jack in my absence. It's not a question of competence, you understand. The fact is that our interests are not entirely congruent. Hunter and Sinan admire Jack and his work very much, they respect what he represents. But his actual well-being is a lesser consideration. Whereas my feelings for Jack are very simple. I love him.' She said it with a finality that brooked no contradiction.

Until this moment, I have always assumed that Vera had her story prepared, but it's not inconceivable that she was improvising expertly. The suggestion of forgery was as convenient a front for her as it had been for Hunter. After all, there is a kind of logic to using a plausible criminal enterprise to conceal a diabolical one.

'Vera,' I said, and began wearily to enumerate my objections to this plan.

She cut me off with a raised palm. 'I do not want to elaborate on the nature of your obligation to me, but I do have a sense of pride. I do not want to speak about what I am giving up.' There was a catch in her voice. Tears started into the corners of her eyes. She dabbed one away with her forefinger. It was clear to me then that her indifference had been a pose. Our recklessness had unearthed her buried wish for a child.

At the corner of Piccadilly and St James's Street she stood on tiptoe to kiss me on both cheeks. She smelled of cigarette smoke and dry-cleaning. She drew back, holding my gaze for a moment, and gave my hand the lightest of touches. 'Nicholas,' she said softly, almost to herself. Then she turned and left, bobbing through the crowd with her unmistakable walk, until she was lost amongst the passers-by.

Did I have a choice? Of course, I did. It was in my power to walk away then. There was no rational reason to be sentimental about the abortion. I didn't have to help Vera. But I think the truth is that I was moved by her plight. I felt guilty about inflaming and then dashing her hope for a child. The least I could do was care for Jack while she was gone.

CHAPTER 15

And so, a week to the day after I'd read my paper in Florence, Vera and Misha Bykov brought Jack to my house. They arrived in a large, black new model Mercedes. Jack lay asleep on the back seat under a tartan blanket.

Bykov's involvement was a particular surprise. It turned out that though he was Malevin's hired muscle, he was unquestioningly loyal to Vera.

He waited in the front garden while Vera followed me into the house. 'Are you sure it's wise to have Bykov in this?' I asked her. Through the gaps in the net curtain, I could see him lighting another cigarette. He rubbed his rumpled face with his hand and poked under the acanthus with the toe of one of his Italian winklepickers.

'Misha is an ally,' Vera said. I must have looked doubtful. She said he was a good man and trustworthy. 'He has formed a sentimental attachment to me,' she added.

'Does he know . . . ?'

'About the pregnancy? Yes.'

From the way Bykov had avoided looking me in the eye when we met, I'd had the feeling that he believed me guilty of some failure of gallantry. Now I knew.

'Vera, I'm so sorry about all this,' I said.

'I am also sorry,' she said. 'Whether I could carry a child to term is doubtful. But I have known too much death to discard life lightly.'

She was uncharacteristically fragile that day. I suppose that even at that early stage of pregnancy, the physiological changes were playing havoc with her mood.

Vera roused Jack from the back seat of the car. Bykov and I each took one of his arms across our shoulders and shuffled him across the threshold like a drunkard. He was less substantial than I anticipated – his body strangely soft and light.

We put him in Lucius's room at the back of the house; it had a door that locked and Vera had made it abundantly clear that the less visible he was, the better.

She waited for him to wake up in order that he might adjust more gently to his new surroundings. She assured me that she would be gone no longer than a week, but it was clear that she was testing the elasticity of my tolerance by progressively revealing the more alarming aspects of my new charge. Virtually the last thing she gave me was a spongebag with his medications, pepper spray and a chemical cosh to use if he became, in her words, 'unruly'. Naturally, she told me the last two were merely a formality, and the likelihood of their being necessary was tiny.

The whole of his worldly goods was in two plastic bags. I left them on top of the empty drawers in Lucius's room for Jack to arrange as he saw fit, and cleared Lucius's desk of its Warhammer figurines. Vera emphasised the importance of keeping him to his room. She said he was in every respect like a traveller from a distant country. The currency baffled him; he found it hard to follow the speech of the natives. He would be happiest simply sitting and reading or writing. I should be concerned to keep him off the streets as much as possible, particularly in the early evenings and at night. He had a healthy appetite but preferred simple, lightly seasoned food. She gave me a list of favoured items.

It reminded me of the detailed instructions that Leonora used to leave me when the children were toddlers and I was at home looking after them. I'd invariably chuck them away. Looking after tiny children is miserable enough without being entirely deprived of your agency. Out would go the schedule, the naps, the tubs of sweet potato and healthy snacks. And more often than not, Leonora would return to a house in chaos, with the children rampaging around it, wired on sugar and sleep deprivation.

Jack stirred in his sleep at about five in the afternoon. Vera sat beside him and woke him up gradually by applying gentle pressure to one of his hands. It moves me to recall her tenderness to him. When he was awake, she helped him upright and immediately gave him two pills and a large mug of warm milk which he took without demur.

'Are you well, Jack?' she asked.

There was no response. He had a toddler's ability to ignore questions he regarded as superfluous.

'I have to leave you for a while.'

Now I saw definite anxiety in his eyes.

'I'm entrusting you to the care of my friend, Dr Slopen.'

His lips issued a muffled noise that sounded like: 'Doctor?'

I used to chastise Lucius and Sarah when they told their friends that I was 'not a real doctor', but privately I've always understood the profound reassurance that the medical qualification brings.

'If you behave yourself, Dr Slopen will let you use his library.'

At this, he brightened and put down the mug of milk. He rubbed his shaved head – it seemed to be a tic, a form of self-comforting.

'Goodbye, Jack.' She inclined her head slightly towards him in farewell. I saw her to the door.

I could tell she was on the brink of framing a question. Then she paused on the threshold and said, 'I need to ask again. I need to be sure this is what you want.'

'This . . . ?'

'The termination, Nicholas.'

'It's impossible, Vera. I've got no money.'

'I have money. Don't let the reason be money.'

'Of course it's more than that. Bringing up kids is hard.'

'I think you and I could make each other happy,

Nicholas. Intellectual companionship is very important. Sexually we are compatible. You have been a good father already.'

'Vera, I'm on my uppers. I don't have the resources – emotional, financial, spiritual. You name it. I'm sorry. I'm so sorry.'

She touched my cheek and smiled. 'I don't need to turn you into a criminal. I just needed to be sure.'

He was up on his feet and scanning the spines of our hardbacks when I returned. Against all my objections, Leonora had arranged the books in the front room by size, resulting in a frankly absurd collocation of volumes: *Rat Pack Confidential* next to Borges's *Collected Poetry*, beside *The Joy of Cooking*.

'You have a fine quantity of books, Dr . . .'

'Slopen.'

'Yes . . .'

I pulled out my Norton Critical Edition of Milton as a kind of offering and gently nudged him with it. He took it, peered at the cover – no sign of the longsightedness you'd expect from a man his age – and handed it back to me. 'We'll have no more Milton, sir. I have a lively appreciation of his merits, but no one would wish *Paradise Lost* to be any longer. I do not share your high opinion of "Lycidas". The diction is harsh, the rhymes uncertain, and the numbers unpleasing.'

'That's Johnson's opinion.'

'That, sir, is my opinion.' He glared at me fiercely.

Written down, Jack's words have a comic quality that was entirely absent at that moment. His size, his deep and grating voice and his belligerent manner made him an intimidating presence.

When I was a boy, I once took home a gull that I found on Wandsworth Common. For some reason, it allowed me to pick it up and carry it to our house. To this day, I don't know what, if anything, was wrong with it. With its fishy eyes and scissor-like beak, it had, at best, an ambiguous pathos. But I was so eager to play the role of saviour that I didn't notice.

After a couple of hours, it grew fed up with being coddled and turned truculent, snapping at my sister's hair and flying around the living room. My dad ended up jamming it in a cardboard box and taking it back to the common.

Jack had something of the same aura, even when he was asleep. With its shaved head and prominent nose, his sleeping visage resembled the death-mask of a Victorian criminal.

Still, he came obediently up the stairs at the promise of being shown the books in my study. He was less steady negotiating the ascent and had to stop on the landing where the staircase turns at a right angle in order to adjust his limbs. When we reached the study, I pointed to the armchair and he sat down heavily. After an instant, he took a small notebook and a Pentel from his pocket; he evidently used them for jotting down memoranda; but, having opened the book, he wrote nothing, simply holding the pen over the page as if their mere presence was a comfort to him.

'Who are the other members of your household?' he asked.

'Just me.'

'What time is it?'

'Five o'clock.'

'How . . . how did I come to this place?' The confidence he'd shown asserting his judgement about Milton had evaporated. In its place was a profound bafflement. Suddenly, he was as vulnerable as a little child. You could see why Vera was so protective of him. I could see there were other questions behind the ones he dared to ask: *Who am I? Who are you? What's going on?* I know from my own experience of reawakening that the sense of amnesia is so total and so distressing that you do everything you can to avoid acknowledging it.

'Why don't you rest here for a while?' I said. 'We can put your things away after supper. I'm going to pop round to the supermarket and get a chicken. Is roast chicken okay with you?'

While I was speaking, it struck me that he was having difficulty following my words. He looked intently at my face, as though he was sorting through a mass of incomprehensible verbiage for a clue to my meaning. Finally, there was a glimmer of understanding. 'Roast fowl?'

'That's right,' I said.

He wagged his head with an odd subcontinental nod that seemed to signify assent.

I had a scintilla of anxiety about leaving him unattended in the house; however, it turned out that he had no intention of being left alone. As I was getting my coat, I heard him labouring down the stairs, and, despite my repeated suggestion that he stay indoors, he walked out with me into the street without a coat, apparently indifferent to the rain which had begun to fall since his sister's departure.

'Why is nothing known of the habits of your country?' he asked.

This dazed but voluble and seemingly reasonable companion bore no relation to the mute lump I'd encountered in the basement of Malevin's London home. For all the oddness of his conversation, he didn't attract a second glance in Costcutter. In his sweatpants and stained T-shirt, he looked like one of the Polish builders who pop in for jars of bigos and sauerkraut.

My country? What was he talking about? I could only think he meant South London. 'That's an exaggeration,' I said, 'but I know what you mean. People are just snobbish about it. My wife was the same way. There's a perception that it's a bit grotty, but, as you can see, it's actually green and quite pleasant. How about you? Where are you from?'

'Lichfield. My father, God rest his memory, was a bookseller there.'

'Of course he was.'

★   ★   ★

Since Leonora had left, there hadn't seemed much point in cooking. It was nice, somehow, to have a guest in the house. We used to roast a chicken most Sundays, when the kids were small, sometimes having it as our evening meal at five so we could eat together. I poured myself and Jack a glass of wine; it was probably contraindicated for both of us: we were both on medication. Behind the day's excitement lurked that nagging feeling of grief, and the simple act of preparing the chicken for the oven – butter, lemon and a sprig of thyme in the cavity, salt and pepper – recalled dozens of happier occasions when I had performed the same task.

It would be a while before the food would be ready so I suggested to Jack that he might like to have some bread and cheese in the meantime.

We kept our bread in a big blue-ware crock that Leonora had found discarded on the pavement about ten years earlier outside a house that was being renovated. Her original idea had been to use it as a planter, but after we had scrubbed it clean, it looked so pretty that it seemed a pity to fill it with dirt again. We used it for storing bread, and I improvised a cover with a wooden chopping board that I cut to fit with a neighbour's jigsaw. The crock itself was decorated with blurry flowers and swags of foliage and pastoral characters frolicking. I'm not sure I ever looked at it with much attention, but, as I rummaged in it for the sliced loaf I'd bought that morning, Jack couldn't take his eyes off it. His lips moved and I heard the rumbly bass voice with its mushy sibilants say: 'I am fallen among *savages*.'

'Savages?' I said.

'Nay, sir, *worse*. Depend upon it.'

He wagged his head at me and his eyes took on their ferocious beadiness. 'Is it not to be supposed that the heathenest savages in Creation, though ignorant of their redemption, know better than to defile the staff of life with *night-soil*?'

His emphasis threw me for a second, but then I grasped the cause of his outrage. 'I know what you're thinking,' I said. 'This isn't a toilet. It's a bread crock.' Then, baffled by the intensity of his outraged eyes, I added, redundantly: 'For putting bread in.'

'Sir, you are refuted by the shape of this vessel which sensibly proclaims it to be a po. Who are you that claim to love the poetry of Milton, yet are so coarse as to make no distinction between nutritive and excrementitious matter?'

It should have been obvious then – if such a profoundly unlikely thing could ever be obvious. His verbal powers and deep curiosity about the world in which he had found himself bore no relation to my – admittedly slight – understanding of autism. Even a savant should have had a trace of his sister's accent, but he had none; he spoke no Russian, but could make himself understood in Dutch, a language which Vera didn't speak at all.

That first night, the misunderstanding about the

bread crock aside, I found him a wise and sympathetic companion. It felt like a long time since I'd been able to unburden myself to someone and after two glasses of wine, I began telling him all about Leonora's departure. He listened silently as I fumbled to find the words to tap my unspoken grief. For a man whose religious faith was so deeply held, he was surprisingly undoctrinaire in his responses.

'These are the burthens of life, Dr Slopen. There is no fortune so large, or wit so keen, or sagacity so provident, that it can obtrude itself between us and the sharp pangs of loss. I know it is of small comfort to know that others have and will suffer just as you do; nevertheless, it is the truth. Furthermore, I am confident that the passage of time will bring the possibility of a close and more cordial connection with your children, Lucius and . . . ?'

'Sarah.'

'. . . and Sarah.' His voice echoed mine with a gratifying finality. '*Lucius.*' He rolled the word around on his tongue. 'A very fine name. Its root is *lux*. While not strictly Christian, by its reference to light it connotes the blessings of our Saviour. And as for this rascal, Gaspard, what is one to make of such a fellow?'

'In fairness to Caspar, I think he really loves my wife and he's able to offer a kind of security and romance that disappeared from our life a long time ago,' I said, preferring to sound magnanimous than dwell on the darkness I really felt. 'Presumably, he could have taken up with any number of floozies in their twenties, but he's chosen to take on a woman in her forties with children. That's a big commitment.'

'Commitment, sirrah? I'll have the fellow committed; aye, and hanged after! I may very well like another man's hat or coat, but does that give me title to it? I think you will find he is one of these restless, covetous men who looks enviously on what he has not got. I fear for your wife when his eye lights – as it will – upon a new interest.'

'Maybe,' I said. 'I'm not so sure.'

Seeing that talking about Leonora was making me gloomy, he tactfully withdrew and went up to his tiny bedroom. Later, I heard the bed creaking as he moved around on it.

CHAPTER 16

I'd got into the habit of rising late after Leonora moved out. Coming to slowly in that big bed, prolonging the moment before I had to confront the adjusted facts of my newly solitary life seemed like the only real pleasure that was left to me. But the following morning, a Monday, the phone rang before seven. It was Leonora. 'It's me,' she said. 'Are you awake? I waited as long as I could.'

'I am now,' I said.

'Thank God for that.' I heard her sigh. The relief in her voice was audible.

My heart leaped. For a second, it seemed as though she was beside me in the half-dark of the bedroom, the glow of her warm yeasty skin against mine. And there was a recognition in some part of my soul that this was inevitable, this was what I'd been waiting for: my wife to return to me. 'I've missed you too,' I said.

'I can't get into all that now, Nicholas,' she said, in a much more familiar tone of icy impatience. 'Lucius has lost his passport. He says he left it in the drawers of the Blido.'

Leonora knew all our flat-pack Swedish furniture by name. This one, the Blido, like a parodic microcosm of the Procedure itself, reconstituted for me a particular rainy afternoon on the Purley Way and two hours' exasperated fumbling with wooden dowels and Allen keys.

'Can you see if it's there? We're supposed to be on a train to Paris at three.'

I hauled myself out of the bed and padded down the corridor to Lucius's room.

Forgetting Jack was inside, I went in without knocking. The sight of him asleep stopped me in my tracks. He had pulled the window open in the night and broken the handle. The roller blind was flapping in the wind. With each gust, a wedge of sunlight briefly illuminated his sleeping face. His head looked grey and monumental against the pillow. His breath came in a deep, stertorous rumble.

'Any sign?'

Leonora's voice surprised me. For a moment, I had been unaware that I had the handset clapped to my ear.

'Just a second,' I said.

'Why are you whispering?'

I told her I'd call her back.

Jack was stirring. My intrusion had wakened him. The lids of his right eye parted with reptilian precision. 'Who art thou?' he asked in a hollow, terrified voice.

There was only a handful of occasions during our

acquaintance when he used this particular archaism. It was always when some emotion overwhelmed him: sometimes a natural human warmth, sometimes anger. At this moment, it was fear.

'It's me. Nicholas. Dr Slopen.'

'And this place?'

'My home.'

'Very well,' he said, in a voice that suggested its opposite.

I apologised for waking him and explained that I needed to fetch something. His hands gripped the top edge of the duvet and his eyes followed me across the room as I went over to Lucius's desk. Its drawers were filled with a number of plastic tubs containing Warhammer paraphernalia. It is, frankly, a kind of progress that Lucius felt able to leave this stuff behind when he moved out. I understood the pleasure he took in it, but I always hoped he'd grow up to be more like Leonora with her talent for sociability and live connection than me, with my bookish solipsism and dead companions.

A sandalwood box in one of the lower drawers held Lucius's passport. I took it out and flipped to the identification page: there was my son, in a scrawny and epicene phase of his early adolescence. In the same box were some cigarette papers, a packet of dried-up rolling tobacco and some condoms. It seemed less like evidence of a secret life than a collection of talismans, an offering to the gods of manhood. I remembered myself at his age, and my own desperate impatience to become an adult. Oh my poor fatherless boy. Momentarily, I was overwhelmed.

'Sir, I observe that you are melancholy.' The voice was resonant and gruff from sleep, but not without compassion. 'Will you tell me the reason for it?'

'I'm just having difficulty getting used to this new reality.'

From the sparkle in Jack's beady eyes, I judged that I had told him something of interest. 'Alas, you are become like me, Dr Slopen,' he said, 'a gloomy gazer on a world to which you have little relation.'

'My son needs this,' I said, wiping my eyes. 'I'm sorry for disturbing you.'

He watched me in silence as I left the room.

Leonora and I agreed to meet in town so that I could hand over the passport. She said she was giving a recital in Paris and wanted to bring the kids. I pressed her for more details. She was reluctant to tell me anything else.

'What about Caspar?'

'What about him?' She sounded defensive. One of the tacit conventions of our new relationship was that we never mentioned Caspar's name.

'Is he coming?'

'What do you want to know, Nicholas? Is he coming to Paris? Yes he is.'

'No,' I said, suddenly conscious of a volcanic pressure in my chest. 'What I want to know is, is he coming inside you?' By the time I'd finished the sentence, I barely recognised the voice as my own. The white heat of sexual jealousy overwhelmed me. I felt – and I say it with no sense of hyperbole – that I was possessed by a demon.

There was a silence at the other end of the line. Just then, I heard an extraordinary noise coming from Lucius's bedroom. It was a bestial sound, a roar of pain and bewilderment, like something from a trapped animal. I told Leonora that I had to go.

As well as the Warhammer figurines, the boxes in Lucius's desk contained the tins of paint and tiny brushes he used for painting them; and at the back of the drawer, a number of old copies of the *Telegraph*, hoarded because its big broadsheet pages made it perfect for shielding the desk from paint splatters. It was one of these that Jack was holding when I entered the room.

There was disarray. It appeared that his curiosity had been piqued by my intrusion and he had decided to investigate the desk. There he had found the newspaper. He was kneeling on the floor, clutching the page, rocking back and forth. As I came through the door, he stood up.

The dimensions of Lucius's tiny bedroom exaggerated Jack's bulk; he seemed vast and as he gesticulated madly with the paper, his arms flapped like the wings of an enormous bird.

I drew back from him with an agility that surprised me, then slipped and fell hard against the doorknob. I don't recall losing consciousness, but in remembering the events I come to a lacuna that foreshadows the much greater and more troubling discontinuity which surrounds the Procedure itself.

My next clear recollection is of lying on the day-bed in the sitting room. I have no memory of going down the stairs.

There was a white fuzz in my peripheral vision on the left side of my head like an out-of-focus cauliflower, an after-effect of my collision with the door. I was aware of that strange, sourceless melancholy that sometimes follows physical injury: the *timor mortis* of a wounded soma. Something heavy and wet lay on my head. I touched it. It was a damp dish-cloth.

'A poultice of rasped carrots,' Jack explained, with a certain tenderness. He gestured at me with the newspaper. 'What means this?'

'What does what mean?'

'Do not push-pin with me, sir! What manner of devil are you and what hell is this?'

'You're staying at my house. Your sister had to go to Moscow. She asked me to look after you for a few days.'

'To *Moscow*?' His voice swooped with incredulity. '*Lies* and *impudence*! I have no sister!'

'Would you sit down? You're being rather aggressive.'

'Aggressive? And who would not be out of countenance to be treated as I have been?'

'Look,' I said, 'I'm sorry if you feel that you've been mistreated, but you're a guest in this house, not a prisoner.'

My words appeared to calm him. 'Aye, mistreated,' he said. He gazed vacantly for a moment at the floor then thrust the newspaper at me. 'What is the meaning of this?'

I scanned the page of headlines for a clue to his question. 'Rail disruption this summer? Choirgirl saved by canopy in Venice hotel fall?'

'Will you not speak the King's English, you dog!'

'I don't understand your question!' I shouted back at him, trying to match the ferocity of his exclamation.

'This, this, what is the meaning of this!' He was stabbing the date on the page with his finger. 'What is twenty hundred and eight?'

'July the twentieth 2008 is the date of that newspaper. Lucius saved it for his painting.' As he turned his uncomprehending stare on me once more, I saw that my tendency to amplify my replies was just confusing him. 'The date. That's the date.'

'By what calendar? The Hebraic?'

'No. The normal one. Whatever it's called. The Julian. The one that counts from the birth of Christ.'

''Tis not possible.' His voice had shrunk to a disbelieving whisper.

'Of course it is.' I felt in my pocket for the passport that had started this trouble. 'Look at this. It's my son's. See – he was born in 1995.'

Jack studied the passport closely and handed it

back to me with a bewildered look. 'Never,' he said. 'It is not possible. Today is not twenty hundred and eight.'

'No,' I said. 'Today is twenty hundred and nine. That's from last year.'

He gave me a look of haunted incredulity.

'Double-check it,' I said. 'Look in any of those books and see when it was printed.'

Cagily, as if he were afraid to take his eyes off me, he glanced around the shelves and helped himself, one by one, to an armful of volumes. The first book he opened was my Everyman's edition of *Parade's End*. Then a couple of Arden Shakespeares and Charles Barber's *Early Modern English*. After those, he went back to the shelves and took off the fifth and final volume of my 1812 edition of the works of Henry Fielding. They were a gift from my mother on my graduation and though not of major bibliographic interest, they're some of the very few books I own that you could call antiquarian. He opened its foxed, yellowing pages; a book that was being printed the year Napoleon invaded Russia; before a single railway line had defaced the countryside; when London was a city of just over a million people, and the hot air balloon was the pinnacle of aviation, before the internal combustion engine or penicillin had ever been thought of, and yet which was to him shocking in its modernity. He studied the title page intently, running his finger over the type, until it reached the final incontrovertible date at its bottom. I remembered how I had done the same the day my poor late mother handed me the books so proudly over lunch the first and last day that she came up to Cambridge. I was full of self-love in those days and had thought ungenerously that she looked small and grey and timorous. And I remembered how I had said something conceited and ungrateful: 'It's a bit out of my period but it'll look good on the shelves.'

His whole demeanour altered. He seemed to slump and grow weary. Almost in a whisper he said: 'Nay, sir. I am deceived.' The book slid out of his hands and flopped onto the floor. He tottered weakly to the armchair and sat down.

'Sir, I pray you, conduct me to those that know me. I am gone out of my wits.' He sat there, staring hopelessly at his big, sallow feet. 'I am a gentleman, sir. If I have done you an unkindness, I will offer you redress as you think fit.'

He didn't move. The silence stretched so long that I wondered if he'd had some kind of stroke, or shut down as he had seemed to that day in the St James's Square mansion.

I approached his motionless bulk. From it rose an odd array of smells: musty clothes, pear drops and a vegetal scent of decay.

Vera had left me with two numbers: one British and one Russian mobile phone. Both diverted me to a recorded message. I called Bykov instead. I have no difficulty being assertive in English, but speaking in Russian, I feel myself quailing and diffident; a handicap made more acute by the natural brusqueness of most Russian interlocutors. Shorn of the assistance of gesture and visual clues, telephone conversations are the hardest linguistic challenge for a non-native speaker, but even given the strange density of the Russian language, our communication was so laconic as to be absurd.

Bykov picked up on the second ring. 'I'm listening,' he said.

I tried to explain the incidents that had taken place that morning, but I ended up sounding more hysterical than genuinely endangered. Bykov told me there was nothing to be afraid of, and he chided me for not giving Jack his medication. He made it gently but firmly plain that we had no option but to go along with Vera's plan until her return. He could sense that I was looking for a way out, and wasn't going to offer me one. 'Give him the pills, Nicholas,' were his parting words. 'Or he will go out of his mind.'

The pills were in the spongebag Vera had given me. After a moment's hesitation, I took the precautionary pepper spray as well, slipping it into the pocket of my dressing gown.

Jack was sitting quietly in my armchair in the front room, reading Volume One of my edition of the *Collected Letters* with the same mixture of delight and recognition that you might feel on looking over an old diary. He was so remorseful about my injury that he required no persuasion to take his medicine. His outburst over, he had the vulnerability and trustingness of a toddler.

He undressed in front of me without embarrassment. The suggestion of physical strength that he presented clothed was revealed, when he stripped, to be largely illusory. He was overweight. The fat on his legs was loose and shambling like the flesh on the hindquarters of a cow. His belly was white and awkwardly protuberant. His muscles were mostly wasted and his knees caved in slightly giving a teepee-like structure to his stance. He was wearing red Y-fronts with white piping. Most strikingly of all, the front of his left thigh bore a harsh and incongruous tattoo – a large black roundel intersected by a cross. He washed, and shaved himself with a disposable razor that Vera had packed into his bag. I glimpsed him through the bathroom door, working the lather over his face with the painstaking and clumsy slowness of a four-year-old icing a cake. For breakfast he ate a couple of bread rolls and a banana, and drank six cups of tea. He had the *Ballymaloe Cookery Book* open in front of him and as he chewed, he moved his eyes over its pages with the joyless and puzzled attention that he gave to everything. Outside the kitchen window, next door's cat stalked proprietorially through the ruins of my vegetable patch.

The medication appeared to work on him so swiftly that its initial effects must have been purely placebo. Its true pharmacological impact was evident after about an hour. I noticed a dimming of his eyes, a loss of co-ordination and a slackness in his facial muscles that was familiar to me from my visits to the mansion. At this point, he became very docile and manageable. I understood Bykov and Vera's insistence on his taking the pills: they were to cushion his responses to the traumas of the everyday.

I helped him to the car, buckled him into the passenger seat and we set off. I thought the journey might send him to sleep, but the view from the window was more stimulant than sedative. Even in his medicated state, he watched the scenery intently.

As we drove, I found myself talking about Leonora – to have a confessor who was incapacitated by drugs and half insane was better than to have no one. He occasionally mumbled something unintelligible. Once he said a phrase I recognised as a quote from Johnson himself: 'Life is a progress from want to want, not from enjoyment to enjoyment.'

The city was a log jam of traffic. I had to stick the car in the car park on Poland Street and we walked to Leicester Square. The medication which held Jack's anxiety in check also affected his balance. He was like a huge, blinkered horse, stumbling through the streets, yet strangely unnoticed by the tourists and passers-by fixated on the self-conscious flamboyance of Soho.

I had texted Leonora to apologise. I had said I was sorry, and that whatever my feelings were, Lucius and Sarah needed us both to maintain some semblance of dignity as parents. But I didn't feel able to introduce Jack to her. For one thing, it breached my oath of confidentiality to Vera. But the second and greater obstacle was his sheer outlandishness. In his unmedicated state, it might have been possible to pass him off as a visiting academic, but the way he was now, his eyes dulled from the drugs and walking unsteadily, he raised too many unanswerable questions.

Brief Encounter was showing in repertory at the Prince Charles Cinema. I got us both tickets and we made our way into the auditorium about ten minutes after the film had started. He was rapt by the spectacle. I'd bought a couple of meat pies and a gargantuan take-out cup of tea which I passed to him in the darkness. He received them warily. 'Is it not opprobrious?' he whispered. 'I have no wish to earn the minister's contumely.'

'We're not in church,' I explained. 'This is a . . . I looked at his puzzled face. I think at some preconscious level I had an inkling of the problem I was dealing with. I understood at least that I would have to compromise on certain elements of our shared reality. 'This', I said, 'is a playhouse.'

Of course, I had misgivings about leaving him, but I reasoned that I would be gone for half an hour at the most. There was over an hour of the film to run. I unwrapped his pie and when I judged that his attention was firmly held by the film and the food, I told him I was slipping out to the toilet.

★   ★   ★

It took me eight minutes to get to the cafe on Charing Cross Road where Leonora and I had arranged to meet. There was no sign of her. I ordered an espresso and waited. Caspar's big SUV finally pulled up, hazard lights flashing, and disgorged Leonora and the children.

There was a bittersweet delight in seeing the kids. Sarah gave me a kiss. Lucius, who appeared to have grown in the weeks since I'd last seen him, consented to an awkward hug. Caspar remained in the car with a sheepish expression on his face.

'What's all this about?' I asked.

'Mum's playing in Paris tonight and we're all going,' said Sarah. 'Der-brain forgot his passport.'

I'd like to think that in other circumstances Leonora and I might have welcomed the chance to talk to one another, but she was all business and eager to get on. Five minutes later, they were off, roaring up Charing Cross Road, like a brief intermission of happiness, a moving oasis of normalcy. You don't need to be in a carcass to see what's best about human existence, but it helps. As I walked back to the cinema, my thoughts circled obsessively around that car, moving off with my family into a future that I played no part in.

When I got back to the Prince Charles he was gone. Pie wrappers and the lingering scent of pear drops marked the place where we had been sitting, but there was no other sign of him. He wasn't in the loo, and the usherette claimed not to have seen anyone leave. I raised my voice. The half-dozen heads in the auditorium turned to register their disapproval. Suddenly, I was hot with shame and panic.

There was a traffic policeman standing next to his motorcycle on the corner of Panton Street. I asked him if he'd seen a vulnerable adult, late fifties, bald, wearing tracksuit trousers and a grey T-shirt.

'You lost someone, sir?'

'I think I might have.' The dyspeptic feeling of anxiety was building in the pit of my stomach.

'Does he know the area, sir?' he asked. 'Is there anywhere he might go?'

'Not really,' I said.

'Can you do any better on the description?'

I felt close to tears. I could find nothing to describe him. It takes detachment and a degree of composure to formulate a description. The quiddity of him was, in any case, hard to pin down. His silence. The odd smell. The eyes.

'Are you a relative, sir?'

I told the officer I would carry on looking myself. For forty-five minutes, I jogged through the streets between Leicester Square, Shaftesbury Avenue and Charing Cross Road, until the fact of his disappearance became unignorable.

CHAPTER 17

Misha Bykov took the news better than I had anticipated. My relief was quickly succeeded by a feeling of chagrin: his calmness stemmed from his assumption that I was incompetent. He'd been expecting something like this to happen.

The irony – again – is that, though I didn't know it, I had very nearly found Jack without Bykov's help. I learned later that he had tried to get into Black's, the members' club on Dean Street, and had been rebuffed. The altercation was considerable and I can only have missed it by a couple of minutes. But by the time I got there, Soho's grimy and dissolute indifference had closed over the recent drama. It was all quiet, and a trio of crack addicts were hunched around a pipe in a doorway, their backs turned to the closed-circuit television cameras which supervised the street. There was no sign that Jack had ever been there.

Bykov met me in Bar Italia and listened in silence while I told him what little I knew. His big Mercedes sat in a loading bay opposite the cafe. Every parking attendant who came past quickened their pace when they saw it and then made the same disappointed swerve at the sight of its diplomatic plates. Bykov stirred three sugars into his espresso with a surprising daintiness and then drained it. 'Come on, let's go,' he said.

I got into the Mercedes, which reeked of Magic Tree air freshener, and we drove to the Poland Street car park, in order, I assumed, to pick up my car. I was wrong. Bykov descended quickly to the deepest, most subterranean levels of the basement, parked in an obscure corner and gestured for me to get into the boot.

'It's a joke?' I said.

'*Ne shutka*,' said Bykov. No joke.

There followed about half an hour of nausea-inducing darkness and joggling which culminated in my being helped out in a gloomy inward courtyard somewhere behind the St James's Square mansion.

Bykov told me this was the only blind spot on the mansion's cameras. He said it was important that Hunter and Sinan knew nothing of our connection. I had already had an inkling of his loyalty to Vera. It was only later that I understood the depth of his support for her.

He cautioned me to stay inside the car and disappeared for five minutes. He came back holding a small box. Its screen showed a digital map of Greater London, a ragged omelette shape which he magnified progressively until we were watching a little red sphere making its way along a side road in the vicinity of Holborn.

'So. That's where the dog is buried,' said Bykov, using a conventional Russian idiom that sounded oddly sinister in the circumstances. 'Let's go.'

He glanced at the boot and I climbed back in.

This time I was in there for no more than a few minutes when I felt the car pull up abruptly. I heard a hasty rap on the lid and Bykov's face appeared, silhouetted by the – to me – dazzling daylight. 'Quick,' he said, 'in front.'

He had stopped on a cul-de-sac near the Haymarket. I took my place in the passenger seat. The smell of air freshener was so strong that for a moment I wondered if I hadn't perhaps been better off in the boot. Bykov passed me the device. 'Where to?' He wanted me to navigate.

I wrestled with my imperfect knowledge of Russian imperatives, aspectual tenses and verbs of motion in order to direct him through the streets in pursuit of the red sphere. At first glance, I had had an intuition about where Jack had gone, but it seemed so absurd that I dismissed it. And yet, as I watched, it became clear that I was right: Jack was making his way to Johnson's old house in Gough Square.

At number 17, boxed in by unprepossessing offices, stands the eighteenth-century building that was once Johnson's home. All creaky floors and odd angles, it's an unlikely time traveller. It escaped the Blitz by a whisker (the roof was burned to ashes in an air raid) and it somehow survived the redevelopment of the City that followed. When you come upon it from Fleet Street, following a finger-post down an unpromising alleyway between a McDonald's and a Starbucks to get there, the age and detail of it transport you to a moment when the city had a more human scale. I've spent much time there myself as a visitor and giving talks. On its top floor, beneath the restored twentieth-century ceiling, is the garret where Johnson and his assistants compiled the dictionary. A swinging wooden partition on the front wall can be pulled out to divide the room into two. There is something both ingenious and jury-rigged about it. This, as much as any of the more conventional memorabilia in the house, gives a flavour of the physical character of Johnson's world.

'He's stopped,' I said. 'I think I know where he is.'

The traffic was heavy, and in spite of Bykov's muscular driving, we got bogged down in the heaving streets around Covent Garden. When we'd finally extricated ourselves and were nearing Chancery Lane, the sphere, which had been motionless for five or so minutes, began to move again, and now very quickly. There was no hope of catching him now. All we could do was watch as he sped up Ludgate Hill, past St Paul's, and shot north, finally coming to a stop about 150 metres south of London Wall.

There was no longer any need to hurry. We resumed our pursuit with a deepening misgiving. On Wood Street, just beyond the sad deconsecrated tower of bomb-ruined St Alban's, we pulled up outside Jack's new location: the City of London Police Headquarters.

Bykov parked the car on the far side of the church, from where we could just see the front door of the police station. 'You'll have to go in and sort it out,' said Bykov.

'Me?'

'He's your responsibility, Nikolai.'

One of the indices of Bykov's growing contempt for me was that he'd started to call me by my first name and use the informal second person singular.

'What about identification for him?' I asked.

He looked uneasy. 'Better without.'

As I opened the car door, there was a thunderclap. It was an instant downpour, pounding out of the gunmetal sky, spattering off the pavements and the exhausted stone of the vestigial church. Entering the police station, I was soaked. I dripped over to the front desk, where I showed my university ID to a shirt-sleeved receptionist with big forearms and a shaven head like a Regency prizefighter.

'How can I help you, Dr Slopen?' he asked, with the hearty confidence of one pillar of the establishment addressing another.

'I believe you may have a patient of mine in custody,' I said, as breezily as I could manage.

The policeman inclined his head slightly towards me. 'What's his name?'

'His name is Jack Telauga.'

Without glancing down at the admissions record in front of him, the policeman said pregnantly: 'I can tell you now that there's no one of that name in the log book.'

'He was in the vicinity of Gough Square. He might have called himself . . .

The man met my hesitation with a blue, unblinking gaze.

'He might have called himself . . . I found myself unable to say it.

'Called himself what, sir?' There was the first hint of impatience in the policeman's voice.

'He's been very confused lately. His name is Jack Telauga. But he may be calling himself . . . I closed my eyes. 'He may be calling himself *Johnson*.'

'Might that be *Doctor* Johnson?'

I nodded.

'If you wouldn't mind taking a seat, I'll see where we are with him.'

I sat, damp and troubled, among the plastic chairs and the routine gloom of the waiting area. For the first time, I had been forced to acknowledge openly the strange and specific character of Jack's delusion.

All madness has a touch of death to it. Here, in the Dennis Hill Unit, I've come to see that reality is not as robust as we think it is. Of course, there are things that are indifferent to human opinion – gravity, the moon-driven motion of the tides, the boiling point of water. But the finer details of reality – the state of a marriage, artistic merit, a person's true nature – have something delicate and consensual about them. That lurch to the wrong, a noble mind overthrown, even Ron Harbottle sacrificing the good judgement he had lived for: it is more than disquieting. Each time someone opts out of our collective reality, it weakens a little.

To me, Johnson's recognition of that is part of his acute modernity as a moralist. I think he saw the relation between individual and collective delusion: the threat of madness to the human mind and the body politic. He knew that it was a small step from religious mania to religious wars. Madness is part of that turn away from the real that Johnson was so vigilant in confronting wherever he found it – not because of his confidence in reason, but because he knew from his own experience how fragile the rule of reason is.

No one more embodies the illuminating potency of reason. Johnson was devastating in his capacity to sniff out the fake in its different guises, to know what the real is, or the *réal*, if you follow Hunter's comical etymology. But this very power was riddled with its opposites: melancholy and uncertainty; fear of his own loosening grip on the nature of reality.

As they fetched Jack up from the cells, he walked like a criminal being led to the scaffold: unsteadily, and with his eyes fixed on the floor. When I said his name, he looked up and his face brightened with relief.

'Dr Slopen? How come you here?' His voice was hoarse and he was wearing unfamiliar clothing.

'Let's get you home,' I said. Jack took my arm. His grip seemed frail and desperate.

The police were only too happy to release him with a caution.

'We'd prefer not to charge him, anyway,' said the shaven-headed policeman. 'In cases like these' – he looked pityingly at Jack – 'the law is a blunt instrument.'

He explained that Jack had made his way into 17 Gough Square, ignored the clerk at the ticket counter and, when challenged by an attendant, had become confrontational. A guide who was showing a group around the house at the time had been so alarmed by his manner that she fetched a policeman.

I understood that Jack's size, his odd manner of speaking and the implied truculence of his peculiar physiognomy had been met not with compassion and gentle handling, but with a misplaced machismo. The upshot was that the police had overpowered him and wrestled him into a van.

And still I wondered what impulse had driven him east, down Fleet Street, towards the dome of St Paul's and into the nest of alleyways around Gough Square.

On our departure, the officer gave me Jack's original clothes in a plastic bag and told me they'd need a wash because the arresting officers had been forced to use pepper spray. He was obliging enough to recommend a particular detergent.

As soon as we were out of sight of the police station, Bykov pulled the car over and undid his seatbelt. He sat for a moment looking in the rear-view mirror. 'What's the matter?' I asked him. 'Are we being followed?'

'*Podozhdi*,' he said. *Wait a second.*

Suddenly, with a speed that I would never have associated with his squat physique, Bykov withdrew something from his top pocket, turned in his seat and stabbed Jack in the leg.

Jack let out a roar of discomfort and surprise. He gripped Bykov's wrist, and then I watched his hands slacken almost instantly and his eyelids grow heavy. He fell forward onto his seatbelt. Bykov shifted him back with his forearm until he slumped against the headrest. It took me a few seconds to recover my composure.

I could see Bykov was enjoying my discomfiture. 'You're feeling sorry for him, aren't you?' he said. 'But it's more cruel to let him get into a state like that: police arresting him, and God knows what. He's crazy, Nikolai. You have to protect him. Take this and use it!'

He handed me the instrument he'd used to dose Jack. It was a hypodermic pen of the sort that insulin-dependent diabetics use. 'It paralyses the soft tissue. It doesn't affect the brain. When you need to, give him one an hour.' A crimson bead of Jack's blood clung to its tip. 'At least I know you can use a pen,' he muttered as he pulled roughly away from the kerb.

CHAPTER 18

Extracted from Dr Webster's Journal

Request from Patient Q this evening for antidepressants. I ask him why; he is reluctant to give me an answer. From his affect, it's clear that he is sad about something. The appearance of unfeigned emotional response seems, in the context of his previous delusional behaviour, a positive outcome. I ask his permission to record the session.

– Why do you think you're sad?
– You wouldn't understand.
– What makes you think I wouldn't?
– Because you've understood fuck all so far.

Q is silent for half a minute and then his manner becomes conciliatory:

– I haven't got long, you know.
– Long?

Q is silent again, then asks if I like haiku. I tell him I do. Q recites.

– *This world of dew is a world of dew. And yet, and yet.*

His recitation is slow and full of affect. For the

first time in our sessions, the countertransference produces a pronounced sense of melancholy. I ask him again why he's sad.

    – I miss my family.

    – Your family?

    – My children, Sarah and Lucius.

    – Dr Slopen's children.

    – [muttering] What's the fucking point?

I explain the reality principle. I tell him that one of my roles is to constantly challenge his delusions. In a sadistic retaliation for my intervention, he corrects my use of the split infinitive. After a pause of several minutes, he makes a fresh attempt to communicate.

    – That's the thing about a carcass. We're like one of those spare tyres that are just supposed to get you to the end of your journey. There's no longevity in them.

    – And what will be at the end of your journey?

    – I'd like to see my children again. I'd like to be able to tell them how much I love them. And I'd like people to know the truth.

    – The truth?

    – The truth.

    – Some people might say that truth is a slippery concept and that there's more than one kind of truth.

Q gazes at me with evident contempt.

    – Who?

I instance cases of so-called alien abduction and suggest to Q that while untrue in one sense the accounts may truly reflect traumatic experiences the victims underwent as children.

– There's only one kind of truth. That's why it's called THE truth. Because there's one of it.

– And what's the truth here?

Q falls silent. His gaze softens.

– [almost to himself] The truth is that Chwang Zoo's [sp?] butterfly is not a metaphor. And I'm a dreamer who has forgotten his waking name.

– That sounds like a riddle.

No further response from Q.

CHAPTER 19

The above is Dr Webster's most recent entry – but dated over a week ago. I can't explain her lack of diligence. 'Chwang Zoo', indeed. Heaven help us: she's turned the Taoist sage into an animal sanctuary.

Though she's added nothing to her journal lately, she appears to have settled on a new tack with me in our sessions – our 'work' together, as she calls it with no trace of irony. Last night, my protective phantasies not only passed unchallenged but were positively encouraged by the doctor.

The atmosphere of the session was different as soon as I entered the room, or 'safe space' as we clients are encouraged to think of it.

She told me she wanted to turn over a new leaf in our work. 'Tell me about this man, this man you claim to be.'

'Nicholas Slopen?'

'Yes. What kind of man is he?'

That threw me completely. I'm not exactly the same man I was before. The Procedure has given me a handle on the old Nicky Slopen, the strained and over-conscientious ice-man, and in doing so, it has altered me. I tried to explain this to her.

'So, you're saying you're not Nicholas Slopen after all? Well, that's a big admission.'

I told her not to be obtuse, adding that one of my regrets in this, one of many, is that I didn't have the chance to be the person I've become with my wife and children. She let that assertion pass without comment and I felt emboldened to ask if she had any children herself.

'My personal life is out of bounds, as you know,' she said; but I know, in any case, that she doesn't.

I attempted to explain to her the pain I felt at being separated from my family, and the pain of being able to recognise my shortcomings as a husband and a parent without being given the concomitant shot at redemption. 'I'm Scrooge with no third act,' I said, 'I'm like a character in Greek myth: the Cassandra of personal development, who knows the truth but isn't believed or allowed to act on it.'

Then the breakthrough. She started asking about Lucius without any prefatory circumlocution to let me know that she knew he wasn't my son. Better than that. After a preliminary foray, he became 'your son, Lucius'. When I realised that was what she'd actually said, I became a little breathless and had to stop. My first thought was *This is it*: Ivan's ticker has had enough and is giving up on me. *Your son, Lucius.* Then my face convulsed and I began to cry. I wept for my little lost boy, and the life I used to have. She pushed a box of tissues towards me. I can't think how long it's been since I've cried like that. I felt ineffable gratitude. Even perched on a grimy pastel bean bag in the DHU, it seemed for one second that I'd had my child given back to me. I told her this after the storm had passed and she looked surprisingly gratified. We sat in silence for a while. My carcass felt an unaccountable sense of peace, as though it and I were joined up, one thing.

'You mentioned that you saw your GP after your wife left you.'

'Did I?'

'Yes, in one of our previous sessions.'

'Don't you mean, after Dr Slopen's wife left me?'

'If you will, yes. Do you recall what he prescribed?'

'It was whatever bog-standard serotonin reuptake inhibitor they're doling out these days. Seroxat, maybe?' I waited for her to make a note, but she didn't, nor was she recording this one. The inference was too tantalising for me not to draw it: 'Does this mean you believe me?'

We sat there for a while without speaking; the plastic shingle inside her bean bag gave a rustle as she crossed her legs.

'I'm taking two weeks' leave,' she said.

Maybe it was the strip-lighting, but she looked sallow and hollow-eyed.

'I usually give some advance warning, but this time it hasn't been possible. I wonder if you'd like to explore how you feel about that.'

I told her that it made me worry slightly for her. These are not salubrious surroundings for anyone's mental health. I didn't mention that it's been over a week since she added anything to her journal; not just silent about me but silent in general. I asked her if she was all right.

'Why do you ask?'

'You seem . . . out of sorts.'

'I'm fine,' she said reflexively and then checked herself, as though she knew she should have said something more therapeutically non-committal.

'I'm obviously not the first to have asked you that,' I said.

'While I am away,' she said, 'you will be able to continue your work with Dr White.'

'Very well,' I said. 'I'll miss you.'

She cleared her throat. 'That's time.'

CHAPTER 20

It's frequently been remarked, by persons more qualified than I to pronounce on it, that the act of caring is a powerful tonic for the care-giver.

In those weeks when Jack Telauga was under my care, our relationship deepened into something that I believe was of comfort to both of us. I wouldn't dare compare the problems I was having then with his. My worries were of the common or garden variety and from the seed catalogue of the average middle-aged melancholic male. My pain was ordinary, though not the less painful for that; while whatever was wrong with Jack was something I could barely describe. And still, it was something to have a companion in those difficult times, however eccentric.

We ate together each evening. He relaxed during meals and enjoyed his food with a touching lack of self-consciousness. At the same time his table manners were so rudimentary that watching him eat could be a stomach-turning experience. Whenever we went to Pizzeria Sette Bello on Mitcham Lane I'd ask for a table in the back where no one could see him attacking his food like a fox going into a dustbin and fouling his clothes with cheese and tomato sauce.

He would get very animated waiting for the order, drumming his fingers on the plastic table-cloth and wagging his head from side to side. 'Depend upon it, sir, many a rich man dining tonight upon roast swan would as lief exchange his vittles for a plate of this cooked cheese!'

In the repletion afterwards, he was as happy as I ever saw him. He could be charming and talkative with a wide variety of people. There was a memorable encounter with a Bobo Ashanti Rastafarian whom we met outside the bingo hall and who tried to sell us a broom. And he had a deep curiosity about things that I took for granted, questioning the shopkeepers around the tube station for hours about mangoes, cassava and plantains.

He loved talking about religion and literature. He knew the names of no writers after 1780 until I lent him some Sherlock Holmes stories, which he devoured almost as voraciously as he went for the pizza. He couldn't make head or tail of a newspaper. We had mixed success with the Indian restaurants on Upper Tooting Road (tandoori chicken he liked; he thought lamb dhansak was some kind of practical joke).

Jack's mood and volubility were highly variable. Sometimes he sat sullenly, speechless; other times he was eager to talk, usually to catechise me on my religious faith, and my lack thereof. Once, he and I walked to the lido – the outdoor swimming pool on the common – in dusty, yellow, late summer sunshine, and he gazed in open-mouthed wonder at the contrails of a plane. One afternoon we even went ice-skating at the rink on Streatham High Road and he was surprisingly adept.

He didn't seem conventionally insane in any way that I could understand. But there was no way of comprehending him. In some eerie and fundamental way, he didn't appear to belong to our world. But that didn't seem the same as being mad.

I tested him, of course. Some part of me believed that the whole thing was an act. It would have been the simplest explanation; but if it was a mask, he never dropped it. He remained perfectly in character. He shed real tears over the death of James Boswell when I showed him a newspaper account of it on microfiche. In fact, his whole reaction was so dramatic – pallor, astonished shaking, two hours of silent brooding before I persuaded him to take a sedative – that I decided to forgo any similar assessments.

You might think that was his intention: to intimidate me into giving up my examination. But the sincerity of his behaviour was such that I just stopped questioning it. The only way I could make any sense of him was to accept that he was in the hold of the profound and irrational belief that he actually *was* Johnson; a belief he never wavered from. His most immediate memories, however wittingly or unwittingly they had been constructed, were identical to Johnson's: of the fatal sickness descending on him, fretting about his pension, about the fractious household of weirdos he'd ended up fostering under his roof, and the almost unbearable thought of the happiness he'd forgone with Hester Thrale, now Piozzi. It was patently absurd, but once accepted, the premise explained so much about him. The letters he'd forged – if that was even the right word – made a queer kind of sense. The years from 1784 to 2009 were a meaningless *entr'acte* to him. From his incarceration in Malevin's dungeon he had scribbled letters in Pentel to the world he believed he belonged to, praying that someone would have the heart to help him. He can't have known the pathos and impossibility of what he asked. *I pray that the gulf between us is not so irremeable that you would neglect a promised kindness.* That wasn't the plea of Johnson in 1784, begging for assistance as he spiralled down into melancholy and death; that was Telauga in 2009, hoping against all probability that someone – his sister; Hester Piozzi; Boswell? – would spring him from his fiercely lit cell. I thought of the book sliding out of his hand, the date on its title page too alarming to digest; too dissonant with his fantasies; the proof that he was centuries out of time. And I think of Webster's words: *That is the very moving aspect of this work. How awful must reality be for the psychotic to take refuge in this?* But of course she doesn't know the half of it.

On the whole, he seemed more comfortable with things that he claimed were wholly new to him than with things that had a flavour of the eighteenth century. Once, I made the mistake of taking him to Morden Hall Park when I needed a new lawn sprinkler from the Garden Centre there.

The sight of the big manor house – very similar in style to the Thrales' – plunged Jack into a deep gloom. It was counterintuitive. You would have thought he'd be happiest of all on the set of a costume drama, taking tea with a lot of people in hoop skirts and britches. But not a bit of it. He was allergic to the very period he believed he belonged to.

It was as though he needed to compartmentalise his competing versions of reality. He could get very obstinate and then aggressive when his internal and external worlds came into conflict. A large instance of this was his behaviour at Gough Square; a smaller one was that I had to stop taking him to the Antelope because he kept asking the Australian barmaid for 'shrub' and became very strident when she told him she had no idea what he was talking about. The notion that London in 2009 was not only related to the London of 1784 but was in some ways the same city, he found extremely threatening. It was this, as much as our experience with the police, that stopped me taking him sightseeing in central London. He never even said the word 'London' in my hearing, but he often talked of 'home' and his 'friends', and how different life was there. And I suppose that my working assumption was that his madness or dysfunction, or whatever you want to call it, was some kind of cosmic homesickness.

I appreciate that Dr Webster would be struck by similarities between the symptoms Jack and I present. But the fact is we are very different cases. I came back to a world I largely recognised. Jack only stayed sane, I believe, by *not recognising* the truth about his situation.

It may seem pointless to take issue with the conceptual shortcomings of the Procedure, given that the most dangerous thing about it is the moral bankruptcy at its heart, but it has struck me many times that it uses an almost fatuously simple set of assumptions about identity. Human personalities are not stable or discrete. They're embedded in, and constructed from, other things: history, societies, cultures, families. Nor are they unitary. Even post-Procedure, I am conscious of multiple Nicky Slopens, not to mention the residual cohabitee we have usurped.

Johnson has the best phrase for it. In one of his letters, he writes that 'in the deaths of those close to us, the continuity of being is lacerated'. *The continuity of being.* The human personality is not an object, it's a process, a constant state of becoming, that depends on a web of interdependencies, binding us to one another with invisible filaments, to our time, to memories and possessions, and back to our changing selves. And even that image probably overstates the solidity and integrity of the human personality. Strip a person away from the relationships that constitute their identity, the friends, the loved ones, the familiar sounds, and the outcome is bound to be breakdown and madness.

And at a deeper philosophical level, the wholeness the Procedure produces is not only illusory. It undersells the scope of the human by restricting it to a single unitary self. Ask Whitman. Ask Shakespeare. Ask any of the major poets. This castle is really a prison. In its dungeons and hidden chambers lie the disregarded slivers that, used right, might complete its divine intelligence. The total human being reflects back to the teeming world a radiant wholeness. No *I*, no *not-I*. *From where we come from, there is no division.*

I had promised to take Lucius and Sarah to Cornwall in the second week of their summer holidays. The date approached with alarming rapidity.

Vera had dropped off the map. I suggested to Bykov that he stay in the house in my absence. He didn't reject the suggestion out of hand. He asked for time to consider it.

Two days later, he rang to say he'd had a better idea. He'd found Jack interim accommodation: a bedsit in a house near Streatham High Road where his landlord would be a middle-aged Pole called Tadeusz.

Both Bykov and I agreed that it would be wise to allow Jack some settling-in time before I left for Cornwall.

Tadeusz raised an eyebrow at Jack's minimal luggage, but Bykov paid him two months' rent in cash, while I explained that Jack would require a certain degree of attentiveness. Tadeusz was unfazed by the special demands. He was gap-toothed, religious, and had the knotty upper body of a weightlifter. He had rebuilt much of the house himself and didn't look like the kind of person who would forget to give Jack his medicine.

I cycled round to check on Jack later that evening. Tadeusz had supplied him with a pile of jigsaw puzzles from a charity shop and when I peered into his room he was assembling a five-hundred-piece version of *The Haywain* with a look of absorption that was the nearest thing I had seen on his face to real happiness. I decided to leave him in peace.

The house seemed unbearable on my return. After ten minutes pacing restlessly, I found myself with the phone in my hand.

She answered after one ring. I'd guessed she would. This abnormal solicitude, her accessibility to me, was part of the conceit that we were both getting exactly what we wanted. 'Nicholas?' But the lack of the diminutive was a kind of hand-off from the start. 'Lou and Sarah are out with friends.'

'It's you I wanted to speak to. I wanted to meet up,' I said.

'Let me have a look in my diary . . . When do you get back from Cornwall?'

'I was thinking of slightly sooner. Like tonight.'

'Tonight? It's almost eight o'clock.'

My pushiness and her keenness to maintain the fiction of amicability meant that the outcome was never in doubt, but I knew that I only had so many of these before she closed herself off from me entirely. We met at Embankment – equidistant from both of us – and ended up walking to Somerset House to sit rather frigidly in the court-yard. We must have looked like a particularly poorly arranged internet date. She was wearing some striking new shoes and a tailored coat, and yet I still had the feeling that she'd dressed down for me.

'It's nice to see you,' I said, with a warmth that was enough akin to desperation to make her seem uncomfortable. She smiled and shivered a little. I suggested we go inside, but she insisted she was fine.

'So. To what do I owe this pleasure?' she said.

'I'm having a strange time at the moment.'

'Of course, love. We both are. It's going to take time.'

'I . . . I had a sort of vision today of how I don't want to end up.'

Her silence was the precise opposite of the therapeutic one that's intended to enable self-revelation: if she gave as little encouragement as possible, perhaps I would simply stop talking of my own accord.

I asked her if she remembered the letters that Hunter had asked me to work on. She said she did.

'They turned out to be forgeries. I didn't mention it at the time because, because the truth is I was a little taken in by them and I felt ashamed.'

My voice trailed off. The fountains had been displaced by an exhibition of public art – big fibreglass snails behind which two small boys were playing hide and seek.

'They're up past their bedtime,' said Leonora.

Trailing off, I vaulted into the deep end of my planned remarks. 'Do you ever think we made the wrong decision?'

'We made a decision,' she said firmly.

'I'm not sure I did. I think I went along with the idea that I had a choice because I didn't want to admit that you were leaving me, but that's what happened, and the fact is, I don't like it. I miss the children, and I miss you. I miss being a family.'

'Oh God, listen to you, Nicky. You sound like the corny bourgeois you always claimed to despise.'

'I was stupid to despise them. I've seen the future and it's doing jigsaw puzzles on your own in a

South London bedsit and having no connection to the outside world.'

'Well, I think it sounds, forgive me, like your idea of heaven.'

'I love you.'

'Please, Nicky. Don't be so boring.' She grimaced. 'Has it occurred to you', she said, 'that this isn't about *you*? It's not you I want to change. I want to be a different *me*. And with Caspar I am. I feel like finally I'm the me I was supposed to be.'

The impact of her words was almost physical, as though a soft part of me had collided with her stony intransigence.

The portents for our holiday were grim. We arrived in rain after a seven-hour drive to a caravan park that seemed ominously full of shaven-headed families in sportswear. The children regressed to a glum, uncommunicative phase of adolescence and I despaired on getting through the week.

The first morning, the sun came up and I booked them both into a surf school. After two hours, they were hooked. We spent six days of uncomplicated bliss together: they were in the sea all morning while I ploughed ahead with the footnotes to the letters, working outside if the wind wasn't too strong, or at the dining table in the caravan. I watched them sometimes from the beach, like dolphins in the surf, all glittering adolescent limbs and laughter. We ate out extravagantly and I let Sarah drink wine. We played board games together in the evening before they dropped off to sleep, exhausted from their watery exertion.

I think in some ways my experience of Jack made me a better parent. I had a better sense of what it was to be truly vulnerable. And I think, having been forced to let go of my children once, I was less prescriptive, more ready to listen, more awed by their independence and their compassion for one another.

There was no mobile phone coverage at the caravan. The three of us would go up on the cliffs to call home, looking out on the uninhabited lime-stone stacks a few hundred yards from shore. I would eavesdrop on the children's gratifyingly monosyllabic conversations with their mother and then check in with Tadeusz, who assured me that all was well with Jack.

But on the drive home, locked into returning traffic on the M4, I received a barrage of text messages in fractured English. I wasn't able to call until I'd dropped off the kids. It's one of my continuing regrets that this farewell was clouded with an irrelevant anxiety. Sarah hugged me with the fierce affection that she had showed me as a toddler and went into the house without letting me see her tears. Lucius was more laconic, but I could tell he was sorry to see me go.

CHAPTER 21

When I finally spoke to Tadeusz, he said Jack was sick and refusing all medication. I drove round immediately.

The first thing I noticed on entering his airless bedroom was the smell of pear drops. Jack lay upright in bed, wearing a grimy yellow dressing gown. He was shockingly transformed. His body seemed to have shrunk. His breath was stertorous.

I hauled open the sash window. The scent of cut grass and sunlight drifted in from the garden. Jack stirred slightly, but his eyes were closed and he seemed delirious. I asked Tadeusz how long he'd been in this condition.

'Two days,' Tadeusz said. 'He needs doctor but . . . He gave me a doubtful and panicky look. 'I worry his visa not good.'

I touched Jack's clammy forehead. He looked at me without recognition. His taste-buds stood out on his dry tongue as he breathed open-mouthed. I told Tadeusz I was calling an ambulance.

The ambulance crew arrived within twenty minutes. They manoeuvred Jack gently down the stairs on a blanket, put him on a saline drip and took him straight to St George's Hospital, where an orderly called Keith with corn-rows and a do-rag wheeled him down to the X-ray department. He shuffled along behind Jack's wheelchair with his baggy navy trousers bunching around his oversized feet. We followed a back route that passed through Accident and Emergency. 'The VIP area,' I joked darkly.

Keith kissed his teeth. 'That's the last place you want to be, bruv.'

The doctor who read the X-rays was an under-slept woman in her early thirties, who wanted to know if I was the next of kin.

I explained that Jack's sister was out of the country and that I was looking after him as a favour.

The doctor asked if there was any way to get hold of her.

'I'm trying,' I said. 'How bad is it?'

'It's pneumonia,' she said. 'We'll give him antibiotics anyway, but we won't know if it's bacterial or viral until we get the lab results.'

They inserted a cannula messily into Jack's bony hand. He flinched as it went in, but submitted to everything with the resignation of a man with no options left.

I stayed at his bedside that night, sleeping only fitfully, watching the saturation probe glowing red on his finger and listening to the sound of water bubbling in the respirator. There were groans from the beds around us. The ward seemed hellish, deathly. And the place had a melancholy personal signficance for me. Two decades before, my sister Emily had died there while I was away at university.

The next morning, we moved him to a cubicle closer to the window. We had a view south as far as the distant green of the North Downs. Leaning back against his pillows, Jack stared out at the sky. It was cloudless. A gull-grey jetliner passed slowly across the arc of the city towards Gatwick. Its engine made the glass in the windows vibrate.

Jack pulled off his oxygen mask. 'Now I am sure I dream,' he said, in a frail and croaky voice.

I'd previously tried and failed to explain to him the principles of aerodynamic lift, my O level in physics being unequal to the task, but I made another attempt: 'I think it's to do with the rate at which the air passes over the top of the wing.'

'Nay, sir, the specific levity of air is too great for the support of such burthens.' He shut his eyes as if the inexplicable sight were causing him pain. 'God have mercy upon me.'

I went home that morning for a change of clothes for both of us and some decent tea bags. Intermittently, I called Vera without any success. I'd either get the long, plaintive foghorn of a European ringtone that told me she was in Moscow, or the clipped recorded Russian operator saying that the *abonent* couldn't be reached and I should try again later.

On my return, Jack had rallied a little. He was sitting up in bed eating boiled eggs. There was something reassuring and homely about their faintly sulphurous smell. He asked about my trip to Cornwall and I showed him pictures of the children on my mobile phone. He lingered fondly over one of Lucius. 'He has a touch of young Davy Garrick about him,' he said.

We did a jigsaw puzzle together until he seemed weary. Just as the doctor had warned, his condition deteriorated again in the night. His breathing slowed, and once his pulse-rate plummeted so low that an alarm sounded and the nurses rushed to inject him with adrenalin.

In his moments of wakefulness, I read to him from *Erasmus* Darwin's epic poem *The Economy of Vegetation*. His face bore no expression, but his hands on the bedspread flexed weakly to the beat of the verse.

Once more, the morning brought an improvement in his breathing. The nurse lowered his oxygen. Outside, the morning sun shone its yellow rays on the rise of the landscape from Tooting Broadway to the imperceptible hill where I knew my house stood, empty. There were no planes, but a contrail was dissipating above Crystal Palace in two lines of fiery dots and dashes, like a communication from the biblical God or a detail in a sublime painting.

As his lucidity returned, Jack's mood grew morbid and wistful. I noticed once again his odd habit of regurgitating lines from the *Life* as though he were speaking them for the first time.

'I would consent to have a limb amputated to recover my spirits,' he said, propped against the pillows, in gloomy contemplation of what we both knew must soon follow. Something began to trouble him. He turned to me and gripped my hand with a sudden insistence. 'I pray you, sir, to burn my journal.' He wouldn't let go of my wrist until I promised to go immediately.

It was a relief to be in the sunshine after those long, immobile hours listening to the rise and fall of Jack's breath. The vigil had left me drained but physically restless so I walked all the way to Streatham. The traffic was strangely light.

Tadeusz answered the door wearing sandals and sweatpants. He was watching an evangelical Christian television programme in Polish. The whole house smelled of beetroot. I realised it was Sunday.

He followed me up the stairs apologising. The poor man had been torturing himself over his decision to delay calling the ambulance. I understood from his fragmentary explanations that he hadn't wanted to take that responsibility himself, fearing that Jack was some kind of illegal immigrant and that he would be deported. 'I should have done some things more,' he said, shaking his head agitatedly.

I told him not to worry. The hastiness of my

response took him aback. 'It will be the end?' he asked. I said I didn't know.

Jack's room, lately vacated, still had the resonance of him. The sheets of the bed were still folded back where the paramedics had left them; the impress of his body still visible on the mattress and pillow. A Bible and a glass of stale water sat on the bedside table.

I found the journal – a hardbacked Silvine notebook – in the drawer of his desk and read the first lines:

> *How the last months have past, I am unwilling to terrify myself with thinking. This day has been past in great perturbation.*

I was struck by the doubling of the word *past*. This wasn't a great prose stylist, moralising with elegant variation. This was a man driven to express his internal suffering with whatever words came to hand. Among the other pages, I recognised verbatim extracts from Johnson's extant autobiographical fragments: reminiscences, prayers, supplications to his creator.

> *Almighty God, heavenly Father, whose mercy is over all thy works, look with pity on my miseries and sins.*

In brief sections in Latin, he had catalogued the varieties of his nocturnal torment: *nox turbatissima*

. . . *nox inquietissima . . . nox molesta.* And from
these entries I gathered that my errand was
motivated by a desire to conceal from the eyes
of posterity a secret no more dreadful than
a guilty habit of masturbation. Poor Jack, I
thought.

Of course, I could never accede to his request
to destroy it. It would be a terrible act of vandalism.
It would go against every instinct I had as a scholar.
But I could bring it to the hospital, and try to
appeal to his better judgement.

As I was flicking though the book, marvelling at
it, a single folded sheet dropped to the floor.

I picked it up. It was a letter, addressed to me,
which he must have written during my absence in
Cornwall.

To Dr Nicholas Slopen

Sir,
  *It is but an ill return for the many kindnesses
with which you were pleased to favour me, to
have delayed my thanks for them till now: I
think myself obliged to you beyond all expression
of gratitude for your care of me.*
  *It is not a Sophistic means of exculpation for
my tardiness in writing to say that one ground
for it was my fear that greater knowledge
would expose you to hazards of which you
cannot conceive.*
  Yet, my own experience now persuades me

that it is better to see dangers early than to be surprized by them. Fear, being the necessary effect of danger, must remain always with us. Therefore, be forewarned – the common task.

You should know of my own experience that after a long illness in my rooms at Bolt Court, I came to myself in circumstances too strange for me easily to explain and later fell under the care of Mr Malevin and Miss Telauga, whom you have been pleased to call my sister.

In the early stages of my recovery the conviction possessed me that I had found myself in Limbo.

However, the operations of time and reason have bestowed light on an unlikely truth. I discover myself the exception to the old adage Mors omnibus communis. *For me, the dream of natural philosophy has become a waking agony.*

And yet, even now, I find Hesiod's maxim holds: that the evil of the worst times has some good mingled with it. A rational man may not doubt it. Your concern and gentleness have mitigated my discomfort and lightened my misery.

I look forward to renewing our conferences on your return. For this, and other debts of kindness to you, I acknowledge my gratitude and declare myself, your obedient humble servant.

SAM. JOHNSON

I was underslept, of course, and vulnerable, but the words touched me deeply. I could see the care he had taken to write it. And I was reminded of qualities that I used to love about Johnson's letters: the sense of his emotional range; his special gentleness to his female correspondents; the kindness that was an essential part of his moral vision. I think kindness, more than anything else, enabled him to transcend the limitations of his historical era. It let him see, for example, the terrible injustice of slavery – which sounds self-evident, but Boswell couldn't see it.

And at that moment, I understood that I had come to share the madman's delusion.

I understood too that for a very long time I had been carrying an intuitive misgiving about everything I had been told. Like the frog in the experiment who fails to perceive the incremental rises in temperature of the water around him and ends up boiling to death, I had been ensnared by a succession of deepening falsehoods, some of which carried barely the whiff of plausibility. Now, when I started to poke holes in Vera's story it came apart in my hands. *Her brother? A savant? A Russian speaker?* None of it stacked up.

When I got back to the ward, the curtains had been drawn around Jack's cubicle. I felt a momentary anxiety about what I'd find there.

Inside, an orderly was stripping the sheets. 'You're too late,' she said. 'He's gone.'

'Gone?' I felt as though the journal was a boulder and the weight of it was pulling me towards the floor.

There was a pause. The woman, who was small and birdlike with an Iberian name, Maria, perhaps, or Luisa, suddenly looked embarrassed. 'Not gone – discharged. He was signed out by his family.'

I was reduced to incredulous babbling. The woman blushed to the roots of her ebony hair.

Sensing some kind of trouble, the head nurse on the ward had appeared at the end of the bed. 'Can I help?' she asked, with a certain wariness in her voice.

'I'm looking for the patient who was here.'

'He's been discharged.'

'Discharged? He was breathing from an oxygen mask last night. He was in no state to leave.'

'I'm sorry, I'm going to have to ask you to lower your voice.'

'Where's he gone?'

'I'm not able to tell you that. That's a matter for the family.'

'The family? What family? He has no family.'

'I think it's better if we discuss this outside.'

She manoeuvred me towards the outer door. I caught a glimpse of myself in a mirror in the corridor, unshaven, pale, wild-eyed.

'Will you be all right getting home, or shall I have someone call you a minicab?' she asked.

I've never been anything other than respectable. Now, for the first time in my life, I was the object of nervous sideways glances. I was an unwelcome troublemaker, a potential threat. I was dangerous.

Detaching my arm from her gentle but insistent grip, I told her I would be fine. But I remember leaving the building in a state of shock. I was mystified. I could make no sense of what had happened. My thoughts turned fruitlessly in circles. Who could have known that Jack was even in there? Malevin? Bykov? Hunter? Vera?

This time I took the bus home. We trawled through the shabby signage of Tooting Broadway, past the marooned statue of Edward VII and the carcass of Komisarjevsky's once beautiful Moorish picture palace, now a bingo hall, and I leafed through Jack's journal, moved by the prayers and the vivid, human texture of his penmanship.

O Lord, my Maker and Protector, who has graciously returned me to this world to work out my salvation, enable me to drive from me all such unquiet and perplexing thoughts as may mislead or hinder me in the practice of those duties which thou hast required. When I behold the works of thy hands and consider the course of thy providence, give me Grace always to remember that my thoughts are not my thoughts, nor my ways my ways.

I felt I understood less and less, even as, intuitively, I was drawing closer to the hidden chamber of the infinitely dark truth.

CHAPTER 22

At home, I began to survey the information I had. The only explanation that made any sense to me was that Hunter and Sinan had arranged Jack's discharge, if not done it themselves. But if that was clear, the reasons for their involvement with him seemed more obscure than ever. Neither needed the money. And I could think of no plausible literary motive.

Insofar as they could be trusted, the hints in Jack's letter went beyond forgery and suggested . . . Well, what?

Back at my desk, I shelved all my other obligations and belatedly undertook my due diligence on Hunter.

Bit by bit, I pieced together an outline of his life from clues on the internet.

His Wikipedia entry said he'd been born in 1948 in Santa Barbara, the only child of Vincent and Betty Gould. That made him about ten years older than I'd imagined. Betty had been a kindergarten teacher. Vincent, who worked for General Electric, had died suddenly when Hunter was seven.

There was no mention of an interest in books.

If there was a key to Hunter, it seemed more likely to be music. In a scratchy interview from the early 1990s that someone had posted on YouTube ('Adding comments has been disabled for this video') Hunter told a Dutch television audience that his earliest memories were of his mother playing German waltzes on an old accordion.

Elsewhere, Hunter himself made the connection between his early bereavement and his immense appetite for work. He boasted to one interviewer that he worked every day of his life, except his birthday, which he spent pedalling his age in miles on a stationary bicycle. He put this drivenness down to his early experience of death. 'I realised early on that time is the greatest blessing there is,' he said.

He'd spent a couple of semesters at an expensive liberal arts college, but decided he couldn't bear the thought of delaying his encounter with real life for four years. He and a friend called Douglas Martens dropped out and went into business together.

'Dougie and I were joined at the hip,' he told a journalist from a music magazine. 'We bonded over the fact that we both lost fathers young. His died in Korea. I remember as freshmen we made a list of everything we wanted to do together, and I mean everything – we filled a yellow legal pad: start companies, explore the world, visit other galaxies. Then we got depressed because we real-ised that we wouldn't live long enough. I remember

Dougie jokingly crossed out everything on the list and wrote: "Cure ageing." We both decided to drop out then.'

So his claim that he'd been to law school turned out to be a lie; he hadn't even finished university. But I learned from other sources that the falsehood was a typical Hunter manoeuvre: bold, self-aggrandising and oddly unnecessary. Several friends and former colleagues spoke warmly about his charisma and his empowering belief in himself. But its flipside was an impatience with the mere facts. 'Sometimes, when you're around Hunter, he can make reality seem a little bendy,' said one ex-employee, who had found himself walking away from a well-paid job to come and work on Hunter's startup for free.

Hunter and Douglas both took drugs and both were in and out of rehab. But Douglas died in a motorcycle accident in 1978 before ever quite managing his own tricky transition from the drug years to the stationary bicycle years.

'I think about Dougie all the time,' Hunter said. 'If I ever feel like playing hookey, I think about him and it's what gives me focus and it's the reason for my longevity in this business.'

By the late 1980s, growing increasingly exasperated with the behaviour of recording artists and with his fortune, in any case, already sizable, Hunter had begun to collaborate with Silicon Valley types to create computer programs that could compose music without any human intervention. Hunter was typically bullish about the potential of these ideas. 'In less than a hundred years,' he was quoted as saying, 'the majority of the music we listen to will be composed by what we now think of as computers.'

It was hard to know what to make of it. Did he really believe this? Or was it one of those loopy enthusiasms that his mania or disinhibition compelled him to share with the interviewer?

Reading about his life, I understood that he was a product of a particular place and moment in American history. The California Hunter had grown up in was the Ironbridge of a second Industrial Revolution. Among his friends and acquaintances were the people who altered the technological circumstances of the twenty-first century. By the time they were in their sixties, they had lived long, contradictory lives. One minute they had been dropping acid and protesting against the Vietnam war. The next, they put on ties and were bidding to design the software for missile guidance systems. Hunter embodied these paradoxes. He had been a barefoot dropout, now he was a notoriously demanding boss. He had embarked noisily on various methods of personal growth, from Zen to EST, but still seemed uncomplicatedly entitled: a pampered mummy's boy who had never had reason to doubt his own importance.

Hunter had been quick to see the business potential of economic liberalisation in the Soviet Union.

At one stage, in the early 1990s, he'd been part owner of a Moscow radio station and an investor in a number of joint enterprises. It was hard not to be impressed by his energy and the breadth of his interests. It was hard too not to wonder if this drivenness was part of his mental instability. Surely there was another Hunter – the enantiodromic partner of the visible one – who stayed in bed for weeks at a time, complaining he was hollow?

And I kept thinking of the question he'd asked at our second meeting, when he had stared across the table at me with that strange, zealous look in his eyes and asked: 'Have you known much death, Nicholas?'

I rang Hunter early on the Monday morning. He sounded surprised to hear from me, but he agreed to see me that afternoon.

The building which houses the UK headquarters of Hunter's various businesses is a converted candle factory beside the Regent's Canal. The side you approach is all yellow stock brick and cast-iron pulleys, but the rear of the building with the canal view has been transformed into a bizarre eruption of asymmetric green glass which partly resembles a collapsing Mayan pyramid.

Inside, there was an air of understated magnificence: behind a long white desk sat an improbably glamorous receptionist with false eyelashes so big and silver that they opened and shut like Venus fly traps. There was a goldfish pond entombed beneath glass bricks by her feet, a Giacometti by the entrance and, most uncannily of all, a naked man lying at full stretch on the heated slate floor of the reception area.

Hunter came to fetch me himself. He was deeply tanned, but he'd lost so much weight that the effect was to make him look sun-dried, like a raisin, and vaguely reptilian. 'Dead dad,' he said, enunciating the words slowly, as he smiled and offered me his hand.

Reading about Hunter, I had learned of his talent for identifying someone's vulnerabilities. A former colleague had told *Rolling Stone* that Hunter's management style was an acutely toxic combination of emotional intelligence and a taste for personal humiliation. But what he had just said was so extraordinarily cruel that I was staggered. The words were barely out of his mouth before I'd seen all the deep and unpleasant layers of significance he had invested in them.

At one level, he was saying that he knew all about me, about the formative experience of my father's death. *I* knew that, but to have him know it was demeaning. And he was going further, making a link between that loss and my feelings about Jack; feelings which he was implying were inappropriately strong. I felt like he'd stabbed me. He must have seen the change in my expression.

'Ron Mueck,' he said, pointing at the naked man. 'The sculpture is called *Dead Dad*. We commissioned a life-size copy from the artist.'

'Of course,' I said, shakily.

'It's always good to see you,' he said, as we got into the lift. 'And I have to say that Sinan and I are both touched by your concern about Jack. He's in safe hands, he's doing very well. There's no need for you to worry.'

I followed Hunter in silence to his office. It was a vast space, transected by enormous cast-iron beams. He took a seat behind a big glass desk that was empty except for a tiny notebook computer and single Post-It note. From somewhere, an ioniser was filling the room with the scent of peppermint. I sat down on a leather couch.

'The last time we spoke about Jack, you told me he was dead,' I said.

It seemed that for the time being, Hunter was sticking with his unflappable, emollient manner. 'I apologise for that. But there are complexities about this situation that you're better off not knowing,' he said.

'For whose benefit?'

'For yours.'

The sky through the windows was full of low, grey clouds. The outline of Trellick Tower, like a modernist version of one of Lucius's marble runs, was visible in the distance. A scarlet narrowboat puttered through the khaki water beneath us.

'I'd like to see him,' I said.

Hunter opened his palms to the ceiling as if relinquishing his responsibilities to some higher power. 'That won't be possible. It's not what Vera wants. And I think you need to consider her welfare.'

I remember being silent for a long time. The building seemed eerily quiet.

'Here's the problem we've got now,' I said. I felt no anger. Instead, there was a strange relief at being able to drop all pretence between us. 'It's this: I no longer believe a single word you say.'

'I'm not sure whose fault that is –'

'Oh, I am.'

For a moment, I had the gratifying feeling that he was cornered.

'I've really enjoyed getting to know you, Nicholas. I feel we've seen the best of each other. I'd like to keep it that way.'

'I don't share your good feelings about our relationship.'

'That's a pity,' he said mildly.

'Who discharged Jack from the hospital?'

'That was a decision we took jointly.'

'With Jack's interests in mind? Last time I saw him, he could barely breathe.'

'I can assure you the medical care he's getting now is second to none.'

The narrowboat had disappeared. There was a pair of joggers on the towpath, their unearthly day-glo shorts and vests flashing by like tropical plumage.

'It may be a fault in me,' Hunter went on, 'but I've never understood the attraction of the moral high ground. It's always struck me as an overpriced piece of real estate. For one thing, the neighbours are a pain in the ass. For another, it's very exposed. It can even be dangerous.'

His mild tone was so far at odds with the tenor of his words that it took a moment for their significance to sink in.

'That's a threat?'

Hunter shrugged. 'I wouldn't say that, exactly, though you don't get far in my business without a ruthless streak. I'd say it was more of a plea. Call it a plea with consequences. I'm just really urging you to butt out.'

He got to his feet. My time was up.

'None of this is personal,' he said. 'I am just acting to protect . . . interests. My interests and your interests. Our common . . . interests.'

Hunter opened the door to his office. 'And by the way, I'll have to ask you if you have any of Jack's papers. They need to be returned if you do. Legally they're his property, and I have power of attorney in his affairs.'

'No,' I said, 'I don't.'

He left me to find my own way out. I went back down in the lift and lingered for a while over the bizarre sculpture in the vestibule, *Dead Dad*. Far from seeming dead, it looked eerily alive. The skin and hair had been rendered with uncanny verisimilitude. I had the feeling that at any moment it might get to its feet and speak.

I tend to have slow-growing academic convictions

about things, not lightning flashes. My insights are more vegetable than meteorological. But something had arisen in my chat with Hunter which caught my attention. I had noticed a peculiar awkwardness about his choice of words; an awkwardness all the more surprising because Hunter was such a glib and accomplished liar. And yet, I had had the feeling, even as he was speaking, that something taboo had entered his mind and he was having to step around it carefully. There was something he was trying hard not to say.

I am just acting to protect . . . interests. My interests and your interests. Our common . . . interests.

Those hesitations stood out. But why? And after a while, it dawned on me that they recalled a phrase from Jack's letter. I couldn't check it there, in the lobby, after the lie I had just told, but as soon as I was on the tube, I took it out of my jacket and reread the phrase that I remembered. It came at the end of the third paragraph, the one in which he had counselled me to be aware of the dangers we faced. This was the sentence: *Be forewarned: the common task.*

Gradually, this line and Hunter's hesitation combined in a single equation which solved itself.

My interests and your interests. Our common . . . interests.

The words became fused with Jack's exhortation. That was what Hunter had been trying not to say, the fence he had balked at. *Our common task.*

And when I understood that, a second meaning

241

emerged from Jack's sentence. On first reading, it had seemed so straightforward: he was urging me to be vigilant, to accept the need for circumspection as our common task.

But there was a grammatically viable alternative. The common task could be what he was warning me about. You could parse the sentence like this: *Beware of the common task.*

This was the thread that I followed to the heart of the labyrinth.

CHAPTER 23

I had a dream about Dr Webster last night: the multiple ironies of that! – not the smallest being that I failed to present her with a single dream during our work together.

We were sitting in the safe space. 'It seems that, very early, you abandoned any hope of being understood,' she was saying.

I disagreed strongly and handed her a book. 'Look,' I told her. 'My biography.' It was hardbound, quarto, with oxblood cloth boards and my name in gilt letters on the spine.

She glanced at a few pages and then, revolving the book in her hands, showed me the words.

The lines and paragraphs had the irregular look of bona fide text, but on closer inspection this was revealed to be an illusion.

It reminded me of the Latin gobbledegook designers use in mocked-up layouts: placeholder text. It's not meant to be read. The real content will be inserted later. They call it 'lorem ipsum' after the fragment of Cicero it's taken from: *dolorem ipsum*, 'pain itself'.

But here the text was formed of a single, repeated word: *mankurt*.

I woke up in my narrow pine bed with the sensation that I had fallen from the sky. This heart was thumping in his chest.

One continuous thread between the broken halves of my life is this: my grasp of the secret kinship between insight and despair. Who said, *There is no hope without the concomitant capacity for tears*? Johnson? Jack? Perhaps I did.

I threw myself into my quest. Every now and again, I would leave messages for Vera, trying to make contact and hinting vaguely at the direction of my researches.

They took me back to St James's Square, to the stacks of the London Library. I wasn't even sure what I was looking for, but I was confident I would know it when I found it. It was two days before I laid my hand on it, shelved on the open stacks under Religion and Philosophy of Religion: a slim, black volume of two hundred pages which had the immodest and doubtlessly sexist title *What Was Man Created For?* Its author was an obscure nineteenth-century Russian philosopher called Nikolai Fedorov. Because of the conventions of Russian transliteration, his last name is usually written 'Fedorov' in English, but pronounced like this, *Fyodorov*.

Fedorov's crazy speculations belong to a hidden tradition in Russian thought. It is a strain of utopian philosophy which left a faint trace on Soviet communism, but which was otherwise expunged from history.

What the Gnostics were to the established church, Fedorov and his disciples were to the commissars who founded the institutions of Soviet power. They were the disavowed mystics, the loopy ones who were finally ruled heretical.

Fedorov was an austere and religious man who published virtually nothing in his lifetime, but whose ideas were venerated by a group of followers. Tolstoy was one of his admirers. He died in 1903. A decade and a half later, some of his adherents became senior figures in the new Bolshevik government. They were communists who were drawn to Fedorov's mystical take on revolution. Fedorov went far beyond political economy. He didn't take aim at class conflict or inequalities of wealth and power. He wanted to abolish death.

'The most general evil affecting all,' he wrote, '– a crime, in fact – is death, and therefore the supreme good, the supreme task, is resuscitation. What we are talking about is universal resurrection . . . To turn all the worlds into worlds guided by the reasoning powers of resurrected generations.'

Fedorov also concluded that, with its numbers swollen by the resurrected dead, humanity would have to colonise other planets. He was a nineteenth-century advocate of space exploration.

Absurd? Naturally. But it was also strangely

compelling. Fedorov had somehow retained the innocence of a child's first speculations. He had no time for the fudged, adult versions of immortality, of vague spiritual realms or reincarnation. His immortality was eternal, physical existence alongside all the people you care about.

When you read it stated in such bald terms, of course it seems ridiculous. But it also chimes with a deep, almost unsayable longing. It is such a painful hope that from childhood on we train ourselves not to indulge it: not to have to leave, never to say goodbye, never to lose anyone.

Fedorov's ideas survived visibly in the quasi-religious cult which formed around Lenin after his death. One of his followers, a man named Leonid Krasin, was part of the team that devised ways to embalm the dead leader. 'I am certain', Krasin said, 'that the time will come when one will be able to use the elements of a person's life to create the physical person.' The inspiration for that thought clearly came from the book I held in my hand.

But Fedorov's vision had been much more radical and more egalitarian: we were all coming back, not just the leaders. 'Even more senseless is the idea that immortality is possible for a few separate individuals,' he wrote, 'when faced with the mortality that is common to all mankind; for this is as absurd as the belief in the possibility of happiness for a few, of personal happiness in the face of general unhappiness, in the face of a common dependence on so many catastrophes and evils.'

Resuscitation was our general destiny, he believed. And figuring out how to achieve it was the scientific and spiritual challenge that should occupy real revolutionaries.

Fedorov had no idea how it would be accomplished. There was no technological basis for his vision. It was a pseudoscience, in fact: religion disguised with a lab coat. Where it was actually attempted, the results were disastrous. After his death, some of his followers tried to rejuvenate themselves with blood transfusions – Lenin's sister Maria was among them. One disciple, Alexander Bogdanov, contracted an illness from a blood transfusion and died. The botched job on Lenin's corpse, where the dream of resuscitation quickly gave way to the less ambitious task of reupholstery, exposed the impossiblity of what Fedorov had preached.

Fedorov's followers died or were executed in the purges that followed Stalin's rise to power. His ideas remained an eccentric footnote to the story of the Soviet Union. They belonged to the philosophical endeavours covered by the Russian term *bogostroitelstvo*: 'god-building'. Spiritual regeneration, eternal life, resuscitation: all these were declared heresy by the designers of a drab and murderous utopia, obsessed with blast furnaces and pig-iron output.

But in his lifetime, Fedorov never wavered from

his central tenet – humanity's need to devise a method of universal resurrection. It's an obsession he returns to again and again in his essays, referring to it everywhere with the same Russian phrase: *Obshchee Delo* – the Common Task.

On the evening of August 14th, as the dog days were ending, and rain was falling on my untended garden, my phone rang. It was a withheld number. I answered it and heard a tired voice, swimming through layers of interference as though it were coming through on a ham radio. I immediately recognised it as Vera's. She was very apologetic. She explained that there had been complications with her operation. 'I am very weak,' she said.

I told her I had some questions that needed answering.

Her tone was grave. 'Nikolasha, I can't speak freely on the phone. You understand? If you want to discuss anything, you will have to come here. To Moscow.'

CHAPTER 24

The expedited visa cost me almost two hundred pounds. As a form of compensation, I bought the cheapest ticket I could, an overnight flight to Domodedovo that got me into Moscow in time to fight my way round the metro with battalions of commuters.

It had been twenty years since I'd last visited, on an academic grant to spend a summer studying at a shabby language institute in one of the city's northern suburbs.

The metro was still the same, but above ground the place had changed beyond recognition. Gone was everything that had made Moscow distinctive: the propaganda posters, the battered Soviet cars and the perfumed smoke of the cardboard-tipped cigarettes, *papirosy*, that had once been ubiquitous. The impoverished, ramshackle city I'd known had turned smart and heartless. There were sushi bars and huge supermarkets where, twenty years earlier, I would have been overjoyed to see an orange. I felt like Rip van Winkle.

Vera had booked me into a refurbished Soviet hotel which overlooked Kazan Station, but she

249

was reluctant to meet me there. Before I left, she'd repeatedly told me how careful we had to be. I remembered this paranoia from my first visit to Moscow, but in this unrecognisable, twenty-first-century city, her fears seemed groundless.

I texted her to say I'd arrived safely. In her reply, she asked me to suggest a meeting place. The only one that sprang to mind was the Exhibition of Economic Achievements, a place at the northern end of one of the metro lines. I knew of it because, in 1989, the foreign currency bar in a nearby hotel had been the only reliable source of beer in the area. I remembered the Exhibition, known by the Soviet acronym VDNKh, being a strange combination of trade fair and Stalinist theme park.

The smell of the metro at least was reassuringly familiar, a distinctive mineral aroma of smoke and damp coal which rises from the long escalators and hits you as soon as you enter.

I was fifteen minutes early. There was a crowd of shabby people waiting by a tram stop. A soft drizzle was falling. Vera Mukhina's famous sculpted giants, the worker and the farm girl, held their hammer and sickle aloft over the entrance to the park.

It was more disreputable than I remembered. Instead of reverent people paying homage, there was a sense of decay. Garish plastic booths had sprouted along the wide paths, offering a bizarre array of attractions: shooting galleries, punch-bags and karaoke. Russians on Segway scooters and rented rollerblades menaced the handful of pedestrians. The Soviet sculptures looked vulgar and the pavilions which had been intended to vaunt the achievements of the USSR and its fifteen constituent republics were falling apart.

Vera was on time. We met by an installation of an enormous Sputnik rocket, the type that had taken Gagarin into space. She was dressed in black and looked very pale, but I was struck by how relaxed and animated she seemed. She kissed me on both cheeks. 'I congratulate you on your choice of rendezvous,' she said, with heavy irony.

'I'm sorry,' I said, 'I didn't remember it being so . . . I gestured at the plastic beer tents, the shashlik vendors, the fairground sideshows, and I fumbled for a word.

'Yes,' she said. '*Poshlyi*'. The word means 'vulgar' or 'common', but when Vera used it, it expressed a special kind of revulsion, encapsulating a sense of aesthetic and intellectual inauthenticity.

'How are you feeling?' I asked.

She shrugged. 'I tire easily. I am still too weak to fly.'

I suggested we sit down. We walked a few yards to a bench that was sheltered from the drizzle. I watched her check that there was no one in earshot. Above us the rocket stretched up into the thunderous sky.

On the far side of the plaza, a sale of cheap fur coats was taking place in the pavilion that had been built to exhibit the achievements of the Soviet people in the sphere of electricity.

'Were you followed?' she asked.

'Are you serious?'

'Of course. We are not in London now.'

'No, I don't think so.'

'You said you had questions.'

'I don't understand why you left Jack with me. I don't believe I was your only resource.'

'You're right,' she said. 'You know the Tyutchev poem?' She quoted its famous first line: '"*Umom Rossiyu ne ponyat*". It's the one where he talks about the eternal enigma of Russia: *it can't be comprehended with the mind . . . it can only be believed*. What am I trying to show you has the same quality. You have to experience this truth to believe it.'

I felt an uncanny chill at her words. Tyutchev had been describing a mystery that was ineffably glorious. This, on the other hand, seemed to be shrouded in an obscurity like the fog round a graveyard.

She took a manila envelope from her handbag. 'I have some things for you.'

Inside was a crumpled mimeograph of an old Soviet research paper, dated 1946, with the text in faded violet ink. Its author was one Yurii Olegovich Malevin.

'A relative of Sinan's?'

'He is Sinan's father.' She saw my eyebrows rise at her use of the present tense. 'He is still alive.'

At the bottom of the envelope I found another piece of paper, soft like old money from repeated foldings. Its age and fragility demanded gentle handling.

It was a photocopy of the identification page from a Kazakh passport. The holder was a Kazakh citizen of Russian origin called Vladimir Efraimovich Trikhonov. He had been born in Baku, Azerbaijan, in 1960. I laid it across my knee.

'You understand?' said Vera.

The photograph in the passport had been coarsened by the photocopier that had been used to make it, but it was plain that Trikhonov bore a strong likeness to Jack.

'Physically, he was Trikhonov,' she said. 'In all other ways . . . She paused. 'He had no recollection of Trikhonov's identity.'

'How is that possible?'

'He underwent . . . a procedure.'

'But the language, his mannerisms? The handwriting?'

'Epiphenomena. By-products of this procedure.'

I told her it was impossible.

She shrugged. 'You knew him as well as I.'

'Knew him?' I said. '*Knew* him?'

'He is certainly dead by now.'

I don't recall feeling anything at all. An elderly lady was laying plastic sheets over the racks of cheap Chinese clothes outside the Belorussian Pavilion. My last memories of Jack, sitting up in bed, gripping my arm fiercely and telling me to destroy his journal, seemed more real and more solid than the scene in front of me. I found it impossible to believe Vera, never mind grieve for Jack. 'How can you be so sure?' I asked.

'Nicholas, I am sure,' she said.

'I want to be clear about this,' I told her. 'You're saying that Jack was not your brother?'

'Correct. He was not of my blood.'

Not of my blood. I had a chilling recollection of the cruel needle Bykov had used to sedate him and the drop of blood that had hung from its point.

'He was this man?' I held up the photocopy.

'Yes. Trikhonov was an experimental subject. He volunteered to undergo the Malevin Procedure.'

'For money?'

'No. He was a *zek*. He was serving a life sentence in a penal colony. This was presented to him as an alternative.'

'So he consented?'

'This issue of consent is one of many differences I have with Hunter and Sinan. The short answer is yes.'

'What's the long answer?'

Vera sighed deeply. 'Nicholas, suppose I offer you a contract in which you, for a million dollars, agree to sell me your soul? Only superstition would prevent you, correct? You would say, it's impossible for them to take it, I don't believe I have a soul, I will take the money. But then you take the money, and I say, "I define the soul as a portion of your

254

limbic system, which I will now remove and you will no longer have your old identity." Now, you vanish and a totally new person comes into being, with no legal identity of its own, with ill-defined rights, and subject to obligations agreed by someone who no longer exists. Was that contract fair?'

'Well, I don't believe such a thing is possible.'

'That, in a way, is my point. As I understand it, the Native Americans had no concept of the private ownership of land. Result? They lost every-thing to people who did.'

Vera extended her palm beyond the shelter of the tree to check that the drizzle had stopped. 'It's not so mysterious. A plant or a basic mechanical object has a rudimentary consciousness – it responds to external stimuli.' She passed her hand over some ragged flowers in a tub beside her. 'These too. And even simple consciousness – grass, a sunflower, a cistern valve – is inscribed with desires. You understand?'

'A sunflower doesn't *want* to turn towards the sun,' I said. 'That's anthropomorphism. That's what we used to call the pathetic fallacy.'

'I disagree,' she said. 'I think you are simply reluctant to acknowledge the miracle. The miracle is self-consciousness. Recursive consciousness. Consciousness that perceives itself.'

She had lowered her voice. I had to move closer to hear. The aura around her seemed to intensify. I felt as though I was being drawn into her crazy bubble.

'And where does that come from?' she asked rhetorically. 'From language. *Logos.* Reason – *the word* – it's the same thing. Why do you have no memories that precede the acquisition of language? Because before you acquired language, *you* didn't exist. There was no *you* for your experiences to adhere to.'

In the sky to the north-west, the rain clouds had parted. A patch of blue became visible and the sunlight conjured an inappropriate rainbow over the damp pavilions. I had a sudden recollection of the park as it had been: the flowerbeds tended, the exhibits proclaiming the tattered but not yet laughable idea of Soviet superiority.

'The article I've given you was published by Sinan's father in 1946. It is the theoretical foundation for the procedure which Trikhonov underwent.'

'Does it work?'

'Yes, but not exactly as he conceived. Malevin's ideas were too far ahead of the technological capabilities of his era – like Babbage and Lovelace. But we can now call upon very sophisticated technology for the application of these theories. You know what I mean by a piano roll?'

I told her I did: they're an antiquated recording technology that captures the melody and dynamics of a particular performance and then allows it to be replayed on a special piano.

'Conceive, if you can, a piano roll that can listen and respond, both to itself and to the music of an

256

orchestra. It would have the distinctive musical identity of the original pianist, but also the capacity to improvise and embellish. A sophisticated enough version would be indistinguishable from its creator.'

I asked if she was saying that Jack was a robot.

She coloured at this suggestion. 'Such terms carry their own baggage and aren't very helpful. The distinction between biological consciousness and what we still tend to think of as machines is increasingly arbitrary.'

'Can they make one of these piano rolls out of anyone?'

'In theory, yes, anyone can be coded.'

'So why Johnson?'

'A number of reasons. The fact that he authored a dictionary is of course an inestimable advantage. Also because of the abundance of written sources – first and third person. And because the hypotactic structure of his sentences lends itself to the forms of logical branching that form the basis of the code.'

'But why involve me?'

'From Hunter and Sinan's point of view, you were well placed to answer the key question.'

'Which is?'

'Authenticity. Was he real? Did he have life, or the simulation of life? Did he merely repeat speech without comprehension, like Montaigne's parrot, or was he an authentic, autonomous subject? The distinction is the crux of the work. It must be the real thing. Otherwise it is not *obshchee delo.*'

'That's what you wanted me for?'

'That is what *they* hoped to achieve.'

'And you?' I asked. 'What about you?'

'For myself . . . Strange as it sounds, perhaps I hoped for something very like this.'

She paused. The rainbow had vanished. A man in filthy jeans had emerged from somewhere and was spreading gravel noisily with a big spade.

'This?' I asked incredulously. 'That bloke? Us sitting here? Jack's death? The . . . the termination?'

'Of course not. Not all these things. But the paper I chose was unlikely to fool a conscientious expert. And I was lucky enough to persuade Hunter to engage the services of someone who spoke Russian.'

'You wanted me to doubt their authenticity.'

'Yes.'

'Why?'

'Because I need an ally.'

I could see her watching my expression as the implications of her words unfolded. I remembered our first meeting, her feet on the staircase; 'You pity him?' – and her eyes averted at the thought of my compassion towards Jack; our drunken intimacy. She had drawn me into the conspiracy. *I need an ally.* I have been living in the shadow of those words ever since.

We sat in silence for a while. Finally, she gestured towards the rocket which rose up in front of us, topped with its tiny capsule. 'Before Gagarin, you remember there was Laika, the dog we sent into space? Afterwards, the chief scientist, Gazenko, said, "We did not learn enough from the mission to justify the death of the dog." Do you understand?' She searched my face for a reaction. 'Some progress has an unacceptable price. For a very long time, I believed that what we were doing was a good thing. This idea of Fedorov, *obshchee delo*, it offers so many possibilities, so much hope. But then we began to apply it. Gradually, I understood that what we were doing was ethically inexcusable. I saw the guilty part I was playing. I became ashamed of myself. This version of *obshchee delo* is wrong. Latterly, they have failed to heed even the most basic moral safeguards. I no longer ask where the bodies come from. Misha says they are using vagrants, *bomzhi*, and deserters. This is not what Fedorov conceived of. He called it *obshchee*, not *tainoe delo*.' The distinction she made in Russian was between a common task and a secret one.

'Why don't you just write a letter to the papers?'

'Do you believe what I have told you?'

I said nothing. It was clear that the answer was no.

She smiled. 'So, what chance do I have to persuade another?'

CHAPTER 25

I spent that evening in the lobby bar of my hotel, eating chilled soup made out of rye beer and cucumbers, trying to untangle the dense and scientific language of Malevin senior's article with the help of a Russian dictionary.

In his paper, so far as I was able to understand it, Malevin argued that certain external records of brain activity could be minutely related to the biological foundations of personality and memory. With judicious and sophisticated handling, he contended, these records – in principle, various, but in practice almost exclusively linguistic – could yield codes which mapped every nuance of what he called the 'core complex' (in Russian, *sushchestvenniy kompleks*). This core complex seemed to be more or less what we consider to be human consciousness. Malevin claimed that with enough material it was theoretically possible to reconstruct the core complex in a new organism. Malevin gave the name 'proxy complex' (*zapasnyi kompleks*) to the theoretical being that would result if an exogenously derived code were inserted into a new subject; it was a cuckoo entity perching inside a new carcass.

The terms were confusing and it was slow work making sense of his argument. I knew Vera would have been horrified if she could have seen me riffling through my dictionary in a public place. It was a small but deliberate act of rebellion on my part. She had insisted on leaving the park first. I was to remain on the bench for five more minutes. I watched her walk away, with that slight limp, past the broken Friendship of the Peoples Fountain, dwarfed by its huge and obscurely sinister gold statues. Vera's paranoia seemed to border on delusion, yet it was far from being the least credible aspect of her claims.

Even if Malevin was a real person and he had advanced his ideas with some sincerity, it seemed deeply unlikely that he could have believed in their application. In 1946, the memory of war was traumatically fresh. The Soviet Union was rebuilding itself. The country surely couldn't afford a costly renewal of Fedorov's flirtation with god-building. My instinct was that the man was a pure research scientist, in love with the elegance of his theories.

I met Vera the next day by the statue of Pushkin in Pushkin Square. It's a traditional spot for romantic assignations, but that wasn't why Vera had chosen it. There was a political rally taking place in a cordoned-off area inside the square.

'More crowds,' she said. 'It's better. We can hide in plain sight.'

I told her what I'd felt about the article.

She granted that I was right about Malevin, but she pointed out that from the 1930s onwards, the personality cults around Lenin and Stalin had distorted the priorities of Soviet science. The most famous example of this is Trofim Lysenko, whose ideas about genetics were championed not because they were right, but because they seemed to confirm Marxist theory.

'And in the case of Malevin,' she said, as we weaved through the angry pensioners waving placards, 'his ideas seemed to offer a possibility of increasing the health and effectiveness of our leaders. As a result it suddenly generated huge interest from our top scientific cadres.'

She said that in 1951, Soviet scientists led by Malevin himself had attempted to apply the principles of his theoretical design to human subjects.

'What happened?'

'It's best for you to ask him yourself.' With a studied casualness, she handed me a small hardback book, a copy of Mandelstam's poems that she had bought for a couple of hundred roubles in the metro. Inside was a train ticket to Arkhangelsk.

'Is it safe for me to see him? You're not worried?'

'Yurii Olegovich is no longer part of this work.' The slightly old-fashioned way she referred to him, by his first name and patronymic, suggested a deep residual respect for the man. 'He's retired, basically forgotten. Travelling by train there is very little risk.'

'Will he speak to me?'

'He's proud of his work, he's furious with his son. He loves an audience.'

Looking back on our conversations, I realise I had never been so comprehensively seduced. Vera not only respected and condoned my scepticism, she said that the nature of what she was telling me was so improbable that she would suspect the sanity of anyone who accepted it unquestioningly. And she was tenacious too, in the most inexorable way: apparently soft, apparently reasonable, but unwavering. She made her case as though her life depended on it. I had a half-formed misgiving about spending more time away from home, far from Lucius and Sarah, but my curiosity was such that I never really hesitated about going.

Yaroslavl Station looked seedy in the evening light. Rumpled men were buying cans of beer from the kiosks as pick-me-ups. Pop music blared out of a snack bar. But inside my designated carriage there was a reassuring Soviet calm. The attendant took my ticket and showed me to a spotless two-berth compartment.

Less than an hour out of Moscow, the suburbs gave way to deep countryside. The train rumbled through it for almost twenty-four hours, crawling through forests and nameless wooden settlements whose quaint exteriors belied the hardscrabble lives of the people who lived in them. It was the middle of August, and by midnight, there was still enough light to read by. I fell asleep in the early hours and slept until lunchtime. At six o'clock the next evening the train pulled into Arkhangelsk.

There was a flavour of Ronald Harbottle about him: his dingy flat with Caucasian rugs on the floor; the joyless balcony with stacked jars of cabbage and its view of the White Sea.

He was ninety years old, though he looked at least twenty years younger. When I attributed his longevity to his genetic endowment, he dismissed it with a flap of his hand. His shirt sleeves were neatly rolled up, revealing forearms as wiry and brown as tree roots.

'Fairy tales for children! Mountain people have this reputation, but it's entirely down to the clean water. Clean water is at the heart of everything. There are two kinds of culture: tea-drinking culture and brewing culture. Why? Water purification!' He shook his finger at the ceiling. 'The tragedy of Russia is that it is an Asiatic tea-drinking culture that believes it can drink alcohol!'

He was an exile from his beloved South, estranged from his son and no longer involved in the work that bore his name. He was not even allowed to examine his own research papers. They were still technically classified, along with all those other arcane Soviet studies that have no respectable western parallel: the psychics and remote viewers, the astroarchaeologists and the inheritors of Kozyrev's woollier dealings with electromagnetism.

'I was a disciple of Fedorov,' he said. 'At that

time, no question seemed impossible. We asked, why must we die?'

I remember asking him in Russian if he would consider submitting to the Procedure himself. His reaction reminded me of the old joke about a competition where the first prize is, say, a week's holiday in Skegness, and the second prize is two weeks' holiday in Skegness. Two existences, he suggested, would be an appreciably worse deal than one. He was from a time and generation for whom existence was something to be survived.

My ne zhivem, my sushchestvuem – we don't live, we exist – is a stoic lament so common in Russia as to verge on cliché.

Malevin said his first life had included forced exile from his homeland, the loss of his parents, the Second World War, eight years in the Gulag. Why should he expect the next one to be any better?

He told me that as a young scientist in the 1940s, his expertise lay in the biological origins of consciousness. In 1946, in a closed session of the Soviet Academy of Sciences, Malevin had presented the paper which drew him to the attention of the most senior members of the scientific establishment.

'It was a beautiful and intuitive idea,' Malevin told me. 'Consciousness is preceded and constructed by language itself.'

His vigour and optimism only faltered twice during our long conversation. The first time was when I mentioned the break-up of the Soviet Union. 'A tragedy,' he said, with the sudden gravity of someone recalling a bereavement. 'A *coup d'état*. The gas and oil industry stepped on the throat of the people. They held the Soviet Union to ransom.'

Earlier, he had proudly showed me his party card and told me he still regarded himself as a Soviet citizen.

The second time was when I asked him if he thought it was possible for his ideas to work in practice.

He fell silent for a while, and sat scratching his forearm. I noticed for the first time that his eyes were different colours: one was blue and the other brown.

When he spoke, there was a note of wistfulness in his voice. 'Undoubtedly. You may know that we attempted something of this kind ourselves.'

I said Vera had referred to it.

Malevin looked grave. He said the first, doomed and premature attempts to apply his ideas took place in a closed research centre near the Aral Sea.

'It was too early,' he said. 'We weren't ready. But by then it was already a political question.' He said that he had argued in his first paper that for the Procedure to be viable, you needed a large quantity of material – he gave the rather arbitrary figure of a hundred thousand words as a minimum. But just as important, he told me, was its range. He rubbed his thumb and forefinger together to emphasise the significance of tone and texture. 'Subtleties,' he said. 'Details.'

This is why, he said, for all their apparent advantages – no ethical oversight to trouble the scientists, a virtually inexhaustible supply of donor bodies – the early experiments were doomed to failure. Even with every word of Stalin's writings coded, the results were insufficiently robust to produce what he called 'a functioning proxy complex'.

The experiment of 1951 created a prototype so monstrous that it earned Malevin ten years in the Gulag – rescinded under Khrushchev – and caused the programme to be mothballed indefinitely.

Malevin told me he knew the project was in trouble even before the crazed and truculent mankurt came round from anaesthesia. He said the impossibility of the scientists' task stemmed from the fact that huge areas of human life are simply not represented in the dictator's writings. They had coded the work in minute detail, but vast tracts of the proxy complex were blank, existential nullities, like the conscience of a psychopath.

As soon as the golem became conscious, it began to attack one of the scientists. Captain Gennadi Hubov, a hero of Stalingrad, was present at the first experiment. While the others stood watching in horror, Hubov calmly drew his gun and shot the golem dead. For this perceived crime, Hubov was himself executed. In his official report on the tests, Malevin blamed the failure on fatal shortcomings in the coding process. All work on the project ceased.

The arctic sun had dipped below the horizon. It was around midnight. Malevin took sips from a glass of warm milk to soothe a stomach ulcer.

I mentioned his mismatched eyes.

'The doctors say it's a birthmark,' he said. 'But my grandmother said I was blessed by God. Not for myself, unfortunately. But to bring good fortune to others.'

'Is that why you chose science?'

He shrugged. 'Perhaps.' Suddenly he looked tired, but I didn't want our conversation to end. I asked him what had set him on this path, what was the inspiration – I used the English word – for his work?

He said that for as long as he could remember, he had been fascinated by repetition, by the way human beings tell the same stories about themselves over and over again.

In his first writings, he had posited that these retellings and recurrences are some of the ways that consciousness undertakes repairs on itself. The human personality as he imagined it was a highly embattled construct: assailed from without by an infinite array of sense-data, attacked from within by a collection of centripetal and contradictory drives and impulses. It constantly needs to groom and restore its sense of integrity. Repetition, he said, is a simple and non-invasive version of the Procedure.

For obvious reasons, neither Malevin nor anyone else in the old Soviet Union was ever allowed to write about the theological implications of his work, but Malevin told me that he believed that the individuated personality was already one step towards a kind of deadness. You couldn't deny our physical separateness from one another, he said, but he felt there was a state before personality, when the pre-verbal sensorium is fully open to the world. The analogy he used was a camera body with no lens attached: light flooding into it. Of course, with nothing to focus the light, the experience is irrational, but, Malevin maintained, closer to the actual energetic state of reality. At this point, he said, the analogy breaks down: there's no way our individuated consciousness can grasp the notion that the camera and the light are actually identical, or that we are a seamless part of the out-there. We can't get there in words, because the job of words is to construct the fiction of our separate identity.

It was as much as I could do to follow him. Listening to Malevin, my Russian, perfectly adequate for a host of day-to-day uses, was like an old locomotive being driven far beyond its tolerance: rivets bursting off the boiler, everything overheating, and yet pounding forward with an exhilarating sensation of speed.

CHAPTER 26

I woke up the next day in my hotel room in Arkhangelsk. Out on the chilly water, a man was fishing in a tiny boat. I longed to be home. At breakfast, a table of Swedish engineers next to me were eating plates of buckwheat porridge and cold meat. I caught the train back to Moscow at lunchtime and arrived the following day.

With hours to kill before my next meeting with Vera, I went to Tolstoy's old house on Prechistenka. I saw the shoes the writer had made himself, his bicycle. I thought of all the people and experiences that made Tolstoy Tolstoy. How would you code all that? And if you did, who would you get? The priapic soldier and nobleman, exercising his *droit de seigneur* upon the serfs on his estate? The writer and paterfamilias of the middle years? The bearded guru of the late ones, who had sublimated his vast ego to the quest for Christ-like perfection? How could you fashion those layers from his words alone, and yet have each one riven with all his authentically human inconsistencies – that old man writing in his final year and experiencing a flash of recollection as he remembers his adored peasant lover: 'to think that Aksinia is still alive!' Could you really inscribe all that in a fresh carcass?

Malevin had seemed to be suggesting that there was a spiritual dimension to the work. One phrase in particular stayed with me. Struggling to understand him, I had tried to paraphrase what he was saying and he shook his head impatiently. 'No, no,' he said. 'It's much simpler. We are the masks God made to know itself!'

I remembered how his eyes had glittered in the half-dark as he nodded with pleasure at the exactness of his words. '*Vot tak.*' *That's how it is.*

Vera was waiting for me outside the brand new Cathedral of Christ the Saviour. We walked across the footbridge over the Moscow River past girls in summer dresses.

'You spoke to Yurii Olegovich? He told you about the 1951 experiment?'

I said he had.

'Yurii Olegovich and I do not agree about the significance of that experiment,' she said. 'Malevin provided only the theoretical basis for the procedure that bears his name. My personal belief is that whatever they made in 1951, it wasn't a true proxy complex. Tell me this: a natural philosopher attaches swan's wings to his arms and plunges to his death from a belfry. This shows what? That flight is impossible? Absolutely not. You understand me? In the Soviet Union of the 1940s and '50s, developments in the west, advances in computing, the Turing Test: these things were still unknown to them. Who knows what shortcuts those terrified men took?'

On the other side of the river, the huge brick structure that I remembered as the Red October chocolate factory had been redeveloped into an urban playground for rich young Russians. It was full of bars and restaurants. We found a gallery cafe that was big and airy enough for us to be isolated from the other customers. Vera chose a table near the entrance, where a giant sculpture of a melted iPod was showing images from Soviet propaganda films. I helped her off with her coat and we both ordered herbal tea.

'Tell me something,' I said. 'How did you get mixed up in this?'

She said nothing until the waitress was out of sight, then she leaned forward and began speaking in a low voice. She explained that she had held an academic position in the Soviet equivalent of artificial intelligence, but had left it in the early 1990s when it became impossible to live on the official salary.

'It was a very chaotic time for my country,' she said. 'Many top scientists were leaving Russia. They were experts in very sensitive areas of study. For example, Ken Alibek, the chief of the Soviet biological weapons programme, went to the US. There were many, many such instances. Can you imagine? If there is no future for him here, what hope is there for a simple academic?

'I was approached in 1998 to do work for Sinan Malevin. During that time, he began dealing with Hunter. In the very early 1990s, maybe 1990, before the break-up, Hunter had invested in a radio station in Moscow.

'From 2001, my work changed. I was present at a meeting with Sinan and his father, Hunter, and both US and Russian officials. Following that meeting, I worked closely with Yurii Olegovich, studying his classified work from the 1940s.'

'But who was paying for all this?'

'What we understood at the time was that Hunter had raised funding from private US sources to see if this work of Malevin's had commercial potential. Now I think it's not the case. Above Hunter, there are others.' She looked meaningfully at me.

The scenario she was describing would have seemed beyond absurd if it had been suggested to me a month earlier. But after my experience with Jack, after talking to Malevin, I wasn't so sure.

'Why isn't Sinan's father involved any more?'

'Yurii Olegovich resigned when the source of our funding became clear. He is an old Soviet idealist. He couldn't bear the thought of his work helping our former enemies. The research is being conducted by a clandestine US and Russian joint venture. You understand that the next technological frontier is the human body itself? I'm speaking of human enhancement. The possibilities are enormous, but so are the costs. Each enhancement is tied to a human subject. Every operation is a risk. There is the danger of accident and injury, and the certainty of ageing. Using the Malevin Procedure, each enhanced subject can be in principle duplicated at relatively low cost. It's the military application of Fedorov's old dream, using science to transcend the limits of the human. In this case, to create the transhuman – the post-human.'

'The *Übermensch*,' I said.

'Of course,' she agreed. 'The fascist overtones are unmistakable. Another of my objections. I have no sympathy with those who idealise human perfection. What place would I have in a world like that?'

There was something very touching about the question, and about Vera's open consciousness of her strangeness and asymmetry. It made me feel protective towards her. And as I stopped fighting the possibility that she might be telling the truth, I began to glimpse her courage. Perhaps she saw some of this in my face, because she reached across the table and took my hand.

'We must not allow it, Nikolasha. We must not allow it.'

The waitress chose that moment to refill our tea-cups and we both fell silent until she was out of earshot.

'There is another thing. I know for a fact that Hunter has an additional personal interest. He was diagnosed with a recurrence of prostate cancer last year. He wants us to speed up the testing of proto-types in the hope of prolonging his own life.'

On the giant iPod screen, an old black-and-white newsreel showed a sturdy Russian woman changing a tractor tyre. The lights in the cafe seemed strangely bright. I closed my eyes for a second and the floor gave a lurch under my feet.

'You don't look very well at all, Nikolasha,' Vera said. She touched my forehead. Her hand felt as cold as marble. 'You have a temperature.'

'I couldn't sleep on the train,' I said.

We walked back to the river bank together and found Vera a taxi. She offered me a lift, but I felt like I could use the fresh air. It was a clear, balmy evening. The absurd, Disneyland sculpture of Peter the Great in a Pirates of the Caribbean galleon was framed by yellow and black clouds. Under this lonely, unfamiliar sky, I was struggling against a life-changing realisation and its consequences.

That night I went down to the fitness centre in the basement of the hotel where there was a sauna.

I remember closing my eyes and hearing the tick of the elements inside the heater. I felt ghastly. I was homesick and I wanted the certainties of my old life, but I knew there was no going back to it. I couldn't seem to calculate how much time had passed since Jack's disappearance. Was it weeks or days? I missed Lucius and Sarah with a terrible, physical yearning. The light in the sauna seemed unnaturally harsh.

I remember getting into the lift and going back up to my room. I remember dialling Vera's number.

For a moment, I see my reflection in the window. Beyond it is the tower of Kazan Station. The hands of its clock advance rapidly before my eyes. The locus of my recollection shifts. I seem to be watching myself. I am watching Nicky Slopen as he answers the door; I cannot see to whom.

The continuous thread of my recollection unravels into an assortment of orphaned memories: a mouthful of gold teeth, an imperial eagle embroidered on a length of cloth, tortellini in the chiller of a supermarket, walking past the statue of Edward VII at Tooting Broadway in darkness; climbing up the creaking ladder to my loft, where under the naked bulb, accompanied by the clinks and hisses of the cold-water tank, I am sorting through the boxes of old papers in which I have saved everything: the English composition books full of murders perpetrated with implements made of ice; morose adolescent diaries ('Frederick came over. We played D and D. I wish my penis was bigger.'); self-conscious teenage ones; and my first long essays for Ron.

My mind begins to unravel. Images of my children strobe and flicker: as they were, as they are, as I've never seen them. I tip headfirst into a pool of coloured mud. This is the red clay from which the biblical God made Adam. Chains of homunculi crawl along cables in an unceasing flow, fighting, laughing, dying. Beneath it all palpates a divine certainty that this is a vision of my place in creation. Life is a profound blessing. My true nature transcends a single unitary ego. Light and tenderness and compassion flood through me. I am all men and women at all times. I am all my mothers and fathers. I am Nicholas Patrick Slopen. Humour and kindness and intelligence will survive death, and God on high is full of generous laughter.

So the pain, when it comes, is a shock.

CHAPTER 27

All my next memories are red: that was the colour of my pain; its sound was like an ambulance siren. I felt like an *écorché*, one of those flayed anatomical cadavers, posed in awful shapes, with bulging eyes and flesh the colour of salt beef. Every fibre of me seemed to have been exposed – a ray of light or a speck of dust could turn me inside out with agony. The contortions of my physical suffering overwhelmed my capacity to think. A few disordered impressions are all that I have of that time: a bucket containing what looked like offal in the corner of the room; a stopped clock with its hands at ten to three; someone wiping my body with a cloth so rough it seemed to be made of shagreen.

One characteristic of pain is that it roots you to the now. It's the flipside of ecstasy – something both saints and deviants are aware of. It says something about human nature, I suppose, that more religions have chosen the flagellant's than the voluptuary's route to the infinite. Or maybe, as my experience suggests, pain just does it more efficiently. It takes you out of the flow of time and pins you in a transcendent present. You forget everything, you become inseparable from your agony, until you emerge from it transformed.

The pain has never entirely left me. It's constant still, like tinnitus; but after a while – months, weeks, days? – it diminished enough for my sense of self to return and for the world around me to swim into focus.

I assumed that I'd been abducted, but if I'd disturbed the workings of a conspiracy that was important enough for my involvement to merit this, why had Hunter and Sinan left me alive at all? How had they moved me? Where was I? And, as I've indicated, there were more troubling inconsistencies between what I seemed to remember of my physical appearance and the body I was confronted with beneath my green hospital gown.

To begin with, my room was kept dark all the time. My neck seemed to lack even the necessary strength to hold my head steady: the sight of the world pitching and yawing whenever I opened my eyes made me seasick. I was fed with some kind of thick orange-flavoured fluid through a tube in my nose; it was changed twice a day by a masked orderly. The bed was made of metal tubing and it creaked when I shifted position. Bowel movements were so traumatically painful that I felt tearful at their onset.

No one ever spoke in my presence. My impression

is that in this period I was attended by one individual of indeterminate gender, but since he or she always wore a gauze mask, I can't be sure.

With hindsight, I can calculate that these events took place around the end of August 2009, but during that period day and night themselves were indistinguishable; other temporal distinctions simply collapsed. I existed in a hopeless present, a stranger in my new body.

I recall, at some point, an attendant dilating my pupils with a pocket torch. This was certainly a man, because he came so close to my face that I could see black eyebrows, brown eyes, greying hair beneath his paper cap. He had olive skin and large pores on the bridge of his nose.

Later, I was given solid food. Someone fed me with a spoon: my arms were useless. I was able to move my jaw, though the food seemed tough and intransigent. My mouth filled with something warm and salty: I had chewed through part of my own insensible tongue.

My incapacity and the lack of stimuli produced a complementary overexcitement in my mental state. My mind roamed through acres of memories. There was a terrible disconnection between my physical surroundings and the world that sprang to life every time I closed my eyes. Inside my head was a richly textured world filled with unaccountable hopefulness, longing and betrayal, and the deep greens of an English spring; outside were the scratched yellow walls of my room, tattered nylon curtains flapping at the windows, and that dusty, bright light.

Some time after the change in my diet, the massages began. The attendant who performed them smelled of garlic and body odour. He would raise me upright, gripping me around the chest with his huge upper arms, and then flip me over onto my stomach. He worked the soles of my feet, pummelled my legs and back; stretched out my arms and cracked the joints of my fingers. When he rotated my feet at the ankles he would wait afterwards for an answering movement from me. On a couple of occasions, my efforts earned a grunt of approbation. Finally, he would turn me back over, laying me out almost tenderly, crossing my arms over my torso before he left, as though I were a corpse he was preparing for burial.

His work produced a perceptible improvement in my vision and co-ordination. Some stage of progress was marked on the day when he hoisted me from the bed and into a vinyl wheelchair with footrests. I was naked beneath my green gown. The corridor was as featureless as my room, unrelieved by any decoration; the only sound the footsteps behind me, their rubber soles squeaking on the linoleum.

The attendant, still masked, removed my shift and lowered me into a murky-looking swimming pool. At first, he merely encouraged me to make my way, crabwise, around the perimeter. On subsequent visits, he used various apparatus – a kind of hoist; parallel bars fixed across the pool – to help me move in ways that were more conventionally human.

As my physical condition improved, I graduated to a series of encounters that seemed intended to test my cognitive abilities.

One of my instructors was the man who had examined me with the torch. The same brown eyes addressed me over the gauze mask. He sat behind a low table; I was in my wheelchair. On the table lay an array of coloured plastic shapes which he mixed and shuffled about with the air of a card sharp. He took out a red square and placed it in a bare space in front of him. Then he examined me intently for a response.

You need to understand who I am, who I have been. An impulse to excel academically has been with me from an early age. Part of me wanted nothing more than to graduate from that purgatory with honours.

Lifting my arm with great care, I extended it across the table. My instructor watched me with a notable expectation. I dropped my arm onto the table and swept the pieces to the floor.

I surprised myself with my spirit of defiance. I've even wondered if it's really mine, and not some trace, some palimpsest of the previous tenant.

My insubordination provoked a fresh battery of diagnostic tests. I was placed in a metal tube for hours with electrodes attached to my head; I was shown montages of nature documentaries while odours – I recall, specifically, cheese, manure and rose petals – were pumped into the room around me. I was made to step over low hurdles, walk along a balance beam, catch tennis balls. The exercises were timetabled with scrupulous exactitude: forty minutes of work; a rest period of ten.

I underwent a form of speech therapy. It was conducted by a masked female instructor in the regulation blue uniform. She used a rather ghastly rubber head, which resembled one of those dolls on which I was taught CPR as a designated first-aider at the university. The tongue, teeth and mouthparts of the doll were pliable and anatomically exact. The instructor manipulated them into a specific shape and then played the relevant sounds on a chunky tape recorder, whose anachronism, even at the time, struck me as absurd. Much of the time my efforts to speak resulted in silence; when noises did emerge from my mouth they were discouragingly bestial. Still, she persevered with no trace of impatience.

One lunchtime, I was taken into a long bright room which, in a more benign context, might have been used for school assembly.

A dark-haired balding man with a fleshy mouth sat on a folding chair behind a table set up in the room's centre.

I was escorted to a chair opposite him. Two masked attendants stood just behind me. One of them inserted a leather strap into my mouth; it lay slightly under my tongue, like a horse's bit.

The novelty of the man's unmasked face preoccupied me. I watched as he shuffled some papers on his desk. I couldn't say with any precision where he was from. He was of vaguely Mediterranean appearance, but when he spoke, he had the indeterminate American accent of a call-centre operator.

'My name is John Smith,' he said, in the tone that Fenella Webster would probably describe as *affectless*. 'It's my job to ensure that you are happy and comfortable here. Please indicate that you have understood.' He made no effort to meet my eye; he was fussing with something in front of him. I remained silent. Now he looked up at me. 'Please indicate that you have understood.' His face was as unreadable as the plastic head on which I was learning to pronounce my vowels.

The attendants stepped slightly away from me and a wave of pain seemed to root me to the floor. When it passed, he was still looking at me. 'Please indicate that you have understood.' This time, I nodded.

'Good job,' he said. 'In front of you, you will see a series of pictures. Please pick the one that most closely describes the idea *fast*. Can you indicate if you've understood the question?'

I nodded. The array in front of me depicted a tortoise, a tree and a bird in flight. I tapped the picture of the bird.

'Good job.' He selected a new array from the box in his lap.

The pictures he laid out in front of me looked like photos from a family album. There was a little girl of about seven, an adult woman in a headscarf smiling and holding a paint roller, and a boy of ten posing in a football strip that I didn't recognise.

'This time, please pick the card that most closely represents the word *Irene*.'

For a moment I thought he was joking. I looked at him in vain for a clue. Time was passing. I decided to pick the little girl, but before I could raise my hand the attendants moved away and another surge of electricity compressed my gut; this one lasted twice as long as the first.

'It's important to me that we do this exercise properly,' he said. 'That means no guessing. Can you indicate that you've understood?'

And so it went on for the remainder of the forty-minute session: facile questions alternating with incomprehensible ones. I became stressed and jumpy each time he changed the array. I attempted every possible approach to the incomprehensible questions: answering, not answering, gazing at him blankly, shaking my head. Nothing made any difference. The shocks seemed to increase in length and intensity.

'It's important to me that we do this exercise properly. Can you indicate that you've understood?'

Finally, he called a halt to the torment. The attendant removed the bit. I took my first unobstructed breaths. 'Thank you for your hard work today,' he said. He flexed his mouth in a perfunctory smile. 'See you tomorrow.'

That evening I watched a mosquito sink its proboscis into the unfamiliar heft of my upper arm, drink its fill, then fly away laden with this alien's blood. I thought of Jack and I experienced a wave of grief that seemed to crash uselessly on the obdurate walls of this vessel.

The next morning I was wheeled down to a common room in a distant wing of the building. The room was dimly lit and it took my eyes a moment to adjust to the darkness. Around me were half a dozen broken figures slumped in wheelchairs. Most of us were inert; one twitched restlessly; another, his eyes shut, the top of his skull ribbed horribly, like a walnut, began speaking. 'We must attend to the difference between what men in general cannot do if they would, and what every man may do if he would,' he said, in a shrill and grating voice. 'Sixteen-string Jack towered above the common mark!'

I listened with an unease that shaded into horror as he repeated himself word for word with identical intonation more than a hundred times.

★　　★　　★

The sessions with John Smith continued each day. On alternate afternoons, I was parked in the common room with the vegetative carcasses and Sixteen-string Jack for two interminable hours.

One afternoon, I began screaming at my orderly as he wheeled me towards my appointment. It was to no avail. Then I felt something like a solid object forming in my mouth. I released it almost involuntarily. It was the word 'book'. Panic and rage gave way to a feeling of wonder. I uttered it again and again, relishing the deliberateness of the sensation; the kick of the terminal consonant on my soft palate. It was almost magical, the sense that I had regained control over a portion of reality. The orderly turned me round and took me back to my room. Tomatoes and fresh fruit appeared beside the stodge on my tray at dinner time.

The sessions with John Smith ceased. In retrospect, it seems likely to me that his questions and the seemingly random punishments were designed to use stress and frustration to knit my consciousness into the new carcass, but that is clearly only my conjecture. The period of convalescence that followed was slower, but more comprehensible, and there were even moments of profound relief as I edged towards more finely co-ordinated use of this body and began to bring its recalcitrant tongue under my control.

A week later, I was walking unassisted and while my active vocabulary still numbered no more than half a dozen words, my comprehension was as lucid as it is now.

One afternoon, a nurse collected me from the swimming pool without a wheelchair and supported me as I walked unsteadily through the harsh light of those corridors. I was sweating from the unfamiliar exertion of navigating that big carcass and I was full of trepidation. I wondered what fresh misery had been prepared for me. A pair of heavy double doors opened ahead of me. Beyond them, I saw a small figure swigging from a plastic bottle of water. Vera Telauga. And beside her, dressed in an unfamiliar linen suit, looking at me with pity and disbelief, was me; or, me as I remembered myself.

'You . . . I faltered. No other words would come.

'Sit down,' he said.

Vera took my arm with a gentleness that was as unexpected as it was welcome. 'We've come to take you home.'

CHAPTER 28

For the first time, I was admitted to the world outside the unit. A basketball court stood in the blazing sun. Beyond the chain-link fence around it, a plateau of desolate yellow grass stretched to the horizon in every direction. The breeze was infused with an unforgettable, slightly medicinal smell that I know now to be wormwood. I know now also that the place where I underwent the Procedure was in the Russian-administered town of Baikonur within Kazakhstan.

There was a local driver waiting in a battered Mercedes just outside the gates of the complex. By the time I reached it, the unaccustomed effort had left me soaked in sweat. The sun overhead was pitiless.

Nicholas, as I suppose I must call him, was unmistakably awkward with me, and yet I couldn't help noticing in him, in spite of everything, a new purposefulness. Whatever he had been engaged upon with Vera had revitalised him.

We drove for hours through miles of desolate desert steppe. Vera remained beside me in the back; Nicholas sat in front with the driver, an

289

Uzbek called Kairat, staring fixedly at the road ahead. Occasionally, he ventured a couple of words to Kairat in Russian that surprised me with its woolliness and grammatical inaccuracy.

Towards lunchtime, Kairat stopped to fill the car with diesel. The four of us ate boiled eggs and *samsa* – baked Uzbek pasties – at a roadside stall. A Kazakh toddler with a wide Eurasian face played in the dust with a toy train and I thought with a pang of Lucius. *My son.* I looked across at Nicholas. He hadn't seen the boy; he was stealing a doubting glance at me.

'I'm not sure how I feel about this,' he muttered to Vera.

Later, returning unsteadily from the washroom in the back, I overheard them talking in whispers. As I approached, they heard my heavy footsteps and fell silent.

'We're sorting out the bill,' Nicholas said. It was only the second time he'd addressed me directly. Of course, I knew he was lying. *Hypocrite lecteur. Mon semblable. Mon frère.*

Whatever human experience offers in the way of analogues for the Procedure, it always comes up short. It's not like parenthood. Nicholas had no instinctive love for his proxy complex. I was ugly and disappointing, confirmation of his worst fears, like a particularly unflattering photograph.

In so many ways, Nicholas and I found ourselves in uncharted territory. *We? He? I? One?* Even the choice of pronoun is vexed. There is no word that captures the distinct but overlapping consciousness of core and proxy complexes like ours. And more and more, that word *proxy* I feel to be a violation of my unique subjectivity.

By contrast with Nicholas, Vera was almost excessively engaged with me. She talked constantly, making conscientious eye contact and pointing out features in the landscape: raptors wheeling over the plain, camels moving slowly through the heat, patches of salt showing through the parched grass.

That night, we stayed at a shabby hotel on the outskirts of a town that I believe was Shymkent. Vera helped me to wash, drying me with a gentleness that this carcass mistook for a lover's touch. She lingered over my arousal and I found myself instantly brought to the pitch of ecstasy. She consoled me so tenderly that nothing about the episode seemed weird or demeaning. 'You cannot be a stranger to joy,' she whispered.

She asked me if I was too tired to eat with them. I felt frail and bewildered but I craved human contact. Vera changed her clothes and put on make-up for our dinner. We ate fatty *shashlik* and raw onion in a private booth in the outside courtyard of a *chaikana*. Nicholas drank several beers and ignored us.

Halfway through the meal, Vera's patience snapped. 'You have to engage with him,' she said to Nicholas. 'For both your sakes.'

He turned slowly and theatrically to meet her angry stare. 'If you can't persuade *me*,' he said, 'how are you going to persuade anyone else?'

A waitress in plastic sandals entered our booth to put a basket of freshly cooked flatbread on the table. As she left, Vera said to Nicholas: 'I told you what to expect.'

Nicholas pulled off a tiny piece of bread and examined it without answering her. I felt his bitterness and disappointment. He was punishing her with his contemptuous silence. I think that I grasped even at the time not only the substance of their disagreement but Vera's profound fear of being disbelieved. She was compelled to try to appease him. 'He may be months away from full rehabilitation,' she said.

'And what if this is as good as it gets?'

She gave him a volcanic stare which he met without speaking. I felt wounded by his contempt. I wanted to tell them that I understood everything; that I grasped, however dimly, the mystery of our overlapping consciousnesses.

I opened my mouth to speak and they both looked at me with a sudden surge of interest. I could feel my eyes rolling back in my head with the effort. 'Book,' I said. 'Book.'

Nicholas shook his head and looked away disgustedly. Vera patted my hand.

The next morning, we set off before dawn and drove for several hours. The flat land had an oceanic scale; shoals of tiny livestock moved slowly in the distance. When the wind blew over the grass, the blades rippled like the surface of an enormous green lake. Gradually, sand and scrub came to dominate the landscape. I saw from a road sign that we were approaching the town of Turkestan. Just beyond it lay our destination: the mausoleum of Akhmet Yassawi, an eleventh-century poet and Sufi mystic.

The building, erected on the command of Timur the Great – Marlowe's Tamburlaine – is one of the treasures of Central Asia. Its huge central dome rises forty metres from the desert floor.

Kairat pulled up in an empty car park on the outskirts of the complex. The structure was dun-coloured in the blazing sunlight.

'This is an odd moment to go sightseeing,' Nicholas said. I looked at him in surprise: the same thought expressed in an identical form had crossed my mind only fractionally before he uttered it. It was my first instance of a phenomenon that soon grew too commonplace to be noteworthy: the weird echoes between our incestuous subjectivities.

Kairat said he would wait for us, but Vera saw him off with a hefty tip and told him we would make our own way back later. When he had left, she explained that she wanted to change vehicles. The chances of our being recognised increased every day we spent with Kairat; she had therefore asked him to take us to the Yassawi mausoleum on the pretext of sightseeing, but in fact so that we could engage the services of a new driver.

'Since we're here anyway, does anyone object if I have a look round?' said Nicholas. I found the constant note of irony in his voice irritating in the extreme. I remembered Leonora's frequent bouts of hostility towards me, which at the time had seemed so inexplicable. Now I wondered how she had put up with him so long.

We watched his rangy figure stalking through the bright sunshine towards the tomb.

Vera took my arm. 'You need to be patient with him,' she said to me. 'This is very difficult for him too.' She spoke to me directly and with warmth. There was none of that falsity or awkwardness that I felt when addressing Jack for the first time.

The two of us made our way to the rear of the structure where a smaller, more exquisite dome tiled in a ravishing shade of aquamarine stands over Yassawi's tomb. I found the colours almost stupefyingly bright; the intricate swastikas in the walls drew my eyes into the brickwork. I recognised it from Soviet-era guidebooks, where it is pictured surrounded by Ladas and Eurasian men sitting on their haunches selling watermelons.

'The selfish gene aspires to immortality,' Vera said softly. 'This is Timur's – and Yassawi's. But we live in more literal-minded times, Nikolasha.'

In the whitewashed interior of the mausoleum, right under the main dome, a newly married couple, the groom in a black suit and the bride in white veil and a meringue of a wedding dress, knelt in prayer with their ushers and bridesmaids. We found Yassawi's tomb – green marble with a green velvet covering – towards the back of the complex behind a wooden screen. A Kazakh man in a white baseball cap was kneeling in front of it and praying in a soft monotone.

Outside, she showed me the underground cavern where she said Yassawi had spent the final years of his life in solitary prayer. We descended the steps to his tiny cell. It was barely large enough to contain a single body. She touched the rough plaster with her tiny hands. '"Though I am bounded in a nutshell, I count myself the King of infinite space,"' she said. There was an eerie buzz as her voice bounced from wall to wall. I suddenly felt dizzy from the closeness of the tiny chamber, the heat, the physical strain of moving my carcass. I lurched forward as my legs began to buckle under me. She redirected my weight against the wall and then helped me back up the stairs. We rested on the grass in the shade of an apricot tree. A guide called Bulat approached us to ask if I was all right, then asked if he could practise his English. Vera told him I was from the Baltics and diverted him into a discussion about Yassawi's works. They weren't available in translation, Bulat said in heavily accented Russian, but it didn't matter. 'God has put a computer chip in your heart,' he said, 'with all knowledge, all languages. If you pray for forty days in that underground mosque, you will know everything.'

Vera helped me to my feet and we walked slowly together towards the car park.

Without the daily practice, my tongue was losing its hard-won facility. I could only make a gargling sound in my throat. Vera stopped and looked at me. 'What is it?'

My eyes pricked with tears of misery and frustration.

'Man,' I said.

'Which man?' She looked around. 'You mean Bulat?'

I shook my head. 'Man . . . man . . . I clenched my fists with the effort of articulation.

She shushed me gently, took one of my hands and stroked the fist into a palm.

'Man . . . Man . . . Mankurt,' I said finally.

She raised my hand to her lips and kissed it.

This stranger's salty tears plopped into the orange dust. I wanted to lay my clumsy, aching head in her tiny lap. Her hand touched my cheek like a feather. Vera spoke softly to me in Russian, as though only her own language could carry the freight of consolation she intended. '*Ty ne mankurt, Nikolasha. U tebya est' sobstvennaya dusha.*'

You are not a mankurt, Nicky. You have a soul of your own.

She shushed me gently until I stopped sobbing.

Thinking about Vera Telauga now, I experience a warmth and affection that is only comparable to what I feel about my own mother. Who knows what percentage of me is in fact not Nicholas Slopen, but Vera herself ? After all, the hand of a master betrays itself in every brushstroke of their creation.

CHAPTER 29

On the morning of our flight out of Almaty, Vera checked in alone, while we loitered at a coffee shop where a neurasthenic Chekhovian *ofitsiantka* with hollow eyes served espresso and dried-out sandwiches. I had my back to the departures hall, but I could deduce the state of proceedings from the play of emotions on Nicholas's face. His increasingly strained expression suggested that things weren't going according to plan.

At first, it seemed as though Vera would breeze through. Her luggage was accepted without a hitch; her seat assigned; then the attendant called her back. It seemed to be a routine query, but as the minutes stretched out, it became clear that something out of the ordinary was taking place. When I finally turned to look, Vera was standing to one side of the desk, where she was tapping her boarding card on her hand in a show of impatience as the attendant checked in some other passengers. There was a ruffle of energy at the distant edge of the hall and the crowd parted for a phalanx of security men headed by a man in a grey suit. Vera threw her passport and boarding pass to the ground in what seemed like a gesture of frustration but was in fact a pre-arranged signal for us to abort the plan.

Nicholas stood up. 'Come on,' he said. 'It's time to go.'

In my haste, I left behind my brand new suitcase, bought in the market that morning, not to hold my possessions – I had none – but to give me more plausibly the appearance of a business traveller.

Nicholas marched grimly towards the main entrance while I stumbled along a few steps behind him. Vera was standing at the check-in desk protesting as the man in the suit, who was holding a walkie-talkie, plucked at her elbow. As I watched, the uniformed security men swarmed around her and ushered her noiselessly away from the other travellers. An American oilman in chinos kicked his bag to the next spot in the line. His daughter swooped across the floor on the roller in the heel of her trainers. The attendant turned her look of infinite exasperation to the next customer. Vera's face became visible again from the far side of the hall as she turned back to remonstrate with one of her handlers; pale and frantic, she looked almost ghostly against the dark suits that surrounded her. I was trying to read the nuances of her expression – beneath the defiance and the fear, was there a hint of resignation? – when the blade of the revolving door severed us completely.

With gruff tenderness, Nicholas took my arm and urged me to hurry. We walked quickly past the old terminal building, with its crumbly and late baroque Stalin-period plasterwork, towards the importuning taxi drivers at the far end of the car park.

Both of us were numb from the loss of Vera. It was an amputation, an incalculable disaster. But the urgency of our predicament prevented our dwelling on it then. In her thoroughness, Vera had prepared a contingency plan for precisely this eventuality. We had a pair of Swiss passports and train tickets for Simferopol, from where the tram service would connect us to Yalta, and a cruise ship called the *Dimitrii Shostakovich* which would drop us in the relatively free air of Trabzon on the Turkish coast.

Nicholas was silent as we made our way nervously through the gloomy marble ticket hall of the main station.

We had second-class tickets for the train but Nicholas bribed the conductor for an upgrade and we found ourselves alone in a first-class compartment with maroon vinyl seats and *café au lait* drapery. Pedlars moved along the corridor selling buckets of apples and foil bags of grilled chicken.

As soon as the train had lurched out of the station, Nicholas left the compartment. Outside the dirty window, the suburbs of Almaty slid by in the afternoon light; beyond them rose the jagged yellow peaks of the Tian Shan mountains.

Nicholas returned an hour later and sprawled untidily on the opposite banquette. 'We'd better talk,' he said. 'I'd better talk. You understand this thing we're in?'

He leaned towards me and looked in my eyes. I could smell alcohol on his breath. I had the awful sensation of being disgusted by the sight of my own face.

'It wasn't an easy decision to make,' he said.

He wasn't being truthful: the decision was easy; what he was finding difficult were the consequences.

'Vera and I spoke about this,' he went on. 'Something happening to her. She was going to write you a letter, but it would have been compromising. I'm supposed to tell you that there will be a gap.'

From the volume of his voice and his awkwardness with me, I got the feeling he thought I was all gap.

'The way the Procedure works, there's a hiatus – it's called an entelechic or mnemonic hiatus. It's scientific periphrasis. They're just nervous about calling it amnesia.' He closed his eyes and covered his face with his hands. It was a gesture of despair. I could hear his drunken breath whistling in his nostrils. 'Just tell me: do you have any idea who I am? Do you remember anything at all?'

I looked at him for a moment, then I shut my eyes and visualised the mouthparts of the anatomical head. I forced my tongue into the gap between my parted teeth and breathed out. I could feel the muscles in my throat tighten. The sound originated somewhere in my abdomen. 'Th-this,' I said. The word faded away into silence like a hiss of steam.

'Well, that's a start,' he said. I opened my eyes and he was looking at me with a new alertness.

Seconds passed. I manoeuvred my lips to make the tiniest possible aperture. After a tentative start, the sound emerged with surprising clarity: 'World.' Now I threw my head back and felt my face contort. My left foot rose on tiptoe from the strain. 'Of.' As I struggled to maintain the muscle tone in my jaw, my hands spontaneously formed fists. I spat all my rage and contempt into the next word: 'Dew.'

The blood was draining from his face as he looked at me in horror, but I was determined to give him the full proof of life. I went on, my articulation decreasing in clarity with every syllable. 'Isaworld. Of. Dew. Andyet. And yet.' The tension finally left me. I flopped against the seat back. It was no longer hot in the carriage, but I had broken out in a sweat from the effort.

With every fibre of my new body, I understood the associations those words evoked for him. It was his favourite poem: Issa's perfect haiku, compressing a glimpse of infinity into a handful of syllables, lamenting the intrusion of death and change into every life, awakening Nicholas's sense of grief for his father, his mother, his sister. He looked as though he had been slapped. He fell back against the banquette and stared at me, open-mouthed, in shock.

What must he have been thinking? To acknowledge intellectually the possibility of the Procedure was one thing, but to be confronted by your double, your *fetch*. We'd both read enough to understand that, in myth at least, such a thing never ends well.

Suddenly, we were interrupted by a noise at the door of our coupé. Outside, someone was wrestling with the handle. Nicholas stiffened for an instant then grabbed the door and held it shut. '*Zanyat!*' he shouted. 'It's occupied. *Occupé! Besetzt!*' The noise stopped. There were footsteps. Nicholas slid open the door a crack. I could see a puzzled Kazakh retreating down the corridor apologetically.

'My nerves are shot,' Nicholas said. And then: 'You must be starving.'

Vera had packed some food – hardboiled eggs, a wheel of Uzbek bread – and at the next stop, Nicholas bought two polystyrene pots of instant noodles on the platform and rehydrated them with water from the guard's samovar. Textured soya chunks floated in the broth. He fed me with a plastic fork as the locomotive tugged us across the steppe with a distinctive uneven rhythm. In the dying light, cows or sheep were just visible on the vast pastures outside the window as tiny, ant-shaped dots.

'It's got to be stopped,' he said. 'Vera and I agreed on that. It's an abomination. Fedorov wanted to help the whole of humanity. But this is just like every other utopian scheme. Something that's supposed to be a gift for humanity in general diminishes the worth of individual humans to zero. You can see what happens next: life itself will become another good that the rich get more of. Vera said they're already talking about having two classes of proxy complex: *zachots* and *pyaterki*. Only the *pyaterki* will have full consciousness. It's unspeakable. They've been stepping up the numbers. The survival rate is abysmal. But each resuscitation makes subsequent ones easier.'

Nicholas was right to be disgusted: there was nothing egalitarian about this version of the Common Task. It was of a piece with the primal unfairness that has seen favoured consciousnesses hogging power, food and opportunities for reproduction since our ancestors crept out of the ocean. I share his moral outrage.

The gap he was talking about had begun for me in the hotel room in Moscow. That was the moment our experience bifurcated. Our consciousness had split in two like a cell undergoing mitosis. From a storm of almost ineffable images, I had emerged into the hospital bed in Baikonur.

For Nicholas there was no comparable break. He said there had been direct threats to him in Moscow. Two men had tried to abduct him from outside his hotel in broad daylight. He had come to the realisation that Vera was telling the truth and had concluded that they had to act. I was his idea: a double who would be tangible evidence of the Common Task.

Vera, he said, had been initially reluctant. She worried that it would compound the ethical lapse of getting involved with the Procedure in the first place. But what else would provide definitive proof? Vera had said it herself: it couldn't be grasped intellectually. Words were not enough. Like the Apostle Thomas, the human mind needs the touch of flesh to assuage its doubts.

Nicholas had supplied her with his journals, his writings, all the supplementary data she needed. She'd generated a code. It was handcarried in a diplomatic bag to Baikonur and slipped into the most recent batch of resuscitations. They'd had to rush. At the time of my release from the facility I was still some way away from full rehabilitation. Judged purely as a medical matter, my discharge was clearly premature, but Vera sanctioned it while she still had the authority to do so. She needed to do it before her subversion came to light.

We lay parallel in our narrow berths. The carriage rocked in the darkness. 'We're going to have to move quickly when we get back,' he said. 'They'll be after us. As soon as you're ready, we'll go to the authorities. If the police won't act, we'll go public. Vera's drawn up a list of the great and the good: scientists, human rights lawyers. The world's got to know what's being done. Can you imagine what Johnson would have made of this, an unholy combination of slavery and forgery?'

There was excitement in his voice, a bracing sense of the importance of his task. I almost didn't recognise him. Nicholas had never done an impetuous thing in his life. Now, he suddenly had a taste of life as a combatant in an honourable cause. There was an elation about him: the same energising change that comes over Hamlet when he returns to Denmark from England towards the end of the play, transformed from worrier to warrior.

It had grown colder in the compartment as we made our way across the steppe. Nicholas finally fell silent. I assumed he'd gone to sleep. He must have been exhausted. A few moments later, I was aware of someone standing on the end of my bunk and reaching up into the cubby-hole above the compartment. I closed my eyes and wondered what he was doing. Something dropped on me. He had covered me up with a blanket.

CHAPTER 30

Vera had provided in her plan for multiple delays in crossing borders, but we made such good time that we reached Simferopol a day ahead of schedule. A procession of worn-out people passed through the train station with wrinkled Asiatic faces and those third-world suitcases: big fake-tartan laundry bags, full of cheap Chinese goods for sale. A sign over the station toilet said 'Washing footwear is prohibited'. Just outside it, an old woman was sitting in the dust selling a single sinister-looking fish. 'Fresh flounder!' she croaked.

It seemed unwise to linger in a town of any size so we took a taxi to Chufut Kale, an abandoned cave village, where the only other visitors were a man called Dimitrii Muranov and his family. Muranov told us he was a poet, and at the slightest hint of incredulity from Nicholas, he went to his car to fetch two volumes of verse from a cardboard box in the boot. One was a book of love poems to his first wife; the other a book of love poems to his second wife, a blonde girl he called his Lolita who looked barely older than her fifteen-year-old stepdaughter. Nicholas thanked him for the books. Muranov inscribed them, explaining as he did so that he was also in real estate. He offered us a ride in his cramped car, but we had the taxi driver waiting for us at the foot of the hill. We crept off without saying goodbye. Nicholas flipped through the books as we drove back to Simferopol.

'She's still with Caspar,' he said, though neither of us had mentioned Leonora's name. 'They've moved into a big house on Chepstow Road. Last time we spoke, Leonora was about to have lunch with Candy Go. Can you imagine? They have the same Pilates teacher.'

In the days we had been travelling, my speech had begun to show marked improvement, and though I was still unable to form whole sentences, our singular connection meant that Nicholas was often able to guess my thoughts after one or two words, and in this case none at all. Muranov's wives, the poetry, the young children in the limestone caves: by some strange alchemy, these things had made both of us think of Leonora.

It meant there was something exhausting about being together. We were open books to one another. We couldn't outrun each other's consciousness. Wherever one of us went to hide, the other was there before him.

Rain was pouring down in Yalta when we finally arrived after the two-and-a-half-hour trolley-bus ride; the mountains obscured by mist and the sea a queasy mass of grey.

Nicholas and I sat in the half-light of a basement bar called the Black Muscatel and drank sticky Crimean wines.

I've lost my liking for alcohol. It just makes me nauseous and more uncoordinated. But Nicholas knocked the tumblers back in the Russian style and it loosened him up. He helped himself to more wine and then offered the bottle to me. I reached out to cover my glass with my hand and sent it crashing to the floor. I felt his disappointment at my clumsiness, his anxiety that no one would believe what I'd gone through, that he would fail and let down Vera.

At 10 p.m., we boarded the ship, queuing in the darkness with the other passengers on the clanking gangway. That night I had my first post-Procedure dream: I saw Vera in the blinding sunshine at the Yassawi mausoleum, but the dome above it was gilded like the Temple of the Rock and Vera was dressed all in white. She beckoned to me and as I leaned over she whispered in my ear: 'The words of a dead man are modified in the guts of the living.' At that instant, I awoke and saw Nicholas in the bed next to mine. Our eyes met and I knew he had woken from the same vision.

The *Dimitrii Shostakovich* was a cruise ship and her route across the Black Sea had a consequent lack of urgency. She put in at Odessa for one night before doubling back on a south-easterly course to Trabzon. A good half of the tour party – many of them Finns and Belgians – disembarked in Odessa to go sightseeing and visit the opera. Nicholas and I remained on board. We played ping-pong in a windowless steel exercise room; sportingly, Nicholas played left-handed to compensate for my disability.

At mealtimes, he ordered dishes from the menu that I knew he didn't like. He ate honeydew melons and pork cutlets with manufactured enthusiasm. His intention was obvious: he wanted to stress our differences.

To say that Nicholas and I had complicated feelings about each other would be an understatement. But I know that in some way my existence was a liberation for him. He didn't know what the future held – who does? – but he was facing it with a new lightness. At times he missed his old life terribly, Leonora and the children; at others he was beginning to glimpse the possibilities that lay ahead. I think he saw that he had come to the end of something. He had burned out a self. Someone else could be Nicholas Slopen. He would start afresh.

At the same time, our sameness, our redundancy and the potential for future conflict gave rise to terrible thoughts. I took heart from the fact that the torment of the Procedure itself, which is one of the constituent experiences of my identity, was to him a blank. The memory of the suffering I had undergone reassured me of my singularity.

Nicholas consoled himself with a different rationalisation. At root, there was always something patronising in his attitude towards me. Being conditioned to the idea of his uniqueness, he had the notion that he was the original, I the copy. He had no understanding of how profoundly I feel that, far from being a copy, I am an enhancement. I am the best of him. Nor could he imagine how powerfully I am attached to Lucius and Sarah. My love for them wasn't, isn't, a simulacrum of his. It's primary, non-negotiable, agonising. Each night, we lay in our cabin in silence as the ship cut slowly across the Black Sea. The darkness was full of unanswerable questions. I thought of my children.

CHAPTER 31

I had my second session with Dr White today and my overriding sense was of how much I miss Dr Webster. White is about fifty, a second-row forward run to seed, but still with all the hearty's machismo and swagger. It makes me wonder once again about the motivation of someone who voluntarily spends their time in the company of lunatics. Who is really suffering from messianic grandiosity?

White bristled with hostility towards me from our first session. Today, he started with almost the same words, warning me that he was no pushover. He accused me of being up to the same tricks that I was with Dr Webster and said I'd find him a tougher customer. 'I'm not going to swallow any of your bullshit,' he threatened.

I asked him what a strict Freudian would make of that declaration. He looked at me sourly.

We spent most of the session in silence. At the end, he suggested that he'd withdraw my computer privileges if I didn't show more sign of complying. He could see this panicked me. 'I want you to think long and hard, my friend,' he said, in a tone that was anything but friendly.

Nicholas and I got back to England on September 25th 2009. We travelled from Southampton to Victoria by train and took a black cab to Colliers Wood. Nicholas and Leonora were in the process of selling the house and Nicholas had rented a tiny one-bedroom flat on the high street. I followed him to the top floor, using the bannister to lever myself up the stairs. Misha Bykov was waiting for us inside. His body seemed to fill the living room. The curtains were drawn.

He and Nicholas exchanged muted greetings in Russian.

'It's not exactly what we hoped for,' Nicholas said. He put his bag in the bedroom and hung our coats in the hall cupboard.

'No?'

A pair of sofas faced each other around a glass coffee table. Misha sat down on one of them. It groaned a little under his weight.

Nicholas shook his head. 'It might be months.' He went to the galley kitchen and poured us both glasses of water.

I felt Misha's eyes on me as I drank carefully. 'We don't have months,' he said. He asked Nicholas to sit down.

Nicholas sat down beside me on the sofa. Misha

looked at each of us in turn, appraising us. 'We need our proof,' he said.

Proof. *Dokazatel'stvo.* That was me.

'We're very short of time,' he went on. 'They know what we're up to now. And if Vera's talking . . .

Nicholas shot me a glance. 'Vera's alive?'

'Of course. They have to take care of her. They need what's up here.' He tapped the side of his head with his forefinger. 'But us . . . He widened his eyes to emphasise the size of the threat we were under. His irises stood out alarmingly, like the bullseye on an archer's target. 'We're just small change.'

Nicholas finished his glass and put it on the table. 'How long do we have?'

'I don't know. I can't ask them. Sooner or later, they're going to figure out that I'm part of this too. But not weeks. Definitely not weeks. Three days, five maybe.'

'I need at least a week,' said Nicholas.

'Why? What's to stop us doing this now? We need to . . . Misha chopped the side of his hand against his palm. The sound it made evoked abrupt severance.

Nicholas hesitated. 'If we go too soon, no one will believe us. They'll think we're mad. And once we break cover, we're all running for our lives. We need to give ourselves a fighting chance. We need his testimony.'

This answer didn't please Misha, but I could see him considering it. He stared at the floor for a

314

while as though he was recalculating a difficult sum. Finally, he nodded. 'Okay. A week.' He got to his feet.

The focal point of the tiny room was a cast-iron fireplace with giant pine cones in the grate. Misha reached up inside the chimney breast and pulled out a plastic bag. It emerged with a patter of broken plaster and dust which he recoiled from with a surprising fastidiousness. He wiped the bag with his handkerchief and took out a dossier of documents and photographs – a paper trail to the Common Task. Nicholas added the Swiss passports on which we'd travelled from Almaty to the dossier and Misha showed him how to secrete it back inside the chimney breast.

'Okay,' Misha said, in English. And in Russian: 'Good luck.' He nodded at me. I heard the unfamiliar clunk of the front door as he left.

Nicholas saw the query in my face.

'Yes, he can take care of himself. He was a maroon beret. Vera said he was one of the last Spetsnaz soldiers to leave Kabul in '89.'

A degree of irrational optimism is necessary for us even to attempt difficult tasks. There are things like war and marriage that we'd just never undertake if we didn't somehow blind ourselves to the real odds against us. But Vera must have always known that our chances of success were remote.

They needed irrefutable evidence: proof that the Common Task was a going concern, proof that the Malevin Procedure was workable, proof of the criminal conspiracy surrounding it, proof that Hunter Gould and Sinan Malevin were among its organisers and beneficiaries.

I was their Exhibit A.

Vera and Nicholas needed to reveal what was going on in Baikonur before the lieutenants of the Common Task learned that Vera was attempting to betray them. They were under pressure to move quickly. This had forced them to collect me well before my rehabilitation was complete. It had been a psychological blow to Nicky. And yet, events at Almaty showed that they had waited too long. Somewhere along the chain, they had been exposed.

For the next thirty-six hours, Nicholas worked to make up lost ground. He pumped me for information about what I'd undergone. He went through Vera's list of contacts, adding names, excising others. He agonised about when to go to the police, about whether to contact people individually or to hold a press conference. He settled on the latter, and booked a room under an assumed name at Conway Hall, the headquarters of the South Place Ethical Society. And he worried about the impact of all this on Vera.

Misha had said Vera's grasp of the Procedure made her indispensable. But was that true?

Malevin's methods always generate a code for the proxy complex, but its reliability and accuracy depend on the subjective judgements of the coder.

316

Malevin identified 167 key markers which can be recombined in a virtually infinite array. So the coding process requires a subjective sense of nuance. It demands both tough-mindedness and compassion from the coder. It is hard to imagine anyone more rich in both than Vera. In the most delicate and profound way, her extraordinary work exposes the false dichotomy between art and science. She is the reason I am here.

And yet, if Hunter was spooked enough, surely he'd dispose of Vera just as ruthlessly as he'd disposed of Jack? We could only hope that Misha was right about her value to the Common Task.

I was desperate to be as much help as possible. Frustratingly, I could feel my rehabilitation progressing, but it wasn't smooth or linear. There were moments of great euphoria. Together Nicholas and I were able to identify the exact location where I had been held and where I underwent the Procedure. I can say with some certainty that it was in a horseshoe-shaped building near the western bank of the Syr Darya river. The co-ordinates given by Google Earth for the structure are 45 degrees 37′ 27.47′ N and 63 degrees 19′ 24.46′ E. Nicholas was overjoyed to bolster his case with this kind of verifiable detail. He gave me an awkward hug, which we both found strangely repellent.

But at other times, I broke down into dismaying bouts of stammering. There were blinding headaches and a degree of physical discomfort along the length of my spinal cord that no painkiller could assuage.

I think my very eagerness to improve was counterproductive. I think I hurried the pace of my convalescence and my carcass rebelled.

On the second afternoon, Nicholas left me alone in the flat and didn't return until late. He came back guiltily, expressing a forced surprise that I was still awake, but without meeting my eye. He didn't say what he'd been doing, but I knew. He'd gone to see Lucius and Sarah. I was desperate for news of them, as he must have known. But he said nothing. I held my tongue. I heard him brushing his teeth, and then the sound of snoring from the bedroom.

Nicholas had made me up the sofa-bed in the living room. I lay down, but I was unable to sleep. The amount of sleep I required dropped markedly after the Procedure. It may be a side-effect of the Procedure itself; an indication of my premature ageing; or the altered requirements of my new carcass.

It seemed pointless to lie there brooding, fretting about my children and my slow rehabilitation. So I got up and went outside.

The streets were empty. It was about 3 a.m. I kept walking. Towards dawn, I had the whine of milkfloats for company. There was also a prize-fighter who passed me in Battersea Park, jogging and shadowboxing with a surprising lightness of step. He planted his feet almost in silence, but I could hear his breathing and the tinny chorus of the headphones he wore under his hooded sweatshirt.

It was in that first pre-dawn walk that I truly began the long and continuing process of reconciliation with this carcass. The steady rhythm of my footsteps, the calm of the waking city and the slight elevation of my heartbeat not only gave me a pronounced sense of well-being but appeared to speed up my convalescence.

That morning I walked beyond Tower Bridge and as far as Billingsgate, which I reached around six o'clock, towards the end of their trading day. There was something invigorating about the smell of fish and the bright lights glittering over scales and crushed ice. I wandered around staring like a yokel until a porter ran into my leg with a trolley. Instead of abusing me, as I thought he might, he apologised and gave me a pair of smoked mackerel which I carried back home in a plastic bag.

The exercise, my sense of pride in my achievement and the unseasonal sunshine produced in me a joy that I had until then never known in this incarnation. I practised my greeting to Nicholas for the last ten minutes of the walk home, articulating the words with increasing facility. As soon as he opened the door to me, I held up my plastic bag and announced proudly: 'Look what I've got. Foked smish.'

He glanced nervously over my shoulder and yanked me in.

Nicholas was naked from the waist up. He had something oblong in the palm of his hand.

'Smoked fish,' I said.

'Give me a hand with this,' he said. 'It's time to call Hunter's bluff. We can't wait any longer. Misha texted me this morning. He says they're closing in on us.'

It was a miniature recorder. I held it in the shallow valley of Nicholas's sternum while he fastened it in place with strips of gaffer tape.

'I've arranged to meet him at Butler's Wharf. He won't be able to try anything there. All I need is some acknowledgement from him of what he's up to. Then we'll go straight to the police.'

At half past ten, Nicholas spread newspaper on the tiles of the hearth in the sitting room and dislodged the package from the chimney. He wiped it clean and put it in his courier's bag. He handed me a piece of paper.

'I need you to memorise these numbers,' he said. 'This is mine, this is Misha's. If anything happens to me, call Misha. But use him sparingly. He's no use to you dead.' He paused at the doorway. 'Wish me luck.'

'Good luck,' I said.

He looked at me. We embraced, this time with genuine warmth. No words were necessary. I understood.

The wait recalled those impotent and anxious

hours before childbirth, tethered to an outcome over which you have no control, trying to cast all the dark possibilities out of your awareness. You would think that at a moment of such tension, Nicholas's proxy complex would feel something, some sympathetic vibration at a cellular level, as twins are supposed to. But there was nothing.

Outside, the sky brightened. I drank Lucozade and felt its bubbles prick my tongue.

At just after 3.30 p.m. the mobile phone handset on the coffee table burst into life. It rattled on the glass like a hostile insect. The caller was Misha. 'Go quickly,' he said. 'Go now.'

So close to my own death, I'm squeamish about dwelling on Nicholas's. I'm sentimental about the body that formed me. I'm not blind to its inadequacies and imperfections, but it's what I was. It's not merely a platitude to say that something of me died that day. And though I'm not superstitious, I find myself recoiling from the details of Nicholas's death as from a harbinger of my own. But completeness demands it.

Nicholas's body was retrieved from the front nearside wheel arch of a lorry that had been turning left from Kennington Park Road onto Harleyford Street at 4.28 p.m. on Monday September 28th 2009.

I avoided using the word 'mangled' in the previous sentence, fearing that it would cheapen the tone, but now I find that making no mention of the body's condition deprives the statement of some of its impact. Perhaps it is enough to ask the reader merely to imagine the likely outcome of such a collision.

The inquest was held in Croydon. I couldn't risk attending, but I was able to find its details online.

The court heard the testimony of a single witness and the collision investigator, a PC Menzies, whose report gives the appearance of scrupulousness. He described the condition of Nicholas's bicycle in detail. 'The front fork, down tubes and pedals were all smashed. A wheel was buckled. Paint was flaked off. There was a long groove in the tarmac where the bicycle had been carried along the ground.' Using careful legal language for quantifying uncertainty, PC Menzies abrogated any responsibility for explaining what might have happened. 'There were no defects of note in the driver's vehicle. The quality of the CCTV is such that it is not possible to determine the speed at which he was driving.'

The driver of the lorry, a Liverpudlian called David Test who was working on a short-term contract to a firm of hauliers called Wexford Dairy Refrigeration, claimed he had checked the nearside mirror twice before the fatal manoeuvre; though not the most clearly false element in his account, there is something about the detail *twice* that stretches credulity with its unlikely excess of driving punctilio.

According to the coroner, life was pronounced

extinct at 4.45 p.m. She recorded a verdict of death by misadventure: '. . . when, just after 4 in the afternoon, amidst a lot of uncertainty, the two came into collision. Nicholas Patrick Slopen, born Singapore, 1970, died of multiple injuries.'

It's not difficult to piece together what really happened. Nietzsche says the liar gives himself away by the shape of his mouth. The story is in the omissions and the minor details as much as the outright untruths.

Leaving aside the strange absence of witnesses on a busy road in South London on a weekday afternoon towards rush hour – with the notable exception of a dubious Serbian called Lenko Voinovic who supported Test's account in every specific, despite claiming to have been on the phone to Belgrade at the time – and ignoring also the mystifying inadequacy of the traffic cameras in the area, there is a further number of puzzling details that raise questions about the verdict of accidental death, and ultimately about the integrity of the coroner herself, Ms Geraldine Passmore.

More than three hours had passed between Nicholas's meeting with Hunter and the accident. Three hours is a long time. It wouldn't take Hunter three hours to say 'Publish and be damned' or 'I don't have any idea what you're talking about.' Three hours, I would say, is just about enough time for Nicholas to have laid out his accusations against Hunter patiently and thoroughly; for him to have overcome all Hunter's attempts at bluff and appeasement; for Hunter to have become genuinely worried that Nicholas had the goods on him; and for Hunter to have set in train the fatal reprisal.

What had he been doing, or rather, *what was being done to him* in those three hours? Clearly, it was something of so violent a nature that only the convenient fiction of a traffic accident could plausibly conceal it. Notably, there was no mention of the recording device, the microphone or the dossier which Misha and Nicholas had taken such pains to compile.

There was no question of staying in the flat. Nicholas's death had left me with no doubt about the reach and resourcefulness of the conspirators. I was certain they would come for me next. I left London and submerged myself in the transient world of flotsam and rejects. I travelled by bus between out-of-the-way towns. I stayed in hostels and shelters. I kept moving.

The people I encountered assumed that I had had some kind of stroke and after a while I began to encourage them in this belief. I concocted an autobiography in which the stroke had given me an opportunity to take time away from my career and re-evaluate my life. Adding that I had previously worked as a civil servant was normally enough to forestall any further enquiry. The rehabilitation that had seemed so elusive before, now took place inexorably. Each day, I felt more rooted in my carcass, my mind seemed increasingly alert and my speech became clearer. And once I became more confident of my survival, it began to dawn on me that Nicholas's sacrifice had not been in vain. Perhaps I could become a sufficiently plausible Nicholas to send a tremor through the Common Task. Perhaps I could sharpen myself into an arrow to pierce the heart of the conspiracy.

Once in a while, I checked through my old email account and in this way learned from a circular sent to all alumni of Downing College that a former girlfriend was running a shop in a market town in the Welsh borders. One morning, I went into her shop unannounced. Of course, there were emotional ties between us. I craved any connection with my old life. But it was also a way of assessing my progress. If she believed I was Nicky Slopen, others might too. I glimpsed a chink of light beneath the door of my prison.

She was taken aback to see me and referred almost immediately to the news of my death, but we shared enough common history for me to be able to persuade her that she was mistaken.

I wonder a little at her readiness to accept my word. But then we had both aged, we were both heavier and clumsier; not the lithe teenage carcasses who had shared narrow single beds at university and slept soundly, entwined like snakes.

She was in the throes of a separation and I couldn't help imagining the life that we might have shared had things turned out differently. In this counterfactual existence, the other Nicholas Slopen lived in this pretty town with this kind and loving woman. I wondered hopelessly as I left her if the last twenty years were simply a terrible mistake, culminating in my being cut adrift in this stranger's carcass, and with no way back to my loved ones.

I returned to London with a renewed appetite for the struggle. What I had not foreseen was the terrible pull that my old life would exert.

Nicholas's death, terrible as it was, had freed me to love my children again. After my sojourn in the Midlands, all I wanted was a glimpse of them: just to see my flesh alive, all that was left of me. The pressure of this old yearning began to dissolve my singlemindedness.

They were living in a big town house, a temple to Poggenpohl and Bose and Aga and all the other deities of Morestuffism, with absurd topiary in zinc bins on the windowsills.

To begin with, I deluded myself that it was reconnaissance. I took to loitering in the area and was rewarded with tantalising glimpses of them through the basement window.

At Notting Hill Gate one Friday afternoon, Sarah took an *Evening Standard* from me with a fragrant gloved hand. I felt a flash of parental concern when I detected the smell of cigarette smoke mingled with her perfume. She had a mobile phone pressed to her ear. She was taller and walked with a woman's poise: so beautiful, so like her mother. Her face was pale. I thought of the grief she had suffered. And underneath it all, there was still a fugitive trace of the face she had had as a child. Even in her early teens, when sleeping, Sarah's face fell into the expression she wore on the ultrasound, twenty weeks from conception, which so enraptured us.

I staggered outside and wept in the slush: the grimy aftermath of this year's extraordinary snow. I should have made my renunciation then, but like any addict I needed a progressively more potent fix.

At this stage, I was homeless and broke. Nicholas's ATM card had stopped functioning in the middle of January.

There was a shelter in Vauxhall with all the anomie of the DHU but less actual insanity. I gave away free papers, took food hand-outs and foraged in bins. My carcass, oddly, seemed to flourish under the abuse. This peasant body is built for suffering. It's slow and clumsy, but indifferent to cold and shocking in its outright strength. One evening at the shelter I came back from the dank bathroom to find someone nosing in the drawer under my bed. I lifted him clean off the ground by the throat until his face went purple, and felt not much more than mild surprise and the detachment of someone operating a powerful crane.

Through January, I stole into their back garden a number of times and watched them in the glass box of the rear extension, performing the number-less mundane rituals that are the weft of family life. I deluded myself that I was in control of my habit, but then the unforeseeable shock came.

Risking the lightening dusk of February to creep along the rear wall around five o'clock one after-noon, I saw Leonora and Lucius and Hunter's girlfriend, Candy Go, sitting at the granite slab of dining table.

Nicholas, of course, had told me in Crimea that Candy and Leonora were friends. They met at the gym after Leonora decamped to West London. Leonora had been quite open about it with Nicholas. But it wasn't a conversation she'd had with me. And the recollection of Nicholas's words did not carry enough force to overbear the injustice of what I seemed to see in front of me: cordiality between Nicholas's family and his killers. It drove me out of my mind.

The betrayal seemed vast and unconscionable. I could only think of Nicholas's death, his broken body in the wheel arch. I seemed to hear the coroner's voice in my head. I smashed my way through the glass, gashing my forehead and hands in the process. I howled at Leonora, my voice horribly changed. 'Why is she here?' I asked her. 'Do you know what they have done to your husband?' Blood dripped from my accusing finger. Candy's painted mouth was frozen in a mute zero of disbelief. I told them who I was. The horror on Lucius's face will live with me forever.

I fled and tried to hide in the communal gardens, but the police tracked me within half an hour by my bloodstains. The section was granted even before they found the CCTV footage of my vigils outside the house. I was in the DHU the following day.

CHAPTER 32

Extracted from Dr Webster's Journal

Cambridge. Strange to be here, but strangest of all to be going for this reason. Dismal cheap hotel. Embarrassed about my own behaviour. I tell myself that I'll only need to go on this wild goose chase once. It's a form of reality testing. There are only three possibilities: one, that Q's is a severe and complex psychotic delusion which bears no relation to reality; two, that it's a severe and complex psychotic delusion which bears some relation to reality; and three. Three is the one that I'm most worried about.

Am I insane to even be, even to be contemplating this? I don't feel mad. As Q would say.

I realise I'm on ethical thin ice – it's a mark of how much Q has got under my skin that I can hear him complaining about that metaphor. The issue around reading his diary. His testimony, he calls it. Maybe this foolish quest simply to assuage my guilt about violating his privacy?

So much militates against Q's story. I've seen

a photo of Dr Slopen and he's physically quite distinctive: lean and tending to fair-haired. It just goes against common sense. So why am I here?

In Q's earliest sessions he talked in more detail about the procedure he claimed to have undergone: I failed to make notes on it as I was following PW's advice to pay attention to underlying affect. In any case, I suspect Q's understanding of science sketchy at best.

Feel like I'm turning into that minicab driver with the smelly car. He looked like Gandalf: 'Conspiracy theories. It's an interesting area if you're mentally stable.'

He's much as I pictured him. Older, but still handsome. The hair a bit thinner than described but just enough of it to coax into a quiff. It helps that I'm a woman. He's the kind of old-fashioned sexist who fusses over the girls and saves his academic crushes for the boys.

I arrive at three thirty and touchingly he's laid out a proper tea for both of us: swiss roll, toast and honey, Tunnock's caramel wafers. 'So rare to get visitors. Life's slowed down since I retired. Can it really be ten years?' he says, sounding theatrically dizzy at the rate time is passing. I wonder out loud how he keeps track of his old students. That makes him terribly serious all of a sudden. 'I remember every one of them, my dear.' I understand that it's important to him to have done his job well. What else is there? No Mrs Harbottle. No little ones to worry about.

'And you say you're a doctor, but the medical kind, Miss Webster?'

I nod. Say how much I enjoyed English A level, but after Dad died . . .

He sweeps the unpleasantness hastily aside. I remember that's one of the reasons I did medicine. All this reading about love, death, insane passions, but when someone presents you with it in real life, you turn away. Hiding away in books, as though the answer's in *The Franklin's Tale*. He asks politely about my work. I tell him.

'It's Bedlam, isn't it?'

'That's right. The Bethlem Hospital. Now part of the Maudsley Trust. You'll be glad to know conditions have improved.'

'I should hope so.' He stirs his tea and dislodges something from his dentures with his tongue. 'Though you probably have more famous alumni than we do.'

I tell him I'm interested in an old student of his.

'He's not a . . . patient of yours?'

Of course not. That would be highly unprofessional. I say the name and he straight-bats it. 'Very talented. I was so sad to hear that he'd died.'

'Were you in touch?'

He shakes his head. 'I can't think when I saw him last. But it was many years ago. What's your interest in him?'

'I've got a patient who says he's Nicholas Slopen reincarnated.'

I'm surprised how easily it comes out. It seems to amuse him.

'The poor fellow must have done something heinous in a previous lifetime.' He drops it like a bon mot but there's also a genuine hint of bitterness towards his old protégé.

I'm aware that at this point I don't much like Harbottle. All that posing as a national treasure. The obvious narcissism. The ingrained sense of entitlement. Quite possibly I'm chippy, reminded of those floppy-haired Oxbridge wazzocks I did my training with, who were always stealing bits off cadavers and throwing bread rolls in restaurants. But it's liberating not to care what he thinks of me. It feels safe to be straight with him. He can't fire me.

'The thing is,' I say it slowly, 'I half believe he is.'

'Believe he's . . . ?'

Something a bit panther-like about him as he lowers his head as though ready to spring on a flaw in my logic.

'I don't *think* he is. But I half believe it. Beliefs aren't rational. They're what we invest our emotions in.'

He looks doubtfully at me but says nothing. I remember my sixth-form English teacher ticking me off for using the word 'empathy' in an essay, as though it was an arcane bit of psychobabble.

'He seems to know a lot about you,' I say.

'Possibly he's an ex-student, or knew Nicholas? It's possible to find out all sorts of things these days. The internet.'

He says 'the internet' like it's a far-off place he's never been, Timbuctoo perhaps, but from where I'm sitting I can see a wifi router half hidden behind four volumes of Gibbon.

'What does he look like?'

'He's six foot, thickset, heavily tattooed.'

'Doesn't sound like a Downing man.'

I set my cup on its saucer and get the print-out from my shoulder-bag. 'Would you mind if I read you something?'

He makes a flourish with his hand.

I begin: 'Ronald Harbottle was then fifty-three . . .

He's much more comfortable with this. This is caressing his ego. And he relates more easily to me now that he can pretend I'm one of his students. He gets a thoughtful look in his eyes, turns his head into the air at an odd angle, fingers his chin, smiles at the familiarity of it. 'Pencilled annotations of the master' makes him close his eyes like a cat getting its back scratched.

I feel oddly nervous as I begin the section about Matilda Swann but I push through. His smile becomes more fixed. I read more quickly and find I've gone further than I intended. At the end, the words 'usurped by an old man's vanity' hang uncomfortably in the room like a fart neither of us will own up to.

Harbottle sips his tea. 'He was a bloodless little shit,' he says with surprising mildness.

The clock on the mantelpiece begins the Westminster half-hour chimes. He gets up and stifles it in annoyance. 'But it's accurate as far as I remember. That's not what you want to hear, is it?'

I shake my head. 'It's not really good for anyone if this man is telling the truth.'

'Well, rest assured, my dear, he isn't. We may no longer be creatures in a Newtonian universe, but there's still gravity and, I don't know, the Laws of Motion to be obeyed. Just because there's an area of uncertainty about the nature of reality, that doesn't mean all bets are off.'

I decline the offer of more tea: my bladder's bursting but I don't want to break the atmosphere. He pours himself another cup. 'We had this kind of problem when post-structuralism came in,' he says. 'I had students telling me that *Timon of Athens* was a play about the inherent contradictions of late capitalism. Self-evidently false, but rather a nuisance to refute. I would say that "I am the reincarnation of an obscure dead academic" is a statement of that sort.'

I try to ask him how Q knows so much, but what comes out is a stumbling, rather confessional sort of question in which I wonder how Q's got me so confused.

'You're confused, young lady, because you're good at your job. You're sensitive and compassionate and he's taking advantage. Not knowing is a gift. Keats knew it. He called it negative capability. You know the expression? "When man is capable of being in uncertainties, mysteries, doubts, without any irritable reaching after fact and reason".

'As to the less interesting question of how he knows – I would say like any illusionist, this man achieves his effect by the most laborious and dull solution on offer. Hard work, cheating and misdirection. In this case, the answer is he probably didn't write it himself. My gut feeling is that he's plagiarised this from Nicky's papers.'

In the end, I'm reassured and surprised by his generosity of spirit. He sees me to the door and presses Swann's book into my hand as a parting gift. It's pristine and unread, but the cheap paper is yellowing with age. I guess that he has boxes of them somewhere.

'Her poems are very underrated. But I'm not expecting to be vindicated in this lifetime.'

Mingled sadness and relief. Sorry for Harbottle somehow. But it doesn't last long. Tonight, back at the hotel, I can't think how Q is doing it. I've watched the document grow in the weeks he's been using the computer. Is he cutting and pasting it from somewhere on the internet?

Frantic Googling turns up nothing. It crosses my mind to go back into the Maudsley. Check what he's added since I left? Might be something I can use.

Back into work for an ad hoc supervision with PW. I explain everything. He's absolutely silent throughout the session. I give him Q's file. Tell him I'm thoroughly puzzled. I don't know what the truth is, but I believe Q is telling more of it than I think we gave him credit for.

'You've read Rank on doubles?' he asks.

'No, but I've read Freud. He says the fantasy is rooted in narcissism.'

'Initially. But then he goes on to say that having been an assurance of immortality, it becomes the uncanny harbinger of death.'

For an instant, it seems like he's threatening me, but then I realise he's talking metaphorically. I say that I've already thought of the chilling effect on my career of all this, but that I promised myself a long time ago that any time I had a conflict between my work and my conscience, I'd follow my conscience.

PW says nothing. I suddenly feel crazed and hollow.

He says he'll need time to figure out how to proceed, but he's glad I've been honest with him. He suggests I take a further week of leave. As I stand up to go, I feel certain he's sad. Walking through the DHU, I see Q stretched out on his bed, reading *The Economist*. He doesn't notice me.

Today a letter from PW. It's typewritten. PW writes that he's regretfully decided to accept my offer of resignation. WTF? I call Rog in panic and email PW. I say it wasn't my intention to resign! At most, I thought this would be handed over to an external agency who could evaluate our work with Q and make a decision about the best way to continue with him. I say that I'm gutted; this is the last thing I wanted to happen. PW replies with a one-line email to say everything being handled now through Human Resources.

CHAPTER 33

The DHU was in uproar tonight. It's a full moon and there are two new patients on the ward. Some shenanigans between them at supper time resulted in one being taken to a seclusion cell. As a result, I was here early, waiting in the corridor for Dr Webster's room to be unlocked.

The calm up here is like paradise after the man-smells and chaos of the DHU. While I was waiting, I heard the opening bars of the first aria of the *Goldberg Variations* drifting up from somewhere on the lower storeys. A patient? It seems unlikely, but perhaps someone's co-operation in the safe space has earned them music privileges.

Dr White unlocked the office for me with obvious reluctance. 'Is there a music room in the building?' I asked.

He pointedly ignored the question. 'We're reviewing your access to the computer,' he said.

'I believe you mentioned that during our work together,' I said. But my attempt at ingratiation came out as sarcasm.

'In the meantime, I'm going to have to ask you

to use it strictly within office hours as it's too disruptive to have you up here at other times.'

'Won't Dr Webster be needing the computer in office hours?' I asked.

'I'll be back at eight fifteen,' he said as he locked me in and left. I listened out for the diminuendo of his heavy tread and the fading jingle of the loose change in his pocket.

Once he was gone, I checked to make sure Webster's spare keys were still in the tin where she keeps her Hobnobs. As it turns out, she's unlikely to be needing either. I've eaten the biscuits, and the keys . . . Well, perhaps better not to say.

I logged on as her tonight and found the extract appended above.

It's going to sound like wisdom after the event, but I rather had the sense that someone was reading my testimony.

She's too smart to say it anywhere in the text, but it's clear that Webster meant for me to read it.

The sense of exoneration makes me almost tearful.

My elation is succeeded by a chastening sense of regret that I was so dilatory in giving my testimony. I can think of half a dozen better witnesses than the ones she was armed with. She jumped the gun, really. If only she'd had my information on the accident.

But imagine: Ron still alive and compos mentis!

Through the window, London is the orange blur in the sky behind the outpatients' unit.

These fragments I have shored against my ruins.
What to do in the time left to me?
Rereading: *I give him Q's file.*
I *give* him Q's file?
Surely, Webster meant to write I *show* him Q's file?
Could she be so soft, so credulous, so daddy-fixated as to *give* those papers to White, a man who is at best an aggrieved quack, at worst . . . ?
Well, no worst, there is none.
Not a hint of softening in White's attitude to me. Just the threat to revoke my use of the computer. He doesn't believe her. Or he can't believe her?
I'm beyond worrying about myself, but Webster has no idea what she's tangling with.
It's the Glenn Gould version. I can hear it clearly now. Someone's opened the window and the music is . . .

KNOWLE COURT

DECEMBER 2010–?

CHAPTER 1

So much has changed since I last looked at these pages that it's hard to know where to begin.

Pages. How tenacious the old metaphors are.

I find myself once more in a library, surrounded by the spines of old books. I recall Pascal Sheldon's cadaverous and self-satisfied face: *the printed book is dead.* Dust rises when I ease one off the shelves. So these are an obsolete technology, like Victrola needles and buggy whips.

It is a volume of Mayakovsky and its unstamped bookplate suggests the students of Knowle Court found nothing of interest here. The cover is of a pretty constructivist design. The poetry has the gritty scent of revolutionary Moscow. I hear the steely timbre of his voice, insisting – what I've grasped myself too late – that words possess the kabbalistic potency of the tetragrammaton:

I know the power of words. They seem a trifle
Fallen petals beneath a dancer's feet
But they hold a man's soul, and lips, and bone.

When I think of my children, I tend to remember them when they were little, before their difficult-to-negotiate passage into altered teenage carcasses. These are two snapshots: Lucius, launching himself into a stumbling run towards some climbing apparatus with the asymmetrical bulge of a sodden nappy halfway down one trouser leg; Sarah, perched naked on a toilet seat, calling imperiously for Leonora to wipe her bum.

But how? My eyes have never seen such things. What other memories have been extirpated to admit these ones? Yet what can I do but express the soul I find imprinted on me? You cannot choose what to love. Beliefs, as Webster said to Ron, are what we invest our emotions in.

The tremor in my left hand is like the ominous grating note of a failing engine. I am growing weaker daily. What is this testimony but the collateral sparkings of a dying consciousness? I am the shadow thrown by a guttering candle. But while the flame still burns, I will complete this task.

Dr Philip Marshall White, Webster's much-admired PW, had stolen up on me while I was working at the computer. I had the presence of mind to turn and shield the screen from him. He insisted on seeing it. I pulled out the power cable from the back of the monitor; the display contracted to a tiny dot and vanished.

This minor act of insubordination was the pretext

he needed to cancel my access to the computer. That wasn't all.

'We think it's counterproductive for you to have therapy at the moment,' he told me. 'You're too unbalanced. We'll be looking for better pharmaceutical outcomes before we risk overstimulating you again.'

They started me off with oral doses of antipsychotic drugs which made me nauseous and confused. For a couple of days, I was able to avoid taking them by concealing the pills under my tongue or palming them and then flushing them down the toilet, but the nurses had the instincts for deception of Las Vegas croupiers. When blood tests confirmed that I hadn't been taking the medicine, Dr White confronted me. This time, I lost my temper with him and called him a fraud and liar. He summoned the restraint team and they forcibly injected me with a massive shot of Acuphase. I was asleep in the seclusion cell for almost seventy-two hours. They didn't bother with pills after that, they simply stuck me with a fortnightly injection of haloperidol and whatever else they thought would keep me pliant.

With no computer access and my mind too washed out with drugs to read, I found the time passed terribly slowly. There was a careful hierarchy of activities for the clients in the DHU: creative writing and pottery for the most biddable, painting for others, but the hard cases, of which I was now one, had to be content with watching daytime television through the fog of antipsychotic medication.

And the drugs had a whole raft of unpleasant physical side-effects. I had muscular spasms, an agonising tightness in my neck and back and uncontrollable twitching in my face. The medication induced a sense of restlessness that could find no outlet. It was intolerable to sit for any length of time. I ate standing up so that I could keep moving, and I spent hours in my cubicle shifting from foot to foot, trying to console myself by muttering poems under my breath. There was a whole number of them in there, intact, that I couldn't remember ever reading: Hopkins, Esenin, Mandelstam; I knew they were among Vera's favourites and it crossed my mind that she'd coded and tossed them in, just as my mother used to sew a five-pound note into the jacket lining of my school uniform for emergencies.

We had a lot of religious nutcases in the DHU. One of the most likeable was the mixed-race man who called himself Caiaphas. He would pad around the unit most afternoons with a tattered stack of *Watchtowers*, the Jehovah's Witness magazine, which he would hand out and then come by to collect about fifteen minutes later. It says something about the basic decency of the loonies in there that everyone colluded with his harmless nuttiness, accepting the magazines and then returning them without complaint almost immediately.

One afternoon, he came by, selected a magazine from the big wad in his hand, changed his mind, selected another and dropped it at the foot of my bed. 'Haven't seen you around much, brother.'

I explained, through my involuntarily clenching jaw, that I'd been in the seclusion cells and that White had put me on a punitive dose of neuro-leptic drugs.

'Someone's been looking for you,' he said. 'He knows your name.'

Dimly, through the hum of interior noise, I could tell that this information ought to be important to me.

'Staff or client?' I asked him.

'Client.'

'Does he know who I am?'

'Not from me, brother.'

'What's his name?'

'Doesn't say.'

It took me so long to formulate my next response that by the time I had, Caiaphas had gone.

In a world as empty of solace as the DHU, the most humanising thing we had was the caress of water. I took showers as often as I could, at least once a day. We couldn't control the temperature, or even the pressure; the shower ran in twenty-second bursts each time you depressed its button. But for each of those twenty seconds, the water on my scalp was an angel's fingers, and I could stand still, and the heat on my spine relieved its constant aching.

The shower rooms themselves were unsupervised. An attendant sat outside, checking us in and out: we had to book our slots in advance.

Two or three evenings later – it's hard to be precise because of the time-bending quality of the drugs I was on – I flapped round to the washrooms in my dressing gown and flipflops. There were six shower cubicles, three on each side at one end of the room, and a changing area with plastic chairs and hooks to hang clothes and towels; but they were rarely, if ever, fully occupied.

Someone came and went in the stall next to mine. Through the steam I was aware of someone in the changing room undressing and folding his clothing scrupulously into a tidy pile.

The hiss of water drowned out the buzz of the chemicals in my head. I closed my eyes and for a brief and blissful moment the carcass was at rest.

In the next instant, I was struck a huge blow across my back and shoulders and fell to my hands and knees. Something closed round my neck. I was able to slip my right hand through it as it tightened and leather bit into my wrist. Yielding to the upward pressure, I allowed my assailant to pull me back onto my feet as he tried to choke me, then I moved with him, adding my bulk to his, and slammed him into the thin partition that divided mine from the neighbouring cubicle; it surrendered and split. We fell together. Someone was cut from the splinters of laminated plywood. Still throttling me from behind, my attacker brought his knees repeatedly into my ribs, encouraging me to drop my right hand to parry them and leave my throat unguarded. As I struggled to shake him off my back, I sensed myself weakening.

'Who are you?' I croaked.

He gave no indication that he had heard. He was breathing more heavily and his kicks had slowed a little, but he continued to tighten the belt. My vision grew strangely sharp: I could see beads of moisture on the wall tiles, mildew on the grouting. I glanced down to my left. For an instant, I mistook his leg for mine. There, on the upper face of his left thigh, was a roundel identical to the one that marked me: the same size, the same pattern, the same location; the colours fresher and more sharply delineated.

The surge of adrenalin that followed brought a measure of lucidity to my drug-clouded brain. I remembered the sessions at the clinic in Baikonur.

I gathered the little breath I had left in a final effort to communicate. 'My name is John Smith,' I said through gasps. 'It's important to me that we do this exercise properly. Do you understand?'

The belt went abruptly slack. I manoeuvred myself around to face him.

We were lying in a heap on the floor of the shower cubicle. Blood and water puddled on the tiles around us.

He wasn't an inmate I'd ever seen before. He

was about the same age as me, slightly shorter and less heavy-set. He might have been chosen for his absence of distinguishing features. His fair hair was cropped or thinning. His face was empty of expression and his eyes held a terrifying blankness.

'Please indicate that you've understood,' I said.

The nod he gave seemed almost involuntary.

'Good job,' I said. 'Now, I'm going to show you an array of pictures and I'm going to ask you to pick one. Do you understand?'

There was no nod this time. He narrowed his eyes, as though I were coming into focus.

'It's important to me that we do this exercise properly,' I said.

His face had the suddenly alert expression of someone who has heard his name called from a distance. In that millisecond of hesitation, I hit him as hard as I could. His head slumped against the partition and I ran.

My injuries weren't severe enough to merit a spell in the medical ward, but the cuts from the splintered wood required stitches, and the assault itself triggered a formal inquiry by Dr White and two approved mental health professionals.

I explained to them, as lucidly as I could, that my assailant, whose name they claimed was either Thomas Roberts or Robert Thomas, had launched his attack on me for no reason that I could fathom. I didn't want to alienate the possibly sympathetic supervisors with what seemed to me undeniable: that the man was a *zachot*, a programmed assassin, who had been inserted into the Dennis Hill Unit in order to kill me, but I did point out the bizarre coincidence of our identical tattoos and I asked that Dr Webster be called to speak on my behalf.

It seemed like a reasonable request, even to Mumford and Kumar, the mental health professionals who made up the quorum with White on the panel and who had, at first glance, given every indication of being precisely the kind of obedient, risk-averse mediocrities one would need to whitewash an assassination attempt.

Mumford, to his credit, even suggested they adjourn the inquiry until Dr Webster could come in. However, as the senior member of staff, White was able to overrule them. He harrumphed at the pointlessness of the idea. Besides, he said, Webster was on indefinite personal leave. In his subsequent questions to me, he played down the significance of the tattoos and played up what he called the sexual component of the incident. The other client, he claimed, was alleging that I'd tried to assault him.

If I hadn't been so heavily medicated, I would have laughed in his face. I asked him how the bruising to my back conformed to that theory; and to explain why, for that matter, I hadn't sodomised the man when I had him at my mercy.

'Didn't you?' he asked. 'I don't know. Why didn't you?' The crude effort to depict me as a sexual predator was clearly intended to provoke me into another outburst. Mumford and Kumar exchanged uncomfortable glances. To them, White's harshness was beginning to look both unprofessional and mean-spirited. To me, it was further confirmation of the scope and resourcefulness of the Common Task. I had no doubt that White had been suborned. I wanted to ask him if he had any pride. Didn't he remember the scandal of Soviet psychiatry? How did he justify putting his profession at the service of a criminal cabal? But I held my tongue for fear of antagonising him.

I cleared my throat with a cough and said meekly that I recognised I had caused trouble in the past, but all I wanted was a chance at rehabilitation. 'I really want to apologise for my prior negative behaviours,' I said. 'I'd like to be able to return to my work in the safe space.'

The plea for therapy clinched it. 'We can certainly see about authorising a decrease in your medication if you're feeling stable,' Kumar conceded, with a glance at White. White wasn't happy about it, but he had backed himself into a corner.

To have my wounds dressed, I had been taken to a medical unit at a different part of the site. At the time, I'd been too brain-fogged to take advantage of the looser security, but the change in medication heralded the return of greater mental acuity and I began thinking that if I were ever to escape, the medical unit would be the likeliest exit. The knowledge that I couldn't avoid Roberts indefinitely was an additional incentive. He'd been sent to the seclusion cells, but in a matter of days he'd be back among us. He would be labouring with the handicap of a depot injection of Largactil and would probably be a lot less sprightly, but sooner or later he would return to finish what he'd been sent to do.

I took a little comfort from the knowledge that Webster had read my testimony. White knew it too. It had increased the pressure on everyone. The arrival of Roberts was the proof of that. But I worried about Webster as well. I hoped she had had the sense to take at least rudimentary precautions for her personal safety.

There were two keys on Webster's key ring. One was for the door of her office, up on the second floor of the DHU and now completely out of bounds to me. The other, it turned out, was for one of the supply rooms close to the common area, which included basic first-aid equipment. I was able to slip in there after one lunchtime and soak my shirt with surgical spirit.

We had a microwave in the common area which was theoretically for the inmates on restricted diets or with food intolerances. It was supposed to be supervised, but, though secure, the DHU was not a penitentiary. Morale among the staff was low. Shifts were often understaffed and personnel from other parts of the hospital, who were more lax in their observance of correct protocol, would be rotated in to fill some of the gaps.

I chose the period after lunch because there was a shift change then. It was also the time of day when a kind of post-prandial ennui settled on the unit, bringing a consequent decline in vigilance. Around two fifteen in the afternoon, stinking of surgical spirit, I put one of Caiaphas's *Watchtowers* in the microwave along with a generous handful of cutlery and turned it on. The arcing from the metal set the thin paper alight. I took out the flaming magazine and held it to my shirt. It lit with an energising whoosh. My intention had been to wrap myself in some curtains as soon as possible to extinguish the flames and minimise the actual damage to me. I had put on a pair of vests underneath the shirt with this in mind. I reasoned that, after a spectacular enough accident, the staff would send me to the infirmary irrespective of the severity of my injuries. From there I could make my escape.

What I hadn't foreseen was Caiaphas's coming into the room as I was holding the burning magazine aloft. When he realised what was alight, he uttered a terrible shriek and tried to jump on me. We wrestled for a moment. My shirt was by now entirely ablaze with leaping flames. I could feel the heat against my torso and smell my burning hair. The fire alarm sounded and Caiaphas snatched the magazine and ran whooping, waving it like a flag across the common area, pleading for God's forgiveness on behalf of both of us.

Far from extinguishing the flames, the curtains turned out to be flammable and I continued to burn until the duty nurse arrived with a blanket. While I lay wreathed in choking black smoke on the floor of the unit, the ward was evacuated and the inmates filed out past me.

I was taken to the medical clinic for treatment, but in other respects it wasn't exactly the outcome I had planned. The injuries were much worse than I had intended. I had partial second-degree burns on the front and back of my torso as well as my upper arms.

What surprised me was that I seemed to be able to tune out the pain. I mentioned this to the nurse.

'It's a side-effect of the nerve damage,' he said gently, as he tweezed out a piece of charred shirt from my skin.

But that wasn't the case. I could feel the action of his tweezers and it certainly wasn't pleasant, but I could disown it in a way that diminished its hold on me. I could make it not mine.

That evening, when I was left on my own to eat my supper, I took my fork and inserted its tines into the top of my right thigh. It hurt, but by the exercise of my will, or perhaps more accurately by an operation of my consciousness which involved withdrawing my identification from the right leg, I was able to discount the pain to the point where I could push the fork all the way in, up to the arch at the top of the prongs. It was the fear of infection and of puncturing a large blood vessel more than the pain itself which persuaded me to pull it out. It emerged from my thigh with a faint squelch.

I've always been a coward, physically – though not, I would hope, morally. Yet here I was, suffering objective physical agony, and finding myself untroubled by it. Something had altered in my relationship to my body. I found myself able to behave with a thrilling disregard for its well-being. This body wasn't there to be cosseted and protected, but to be flung with abandon into every calamity, to be bounced like a rubber ball on concrete, hurled like a racing car around hairpin corners. What was it Leonora said when I pranged the Renault on our second worst holiday ever, in Salies-de-Béarn? Yes – nothing handles like a rental. And this disregard for my physical integrity held out the possibility of freedom. For all that I loved my old carcass, it wouldn't have been up to what came next.

The drop from the clinic window was about twenty-five feet, but I cut off six of them by hanging from the sill before I let go. A change of clothes, a spongebag with fourteen pounds in loose change inside it, and a travel-card that I'd stolen from one of the nurses preceded me. I went out just after midnight and lost consciousness on impact. I had sprained my right ankle, fallen backwards and knocked myself out cold.

For a brief moment I dreamed of flying. I was

pulling the trigger of a rifle and a white bird was dropping from a branch. I was the bullet. I was the bird falling. I swooped through space, past blurring starlight, and seemed to hear a strange, consoling music and soft human voices. I was on an armchair in Ron Harbottle's study; a carriage clock ticked heavily in the silence; I was squeezing up a tiny climbing frame to rescue an infant Lucius from the top of a slide; I was breaking apart a dried fish with my fingers; I was on parade with shaven-headed conscripts; a woman I'd never seen before was admonishing me outside a metro station in Russian: '*Tebya sglazili!*' *Someone has laid a curse on you!*

I woke to find that I had landed in a puddle. The icy water brought me round and the pain – my ankle, the burns, the ache at the back of my head – focused my consciousness. In the sky above me, the Plough and the Bear gleamed faintly through the light pollution. The air was, in that evocative phrase of Lermontov's, as fresh and clean as the kiss of a child. After the stink of the DHU and the neon and antisepsis of the medical clinic, it was like being born anew.

The first police siren wasn't audible for almost fifteen minutes, which suggests a blameworthy lack of vigilance on the part of whomever was monitoring the security cameras. No doubt they unpicked the footage fully later that morning. I like to think of White in attendance as they screened the pictures to the staff responsible and the police. The images would have shown a bundle coming out of the second-storey window of the clinic, followed a beat later by a long figure dropping and lying still for a moment. He gets slowly to his feet and hops awkwardly around to the delivery entrance at the rear of the unit. There he equips himself with a broom for a crutch, takes a loaf of white sliced bread from the pallet of deliveries to the kitchen, and disappears into the early morning darkness.

I would have gone off their screens at that point. I was changing out of my gown and using it to strap the ankle in order to move with more alacrity.

The Bethlem sits in large and pretty grounds. It was moved in the 1930s to a former estate. Each department is housed in a separate building. Between them lies an expanse of lawn, criss-crossed with roads and dotted with mature trees. I crouched in the tentlike shelter of a huge fir. It was heady with the stink of fox. I changed swiftly, jarring my sprained ankle as I pulled on the trousers. The wave of pain was remote, like a flash of lightning on the horizon. Someone called out as I hobbled off site; I didn't know if they'd seen me or not.

I was under no illusions about the extent and minute accuracy of twenty-first-century surveillance. Footage taken from the camera onboard the 119 that I took from the end of Monks Orchard Road would have been corroborated by the usage record of the travelcard, and there were four or five other passengers on the night bus if they needed witnesses. But I was gambling that I was ten or fifteen minutes ahead of them, and that there was still one place where I could count on hiding.

Mitcham Common in the darkness was as remote and quiet as the Peak District. It was almost daylight by the time I got home and I was half afraid that I would run into the Mauritian milkman. There was a For Sale sign outside the house. The spare keys were in their plastic bag under the acanthus.

I lay down to sleep in the cupboard under the eaves, but before going to sleep, I couldn't stop myself wandering round the house. The downstairs and the children's rooms had been emptied. It looked bigger without the furniture. There were ghostly negatives on the walls where Lucius and Sarah's posters had once hung. My study was largely untouched. There was still a hundred pounds in my copy of Borras and Christian's *Russian Syntax*. I picked up my father's Parker 45 and was shocked how small it seemed in my adapted hand. 'My name is Nicky Slopen,' I wrote on the back of an envelope in faltering ink.

Later that day, I was woken by muffled sounds and the ingratiating voice of an estate agent: '. . . plenty of storage space,' he said, as he opened the door close to my feet. There was a flash of sunlight and he shut it again. I held my breath. 'The couple who lived here have sadly split up.' He made no mention of my murder. He didn't want to trouble them with the gloomy association. The woman asked if it was in the catchment area of Lucius's old school. And down they went. I waited for the clump of the front door before venturing out of the cupboard.

I wondered if the police would bring themselves to look for me here. It was in a sense the obvious place, but in another it presented a problem for Dr White. He had to disparage my claims that I was who I said I was. It would be politically difficult for him to admit that I might be in here.

As it turned out, they didn't check the house for five days, by which time I had created a false back for the cupboard with sheets of plywood. I slept during the day and only emerged after nine to buy vacuum-packed food from the Tamil grocers, whom I trusted because their support for the Sri Lankan separatist movement made them constitutionally hostile to the police. I also brought home bags of ice for my ankle. I went in and out along the alleyway between the houses to avoid the neighbours.

The police made a perfunctory search of the premises around noon on the day they came. Nothing they might have seen would have aroused suspicion. I could see one of them through the keyhole. I could even smell his aftershave. That evening, I slipped out of the house for good.

Moving there had been one of those haphazard decisions that we took in haste, but which coloured our whole subsequent lives. Lucius would have been born in the front room, but for a last-minute change of heart that saw Leonora heading via ambulance to St George's. In that house, Leonora and I raised our children and made the billion mundane bargains out of which family life is constructed, arguing about curtains and bedtimes and whose turn it was to put out the recycling. Two years before, in the spare bedroom, we had made love for the last time before going out to dinner; hasty and almost perfunctory, the act still seemed somehow to hold the possibility of future closeness. Leonora straightened her skirt and smoothed the front of her blouse with both hands.

'We could always have another child,' I said.

She gave a wry laugh. We both knew that our resources and our relationship were too tenuous to support it.

Even now, the house was charged with an indefinable, heartbreaking scent that constantly brought to mind my children. And while I was in it, I could still pretend I had some kind of link to my old life.

CHAPTER 2

I called Misha Bykov from a payphone the day I left the house.

He met me in Richmond Park, just inside the Sheen Gate, where two under-eleven teams of boys were playing rugby in hooped shirts.

By the time he arrived, I had been waiting for him on a bench for almost an hour. It was a bright but raw day. I watched him make his way on foot through the gate. He had on a huge overcoat but no hat and his cheeks were inflamed with the cold.

He didn't acknowledge me, choosing to stand some distance away, smoking a cigarette, as though we had nothing to do with one another. I began by asking if he'd heard anything of Vera.

'She's in a psychiatric hospital in Chita.'

'Chita? Where's that?'

'Siberia.' He shook his head. '*Mnogo vody uteklo,*' he said wearily. It's one of those deceptively simple but dense expressions that's characteristic of Russian. It literally means 'a lot of water has flowed' but carries the sense of belatedness and irreversible change. His face looked more rumpled and underslept than usual. I took it to mean that he'd concluded that our abortive resistance must come to an end.

'I have a few things for you,' he said.

It was money, which I accepted gratefully, and an A4 envelope of papers, which I opened in front of him.

Another grainy photocopied passport, this time of a man called Viktor Koryakin. He had thin, fair hair and was fuller in the face, but I recognised something in the furious intensity of his pale eyes, although for a moment I couldn't remember where I'd seen them. His place and date of birth were given as Krasnodar, September 19th 1978. There were discharge papers from the army, and some police photographs of the same face, this time with a black eye and a bloodstained shirtfront; close-ups of the familiar tattoos.

'It's you,' he said. 'A roughneck from the Kuban. A real Cossack.'

I felt strangely empty. 'Does he have children?'

'I didn't know him,' said Misha.

'What do I do?'

'You have to live,' he said. 'We all do.'

I could hear shrill voices as one of the boys broke away for a try and the sound of the whistle as he touched the ball down to score.

'There's more,' he said.

The envelope seemed empty, but when I turned it out, what looked like a small clear plastic dogtag dropped into the palm of my hand. It was a polygon about an inch and a half in diameter and roughly a quarter of an inch thick. There was a hole bored through the middle. On closer inspection, it was too heavy to be plastic, and there was a strange iridescence around its edges.

'Quartz,' he said.

'Jewellery?'

'Your *klyuchka*.'

I knew the word – it's the diminutive of *klyuch*, which means 'key' in Russian, in a range of senses including a key to a door, a musical key and the key to a cipher. It can also mean a clue, and a spring or source of water.

'To what?'

'To you,' he said. 'It's your code. The one Vera wrote.'

'Like a disc?'

'That kind of thing.'

I turned it over in my hand: my little key, my source, my secret clue. It glittered prettily where the light struck it, magnifying the weak October sun into deep yellow and blue flashes. It was the irreducible content of me, thirty-nine years of my life captured on a three-centimetre disc of quartz. 'There's not much to me,' I said.

'So it turns out.'

I put it in my pocket. 'I was attacked in the hospital. The man had a tattoo like mine. Do you think he was a mankurt?'

He nodded.

'But who was the original?'

Perhaps because he couldn't shake himself free

of the assumption that I was mentally defective, perhaps because Russian wasn't my first language, he addressed me as though I was a child: slowly and with explanatory hand gestures.

'No original. There are two variants. *Zachot* and *pyaterka*. You're a *pyaterka*.'

'And Jack?'

'Also a *pyaterka*.'

'What's the difference?'

'*Soznaniye*.' He enunciated each of the four syllables as he tapped the side of his head. *Consciousness*. 'Vera only works with *pyaterki*,' he added with a note of pride in his voice.

'*Works?*' I picked him up on his use of the tense.

'Of course. The others sew mailbags, Vera makes mankurts. No one else can do what she does. They'll keep her there until she dies, or until I get her out.'

'You might die trying.'

He smiled ruefully at me and the sun flashed on his gold bridgework. 'I've done terrible things in this life, Nikolai. Terrible things.' He turned away and narrowed his eyes at the horizon, as though contemplating his past enormities. 'Yet somehow, I didn't feel I was a bad person. Do you understand? When Vera told me what they were doing, I understood it was wrong and I understood that God was giving me a chance to make up for my old life. He asked and I obeyed. That's how it was.' Listening to him, I understood that both priests and criminals can be men of straightforward morality.

A sharp whistle ended the game. There was a smattering of applause from the handful of watching parents. The boys began filing off the pitch. They looked tiny and knock-kneed.

'You're not worried about betraying Sinan?'

He waved his hand in disdain. 'No way, he's a moron' – the Russian word literally means 'radish'. 'Sinan's not someone to worry about. There are some serious people in the upward chain of command, but not him.'

That phrase that sounds so un-Misha-like, *upward chain of command*, is the best I can do with the evocative noun he used: *vertikal'*.

'Are there many?'

He finished his cigarette. 'Enough to keep me busy,' he said. He patted me on the shoulder and got up. 'Time to go.'

'One thing,' I said. 'Do you know where Hunter is?'

'I can find out,' he said. 'But after that . . . He raised his forefinger to his lips. I understood. It would be our last communication.

'What will you do?' I asked.

He winked at me. '*Men'she znaesh', luchshe spish'.*'
The less you know, the better you sleep.

He turned and walked away.

I knew I couldn't trust myself to stay in London for more than a few days. It was too much temptation. I would come up with some excuse to go and see Lucius and Sarah and it would end up putting them at risk. I needed to put some distance between us, for their sake. There was no hope of connecting the broken thread of my life. But I couldn't shake the feeling that there was one meaningful task remaining to me.

CHAPTER 3

I spent my last days in London in a room above a pub in Streatham, vacillating between the necessity of leaving and my desire to settle scores with Hunter.

It felt safer to be in a neighbourhood I knew and where I had an instinctive sense of what was ordinary. But it had its own form of peril. One afternoon, I saw Tadeusz, Jack's old landlord, unloading crates from a van parked outside the pet shop. Unthinkingly, I went up to greet him. His body tensed as he caught sight of me. He set down his crate. The coldness in his face reminded me who I was. I lowered my eyes and turned away from him.

I learned that night from Misha that Hunter was in a hospice near Richmond Park, a private one, with a Zen garden in its grounds.

I made a couple of speculative visits. Misha had told me that Hunter, a crank to the last, was having his meals delivered from outside, by a company called Raw Genius that specialised in raw food. Each morning before seven, a man on a moped dropped off an array of bizarre juices, buckwheat groats, weird fruits and spiralised and dehydrated vegetables.

One chilly November day I arrived around midmorning, wearing a chef's jacket and carrying a hemp bag of items from a health-food shop.

The place was more like an exclusive hotel than a hospital. The reception area was warm, and heady with the smell of aromatherapy candles and gourmet cooking. 'Clair de Lune' was playing quietly through discreet speakers behind the desk.

I couldn't help comparing it all to the DHU. The basic economic injustice of the world struck me: that the rich don't live the same lives as us, or die the same deaths. Some, like Hunter, don't intend to die at all.

The receptionist spoke to me in a hushed voice that somehow made my deception easier.

I identified myself as a member of the Raw Genius team and told her that we'd delivered the wrong items. It was the only occasion in two lifetimes that I've had reason to be grateful to Caspar's wife Hilary and her obsession with fad diets.

'Entirely our fault,' I said. 'We've got four clients on two different restricted diets and we got mixed up. We delivered one here with a soy lecithin supplement. I don't think he's intolerant, but it's better not to take the risk.'

Soy lecithin. I felt an abstract, almost parental pride in the smoothness of my articulation.

She told me where to find him.

*   *   *

Hunter had a suite of rooms with a verandah. He was shrunken, coughing, his hands frail and liver-spotted. He walked unsteadily, supporting his weight with a frame. His expensive clothes hung loosely.

'Just put them down over there,' he said with a vague gesture in the direction of the galley kitchen.

'I need to remove the other items,' I said.

'They're in the fridge.'

I opened the fridge door.

'How are you enjoying the meals?' I said.

'Good enough. Are you waiting for a tip?'

'I take it you don't recognise me.'

He moved his frame towards me and peered into my face with no trace of fear. 'Why? Should I know you?'

I told him who I was. He appraised me for a moment.

'Let's go for a walk,' he said.

I helped him into a big coat, fur hat and muffler. He manoeuvred his walking frame out onto the baize-green lawn, which was crisp with frost.

'Nicholas said you could barely speak,' he said.

'It came back gradually.'

'A miracle. Look at you.' He was racked by one of his periodic fits of coughing. 'But what's wrong with your hands?'

'They do this in the cold,' I said, struggling to straighten my fingers.

I had to slow to a shuffle to keep pace with him.

The rubber feet of his frame left scuff-marks in the gravel.

Ducks huddled round a water outflow in the middle of the frozen pond. Hunter dropped heavily onto a wooden bench by the side of the gravel path and gave a sigh.

For a few minutes we sat in silence, watching the ice creep imperceptibly across the water.

I was the first to speak. 'I'm surprised you . . .

'What?' he said. 'Thought I'd be scared of you? There's not much you can do to me now. I'm dying anyway. If I was a car, they'd scrap me. Cancer. Secondaries everywhere. I'm riddled with it. The upside is the drugs they've got me on. I'm higher than I've been for years.'

'I thought the upside of being ill was that you were close to it.'

'Close to what?'

'Your higher spiritual life.'

He lowered his voice to an intoxicated hush. 'Jesus Christ, it really is you.' He gave me a sideways glance that had something curious and greedy in it. 'Tell me something: what's it like?'

What's it like? The physical ache, the loneliness, the high clouds, Vera's face as she twisted in the hands of her captors, Jack letting the Fielding novel slip from his hands, Caiaphas, the anonymous misery of the DHU. To know all this, to be me and not me; to be reflected in the frightened eyes of my son and see a monster. 'It's a miracle,' I said quietly. 'You're going to love it.'

I was staring towards the water, remembering a cold winter when I'd pulled out big panes of ice from the pond on Tooting Common and given them to Lucius and Sarah to jump on. The ice had left a weedy, riverine smell on my hands.

Hunter's eyes glittered as he tried to suppress his excitement. I could see him struggling to keep his emotions in check: the thought of what I represented. The hope! And imagine the carcass they'd set aside for him!

He pointed towards the pond. 'They have geese here in the summer,' he said. 'You know, when I was a kid, I had a pet goose called Snoopy. A dog killed it. My mother got me another one. Called that one Snoopy too.'

'You didn't miss the other one?'

Hunter shrugged. 'A goose is a goose.' He reached inside his overcoat for something that he couldn't find. 'Will you remind me of that when we get back? I haven't got my notebook with me.'

He levered himself up onto his frame. 'Come on. I'm getting cold.'

I followed him back across the silent garden.

He leaned against my arm as he negotiated the step up to the French windows.

After the cold, the warmth in his rooms seemed intense and soporific. At Hunter's request, I fetched his notebook from the bedside table. It was in the first drawer: a fat leatherbound Smythson's with onionskin pages.

While he was writing down his memory of the

goose, I made a pot of redbush tea and set it down on the coffee table.

'Do you know where I've been?' I said.

He looked up from his writing and for the first time, I think I saw a trace of fear in his eyes.

'If I said the name Dr Philip White, would that mean anything to you?' I said.

'Not unless he's an oncologist.'

'Dr White's my psychiatrist.'

'I know things haven't been easy for you,' he said.

'That's one way of putting it.'

'You've got to understand, I relinquished any day-today responsibilities some time ago. I've been here, getting my head straight. There was a view that we simply couldn't risk work of this importance being jeopardised.'

'Hence Nicky's murder?'

Hunter suddenly blazed with a flash of anger. 'I'm ill but don't take me for a dumb fuck. What are you, wired up like he was? We all understood the complexity of this work. Vera did. Okay, Sinan's dad had a problem with it, but the rest of us were on board from the get-go. Ethically – I won't kid you – it's not simple. But the upside is, literally, infinite. We're not choosing to be in the business of death. With insights this rich, with the backing we've got, we are on the brink of something incredible. I'm talking about the deepest wish, Nicholas. Time is the great blessing. We're going to get more time. All of us.'

'And Nicholas?'

'Here you are, Nicholas! You're right here.' His anger had subsided and now he gave me a look of calm, transcendent love. I understood the joy I had given him. He was thinking of himself.

There were steps in the corridor. They seemed to be approaching the door, then they died away. Outside, the garden was suddenly bathed in light. A squirrel ventured right up to the French doors with brisk, staccato movements as though it were driven by clockwork. I thought of the wind-up ballerina on the South Bank, and the tragic life-lessness of her dancing. I saw Sarah barely hours old; her eyes milky and unaccustomed to the light; her arms and legs paddling the air. I remembered Lucius, as a child, leaning sleepily against the toilet as he peed in the middle of the night, and then collapsing into my arms. But not into these arms, into Nicky Slopen's arms, not these counterfeits.

'One day, we'll look back at this time the way we look back at the era of surgery without anaesthesia, or before antibiotics. We're going to make death optional.'

'Not for Nicholas.'

'And yet you're here, aren't you?'

'I'm here because Vera felt things had got out of control,' I said.

Hunter smiled. 'Vera accepted what we needed to do. We were clear with each other at the outset. We can't stop this thing because someone's gotten squeamish. There's too much at stake now. We're at war, Nicholas . . . He was struggling to keep his eyes open. The walk in the cold had exhausted him. 'We're at war with death.'

The book slid to the floor. A moment later he was asleep.

I picked up his notebook and leafed through it. His handwriting was surprisingly characterful, very masculine, with a Greek *e* and a long flat tail on his *y*s and *g*s. He'd filled it with page after page of personal trivia.

So, for example: *mom's meat loaf. wrapped in greaseproof paper. grey slabs covered in ketchup.*

Or: *clap clinic 1967 – Deirdre, Phoebe, the Vassar girl?*

I turned another page.

That afternoon at the Barbican. Who's Afraid of Virginia Woolf? Tricia morose about my affair with C. I say we can have another kid if she really wants them, but what about the complications? Her age, etc.

It was just past one o'clock. I wasn't sure how much longer I would be alone with him. I warmed my hands on the radiators to relax the muscles and take the chill off my fingers. I didn't want the cold of them to wake him.

I had envisaged this moment so many times that the act was something of a let-down. In my fantasy it was always a haler Hunter, a more worthy adversary. And there was a particular shamefulness attached to killing such an attenuated version of the man. On what I'd based them, I don't know, but I'd had such vividly different hopes for how

377

things would turn out. Very briefly he opened his eyes, there was the slightest of struggles, and then his life left him, almost willingly, like a bird flying out of a thicket.

CHAPTER 4

My wanderings since are not exactly pertinent to this testimony. But once you've acquired the habit of reminiscence, it gets harder and harder to decide what merits exclusion.

I hitchhiked from London to Swindon. Strange as it seems, in 2010 someone was willing to pick up a large, rather intimidating, heavily built man who was not only an escapee from a secure hospital with an outstanding section under the Mental Health Act, but a murderer.

The Good Samaritan's name was Gordon Swanage. He was an ex-soldier from Newcastle. When I hungrily eyed the chicken salad sandwich in his glove box he pulled over and bought me gammon, egg and chips from a Little Chef on the M4. I told him I had been a teacher.

'I went through hard times myself when I got back from Iraq,' he said, as though he had heard nothing of what I had just said to him. The abrupt syllables of his Geordie accent made him sound, to my ear, like he was speaking Danish. 'We're still suing the Ministry of Defence. When I get the money I'm going to give all this up. Move to Spain. How about you? What's your dream?'

'Just living day to day,' I said through a mouthful of food. 'You know.'

'I do indeed, my friend. I do.'

His kindness to me seemed almost without limit. I find it as mystifying – more, in fact – than the reasoned cruelties of Hunter and whoever or whatever stands behind him.

At Swindon, he went out of his way to set me down at a hand car wash where, he said, the manager was always looking out for good people and didn't ask too many questions, if I knew what he meant.

The car wash was jerry-built out of timber and plywood. A couple of Union Jacks hung over it as a form of camouflage. Everyone there was from Eastern Europe. The workers slept in a condemned building behind it. Sunk in the world of the labouring poor, I began to believe that Nicholas Slopen had never existed.

What I had now was a terribly truncated version of a life, but it was better than the DHU and it wasn't unsafe. With an effort of will, I compelled my thoughts away from anything to do with my past, Nicky's past. I thought about calling myself Viktor, but the name stuck in my throat. I told people my name was Stan, my father's name, and no one ever asked more of me.

After I'd been there ten days, a Volkswagen camper van pulled in. It was so battered and rusty that it seemed odd that anyone would want to clean it; and in fact, its driver, a young woman with dirty blonde dreadlocks held back in a headscarf, was having trouble with the engine and wanted someone to take a look at it. I recused myself on the grounds of total engineering ignorance, which she found funny. While one of the other washers was checking her vehicle, she told me I looked familiar. I said that was unlikely and asked her where she was headed. She told me she lived in a commune on the border of Devon and Dorset. They had cows and grew much of their own food, she said. She had been on her way to fetch a couple of volunteer workers, but they'd called to say they had swine flu and then the van had broken down on the way back.

'So I'm going back empty-handed if I get there at all.'

We'd had a slow week and Alex, our boss, was happy to lose me for a while. I went there with her that afternoon.

It had been a school for half a century – an experimental one that was closed down by the inspectors – and before that a vicarage. It still had a vaguely scholastic atmosphere. There was a library on the second floor which no one used. The books on the shelves were still alphabetised, not because of the diligence of the communards, but because none of them read any more. Firbank, Forster, Galsworthy, Gissing, Golding, it went, and so on, through all the other dead white men, like me. At times, I felt like the Time Traveller among the unlettered Eloi.

Mixed in with them were scatterings of more predictable volumes: *What Colour is Your Parachute?*, *The Tao of Physics*, absurd speculations about the Turin Shroud or the Templars.

Willow – the girl with dreadlocks – was about right when she described it as a commune. They were ineffectual at self-sufficiency, but they did their best and supported themselves by offering the place as a centre for retreats: dance, sacred drumming, all the stuff the old Nicholas thought was nonsense. Come to think of it, the new Nicholas also thinks it's nonsense. But he liked the people themselves. I have to fight the urge to call them kids, but it's how I think of them.

I want to avoid the obvious characterisations of it. There was more than a hint of dippiness about them. And there was an incuriousness, a complacency that you probably find among any people who feel they're getting through life without making any compromises. But the thing to say is that they were so kind to me. There were even children there, with all the optimism that implies.

Willow had an old laptop with a sporadic internet connection. Their commitment to utopian mediaevalism was inconsistent at best. She talked me through Facebook and I was able to use her account to peek at Lucius's. It was strange to see it – I still think of him as a little boy, which he is, but he passed himself off as a kind of sophisticate on it. I wanted to send him a message, but I knew that way lay madness, or worse, so I asked Willow to change her password to remove the temptation.

Everyone there was reinventing something about themselves, even if all they were running away from was just a background that seemed reprehensibly ordinary. My air of authentic disaster gave me a kind of kudos.

I ended up with a bed in what must have once been a broom cupboard on the second floor. Willow came past with dandelion coffee each evening, and scrupulously said goodnight.

'You love to read,' she said, one night soon after I'd arrived.

'It's my life.'

The following night, she asked if she could read with me.

She sat heavily on the edge of the bed with a copy of *Dr Zhivago*. I could tell she was dissatisfied with her book. There was something forlorn and fidgety about her. It made it difficult for me to concentrate.

Eventually she sighed. 'I'm cold,' she said. 'Give me a bit of your blanket.'

'Please don't take this the wrong way,' I said, 'but are you trying to seduce me?'

'No,' she laughed. 'Maybe.'

She kissed me and her tongue flickered in my mouth like a tiny bird.

I pulled away.

'Don't you like me?'

'It's been a very long time since I was with anyone,' I said.

'How long?'

'Longer than I can remember.'

'That's okay. We can just cuddle.'

She moved up awkwardly next to me. I admired her persistence. I held her close to me and breathed in her smell of hand-rolled cigarettes and patchouli.

'What are you thinking about?' she asked.

'I'm thinking about all the people who never get held like this.'

She stroked my face. 'Read me something.'

'It's Edmund Gosse,' I said. 'It doesn't excerpt terribly well. But I can tell you a poem if you like.'

'I'd like that.'

The opening lines of 'Lycidas' floated through my head.

'Why are you smiling?' she asked.

'I'm thinking about an old friend who loved poems.'

The bed frame creaked under us as she nestled closer with her back towards me. 'Whisper it,' she said. She put her ear close to my lips. It was as small and pretty as a seashell and smelled of gingerbread.

I didn't even voice the words, I let my breath

alone carry them across the four inches of silence between us.

'Who would not sing for Lycidas? He knew Himself to sing and build the lofty rhyme.'

She wriggled around to face me delightedly. 'Go on,' she said.

The ankle knitted up completely, though it remained swollen-looking. It turned out that I had the knack of outdoor work, particularly scything – they're scrupulous about their carbon footprint at Knowle Court. Leonora would have found it hilarious. Some muscle-memory in me seemed tuned to its rhythm. The blade snicked back and forth across the pasture and the cut grass fell in windrows beside the swath. 'You're a natural,' said the livestock man.

They were all gentle ruminants there, Willow and the rest of them. I feared for them. Centuries on a more or less peaceable island had left them without any instinct for self-preservation. I found their lack of intellectual acuity frustrating, but their optimism and good faith moving in the extreme.

The sun came out strongly one day towards the beginning of December. Half a dozen of the residents got into the stockman's Land Rover and went to the beach for a barbecue. It was stony and the water was freezing, but there was a competitive bravado about going in. I felt self-conscious about my tattoos and scarring, but they were, if anything, approved of. The displacement of light through the water made my swollen ankle look huge and kinked. I stared at my white feet in the green murk thinking: *whose are these?* Then I plunged in. The cold was so intense I experienced it as heat. I swam away from the shore, pulling strongly. On my shoulders, the water felt like broken glass or jellyfish tentacles. I thought: death can't be more painful.

It seemed as though the others had been happy to immerse themselves and then return to the shore and the fire, but I became aware of someone swimming near me. A shiny dark head broke the water. A seal. For a second, it spared me a curious look and then plunged into the icy depths below my feet.

Willow helped me dry off. The after-effect of the freezing water was a rush of endorphins.

After we'd eaten, someone lit a joint. I demurred. I mentioned its association with mental health problems. That raised a few ironic eyebrows. Of course, in their eyes I'm a baffling square.

On the way back, Willow fell asleep in the car with her head on my shoulder.

I knew the best thing I could do was disappear. So why was I staying? Addressing her body with my carcass that night, I understood the answer. It wasn't the wild, hopeless love I felt for Leonora, but it was love all the same.

'What do you think you know about me?' I asked

her as we lay in my tiny bed staring at the luminous paper stars someone had pasted to the ceiling.

'I know you have children. I saw your son's Facebook page. He looks like you.'

'Really?'

She affirmed the remark, but with noticeably diminishing conviction.

It puzzles me. I can't see any physical resemblance between us. It's true that Malevin claimed that eighty per cent of what we recognise in a face originates from the core complex and isn't somatic at all. But on reflection, I think Willow was just trying to be nice.

At night, I come to the library with her computer. There is a poetic justice in finding myself here.

My most passionate friendships have been with people who are biologically dead. I call on them for succour and advice. I discuss my life with them. I feel I really *know* them in ways they would undoubtedly have found surprising.

But the dead are dead. That may be the truest and most definite fact about human existence. Death is the bass ground that gives everything else point. Every generation seems to know this except ours. I feel I'm entitled to say this. Who on earth is deader than me?

And the dead are dead for good reasons, profound reasons, that we ignore at our peril. There's a reason why the old father in *The Monkey's Paw* turns away his dead son when he comes knocking. The world belongs to the living: to Lucius and Sarah, to Leonora and, though it pains me to say it, to Caspar.

In the past few weeks, I've noticed the clock on this carcass ticking down. The first signs were episodes when I briefly lost all sense of time. These days I can see from my handwriting that my fine motor skills are deteriorating. Working outside in the cold, my hands constantly seize up into claws. One morning, I blacked out in the shower and lost a tooth from the fall.

I didn't – I don't – expect to see the turn of the year.

Weighing it all up, the complications that would arise from my death, the attention it would focus on these gentle people, I think it would be best for me to leave.

CHAPTER 5

Three days ago, before dawn, I took the van that was parked on the narrow drive that leads up to the old entrance hall. It sat in the shadow of the untamed trees that make Knowle Court feel so dark and inward-looking. Willow had left the keys in the kitchen. I wrote her a note, but I wasn't able to tell her anything that I felt could sufficiently explain the betrayal.

The van filled the B roads with the sound of its hoarse engine and strained to keep pace in the slow lane of the motorway. The steering was a little loose and eerily slow to respond. But you get used to anything.

Yesterday, I drove up to the Lake District for a valediction.

Before I abandoned the van, I went to visit the tiny whitewashed cottage where Leonora and Nicholas spent their honeymoon. It's down two miles of single track on the side of an obscure fell. A wisp of smoke was escaping from the chimney. I remembered the two upstairs rooms and the dark kitchen where they read to each other and played board games. No part of me accepts the rational truth: that I was seeing it for the first time.

Sitting on the bonnet of the van, I tied rope around my shoes to give me grip on the snow which covered the slopes above the tawny moorland. On the summit of the fell, with the wind in my ears, I flipped Hunter's *klyuchka* into the air and watched it flash in the weak midwinter light before splashing into a black hillside tarn. I don't know if I'm coming back, but he definitely isn't.

From the moment I saw them, I had no doubt that his rambling journals were intended to be coded. I searched his room for every scrap of paper I could lay my hands on, determined to destroy them.

In the lowest drawer of his bedside table, I found his birth certificate, his navy blue US passport and a copy of his will. Underneath them all was a small black velvet bag with a quartz disc in it. *Of course*, I remember thinking. *It's already done.* Hunter was keeping notes to reduce the gap, to make his own resuscitation less jarring. Had he learned about that from Nicky, before he killed him? Did he have Vera standing by in the mental hospital in Chita to fine-tune the code?

Hunter's *klyuchka* will never reach Baikonur. I made sure of that. I took his and left mine in its place. I put a cuckoo's egg in the nest of the Common Task.

Somewhere, perhaps, the other I am is stirring,

another Nikolasha blinking into life, harbouring all the old hopes, facing all the zappings, the coercive instructions to adjust him to his new carcass. And maybe for him there's a way home that never opened up for me. Whatever happens, I'll make sure he has the advantage of this testimony.

But for me, it's almost over.

Even a mankurt like me is sad to leave this world of dew. Nothing that was done to me makes me believe my sojourn here was abject and meaningless. And I, in a strange body, the fragments of another man's memories, have so many things to speak of: that seal's head breaking the waters of the bay, the light on Rossett Gill yesterday morning, mist in ribbons on Tooting Common, the dead weight of one of my children on my shoulder as I carried them sleeping from the car, my father's dying words to me, as he clutched his own father's medal, telling me he loved me.

This stranger inside me is a creature like every other: obsessed with the limits of his existence, haunted by the spectacle of his passage through time, the blossoming and deterioration of his relationships with other creatures, the unutterable sadness of a finite life on a beautiful planet. And as he's aged, a second world has appeared beside him, compounded of memories and recollected emotion. To this world I will turn in my last days. All my pain and beauty is here.

Looking around this place – an internet cafe beside a minicab office in a northern city – with its wet lino and jingling doorbell, I find it hard to consent to my departure. There is so much still that is sacred and beautiful: the man in headphones typing to the *tsk* of its secret rhythms, the woman with her backpack on the floor and her inadvertent smile, so absorbed in their tappings, their promises and farewells, weaving themselves from shreds of something, the words that were made by the dead, fending off the great oblivion; but, yes, *goodbye my pretty ones, goodbye.*